Peas, Carrots
and an
Aston Martin

HANNAH LYNN

ALSO BY HANNAH LYNN

Standalone Feel Good Novels

The Afterlife of Walter Augustus

Treading Water

Erotic Fiction?

The Complete Peas and Carrots Series

Peas, Carrots and an Aston Martin

Peas, Carrots and a Red Feather Boa

Peas, Carrots and Six More Feet

Peas, Carrots and Lessons in Life

Peas, Carrots and Panic at the Plot

Peas, Carrots and Happily Ever After

The Holly Berry Sweet Shop Series

The Sweet Shop of Second Chances

Romance at the Sweet Shop of Second Chances

Turmoil at the Sweet Shop of Second Chances

High Hopes at the Sweet Shop of Second Chances

The Grecian Women Series

Athena's Child

A Spartan's Sorrow

Queens of Themiscyra

This story is a work of fiction. All names, characters, organisations, places, events and incidents are products of the author's imagination or are used fictitiously. Any resemblance to any persons, alive or dead, events or locals is *almost* entirely coincidental.

Text copyright © 2018 Hannah Lynn

First published 2018

ISBN: 9781718093102

Imprint: Independently published
Edited by Emma Mitchell @ Creating Perfection and Jessica Nelson @ Indie Books Gone Wild

For Sally,

Wherever you are...

CHAPTER 1

ERIC SIBLEY SAT across from the solicitor. He was unsure as to what the appropriate or expected response was, given the current situation. He blinked a few times and rubbed the bridge of his nose, then shuffled around on the chair and tried to find a more comfortable seating position. The shuffling included a solid minute of switching his weight from one buttock to the other, adjusting his legs from crossed to uncrossed, and sliding forwards and back on the cement-hard plastic, after which he concluded no comfortable position could ever be obtained in a chair so cheap and badly built. It simply wasn't possible.

In Eric's opinion, the chair wasn't the only cheap thing in the solicitor's office. The entire room, from the Blu-Tacked A3 posters on the window to the laminate desk, worn blue carpet and instant freeze-dried coffee, reeked of skinny budgets and cutting corners. There was no class, no style. On the other side of the desk, the solicitor looked just as cheap, with his polyester jacket, comic tie and supermarket aftershave.

'Just explain it to me again,' Eric said. 'You're saying I get nothing? None of it? Nothing at all?'

'No.' The solicitor removed his glasses and rubbed his eyes. 'As I have explained, your father has left you the remaining tenancy on his allotment and his 1962 limited-edition Aston Martin DB4 series four, affectionately known as Sally, on the condition that you fully tend to the allotment on a weekly basis for the next two years.'

Eric shook his head.

'But the house? Everything in the house. The paintings, my mother's jewellery, all of that, it ... it's ...'

'It's been left to the church,' the solicitor finished for him.

'But he didn't even go to church!' Eric thumped the table with his fist. 'He was a bloody atheist!'

The solicitor – who was presumably named Eaves or Doyle, judging from the sign above the door – shuffled the papers in front of him, then returned his glasses to the end of his nose.

'I realise that this is a difficult time for you. But your father was very specific about his wishes. The car will remain in your possession, permanently, provided you adhere to the specified conditions.'

'And if I don't?'

'Then your father has made provisions for that situation too.'

Eric drew in a lungful of air, which he let out with a hiss.

'But Abi? He must have left something to Abi? She's his only grandchild for Christ's sake.'

Eaves-possibly-Doyle massaged his temples with his knuckles.

'I'm very sorry, Mr Sibley, I don't know what to tell you. Perhaps your father felt you'd value these gifts more than the house or money.'

'Like hell he did.'

Eric pushed back the chair, snatched the papers from the table, and strode over to the door. When his hand was on the handle, Eaves-possibly-Doyle coughed. Eric spun around.

'Mr Sibley, before you leave, I have to tell you that it would be considered trespassing if you were to step on your father's property from now on.'

Eric's lungs quivered.

'Exactly how am I supposed to collect the car without going on the property?' he said through clenched teeth.

'Your father has seen to that as well.'

The car was being stored in a garage on the outskirts of town. Fortunately, it was a walkable distance as, having travelled from London by train, Eric's only mode of transport was by foot or taxi, and you had as much chance of finding a taxi in Burnham as you did hailing Father Christmas for a lift home from the pub at midnight on Christmas Eve.

The sky was blanketed in dense grey clouds, although for mid-November it was relatively mild. As he walked, a cool breeze pushed him from behind, carrying the scent of damp grass and river water. Eric's feet skidded on the wet autumn slush. So much for crisp copper leaves and frolicking squirrels. His insides lurched. What was he going to tell Suzy? Only last night they'd been discussing what they would do with the money. Their mortgage would've been paid off for sure, with more than a bit to spare. They talked about buying a holiday house, somewhere in Italy, Tuscany perhaps, maybe a skiing holiday, or the Maldives even. She'd been so excited.

Eric bit back the resentment. He wasn't being callous, he wasn't. Yes, his father had died, and that was all very sad, but he was an old man who'd lived a long life. Far longer than he probably deserved. Old people die, there's no getting around it, Eric told himself, and the fact remained, he deserved the house. Growing up as an only child with his father, he deserved a dozen houses. How many other children began doing spelling tests at three? Or couldn't have dinner before they'd recited all the imperfect and perfect past participles in Latin, French, and Spanish? How many teenagers were made to run three miles every weekend morning to earn ten minutes as a passenger in his father's car? A car that he'd got by swindling a ninety-year-old widow four decades earlier. What kind of normal person did that? There was a traffic cone on the side of the pavement. Eric stopped and kicked it.

'Screw you. I hope you burn,' he yelled.

Then, noticing an old woman walking her Jack Russell on the other side of the street, waved his hand apologetically and carried on walking.

The workshop was littered with tools, reeked of petrol, and was run by men who wiped their hands on their work trousers. It was not the type of place you'd expect to find a half-million-pound vintage sports car, stored away in the corner with only a half-on dust sheet for protection.

Eric's lungs seized with terror as a bald mechanic ran his hand along the bonnet of the car, stroking and caressing the bodywork like it was his own personal prized possession. Eric flinched at each and every movement.

'She runs like a dream,' the mechanic said.

'You've driven her?'

'Aye. Never thought I'd get behind the wheel of one of these in my lifetime. But I'd see 'er goin' up and down them roads. And then when your dad's 'ands went, he came an' asked me one day. Just like that. Wanted to be in her again I guess. Can't blame 'im. Sally, ain't it?' Eric nodded. 'Anyways, we made it pretty regular since then. He had me coming up to the house, taking him out on the bends near every week. I guess that's been what, ten months?'

Eric blushed. He hadn't seen his dad since last Christmas, and he certainly couldn't remember anything wrong with his hands then, although he did remember something vague about letting Abi tear the wrapping paper off his Christmas present.

'Somewhere around then,' Eric said, then straightened his shoulders and asserted himself to the matter in hand. 'If you could just get the keys, I'm in a bit of a rush. I've got rather a lot of things to be getting on with.'

''Course, 'course. I'll get them rightly. I take it you'll be heading up to the allotment?' he said.

'How do you know ...' Eric started, but cut himself short. Of course the mechanic knew about the allotment, everyone knew. This was Burnham-on-Crouch.

Eric's parents had moved to Burnham when he was eleven and already at boarding school. As such, the place had never been anything more than an unpleasant vacation home that he was thrust into for three holidays, three half terms, and six exeats a year. He abhorred it. Only an hour from London by train, it was the antithesis of culture and class. In the summer it was full of tourists who wandered along the riverfront, nosing in the quaint shops that sold nothing but tat, while protecting their fish and chips from opportunistic seagulls. In the winter Burnham was a ghost town, other than on the occasional weekend when good weather yielded hordes of bikers to gather at the local greasy spoon and belt around the narrow, twisting lanes, causing havoc to anyone on four wheels. It was not a place Eric liked to be associated with.

Suzy, on the other hand, adored it. She spent her mornings strolling around the marina, taking in the air, and revelling in the grudgingly slow pace. Once or twice she'd suggested they move there, or at least buy a holiday cottage and give Abi the chance to grow up knowing her granddad better. Eric never pandered to the discussion.

He started the engine and closed his eyes. The vibrations buzzed up through the leather work. Tending an allotment for two years? Easy. Eric would tend to a whole farm if he had to. No one was getting their hands on this car. Not in his lifetime.

The car drove exactly as Eric remembered. Loud and stylish and still as argumentative as ever in third gear. The sills looked as though they would need an overhaul in the next twelve months, but apart from that and a little rusting around the inside of the bumper, she was in perfect nick; the way his father had always kept her. Cars had been George Sibley's life-long love. Gardening, by contrast, was an exceptionally ridiculous dalliance.

This was Eric's first trip to the allotment. Part of the reason was time; visits to George were usually planned in conjunction with a visit to Suzy's sister, Lydia, in nearby Woodham, and thus adhered to a somewhat rigid schedule. Arriving at Lydia's late often resulted in her offering a bed for the night in their tie-dye clad spare room that smelt somewhere between a chiropractor's office and a compost heap. To Eric, spending the night there was only marginally better than spending the night on the toilet floor of a seedy sports bar in Wales the night after a Six Nations rugby match. Better to be in and out quick where his relatives were concerned.

The other reason he'd not visited the allotment was that Eric had no interest in it. He had no interest in feigning enthusiasm over rows and rows of green leaves, each one no different to the next. Nor did he want to hear about what potato blight was. Or how the aphids had ravaged this bean or that bean, or how important it was to get your strawberries covered before the birds came and got them all. And more importantly, he had no interest in spending time alone with his father. After all, it wasn't like he bothered taking an interest in Eric's life.

It had been bearable when Eric's mother was still alive. She'd been the link, the tie, his father's one redeeming feature that allowed Eric to see him as more than merely a dictator who had strived to control every aspect of Eric's life, from his university choice to the houses he lived in, and even the colour that his best man wore at his wedding. After all, if she could love George Sibley, there had to be good in him somewhere, right?

His mother, Josephine, had been the polar opposite of his father. While in public she supported her husband's decisions, privately she'd nourished Eric's creativity. It was she who convinced George that Eric did not need to attend remedial maths classes after he received his first B grade in a test. It was she who persuaded George to allow Eric to play lead trumpet in the school jazz band as opposed to screeching away at his second-hand violin in the back row of the orchestra. Josephine vocally and controversially supported Eric's choice to study anthropology at university rather than economics or accounting, and had wept with joy, rather than disdain, when he told them that he'd proposed to Suzy, a divorced writer. Josephine was the link, the bond, the elucidation. And when she died, all that was gone.

The allotment was at the far end of town, behind a cul-de-sac of 1970s pebble-dashed semis. The land backed onto marshes and was apparently a hive of activity for the Burnham over-sixties. Although at that moment in time, the only inhabitant of the street Eric encountered was a sour-faced cat with a gammy leg that forced him to lean more on Sally's brakes more than he would have liked so soon after getting back behind the wheel.

With a vision of flying chickens and rampaging goats already bustling around his head, Eric parked the Aston at the far end of the cul-de-sac, where the houses were slightly larger and the number plates on the cars a little newer. He triple-checked the lock, took a photo of the car – in case it was robbed and evidence was needed for the police – and walked the rest of the way.

The path to the allotment was more dirt track than road. Bramble bushes lined the sides of the track and a scent of sodden autumn and manure pervaded his lungs. He glanced down and groaned. Two steps in and his handstitched shoes were already caked in a layer of tar-like mud. Had he known, he would have brought a pair of trainers, or better still hiking boots, but then how could he have known that he would inherit a sixty-square-metre patch of potatoes, as opposed to an eight-hundred-thousand-pound house? Clenching his teeth, Eric tried not to focus on the ear-wrenching squelch of his feet and walked on.

By the time he reached the gate, it was not only his shoes but his socks and bespoke tailored trousers that were black with mud. He bent down, as if to sniff, before he changed his mind, took a deep breath, and kept walking.

A wooden hut, a little longer than a caravan, was situated by the large metal gates. The wood was aged, crumbling, and splintered and emitted a smell of extreme damp and overripe cabbages. A small window was positioned around five feet off the ground, and a glass-covered notice board was nailed to the side of it. Various subject issues were covered on the notices, from Labrador retriever puppies needing homes to information about a beekeeping workshop which was dated three months back.

Eric took a few steps forwards and paused. The area behind the hut was far bigger than he'd expected. Five acres? Ten? He scoured the view. Really, he had no idea. Rows and rows of tended plots disappeared off into the distance. Hundreds of poles stood teepeed with vines coiled up around the outside while dozens of sheds marked out one border from another. There were greenhouses, polytunnels, and scarecrows, along with tarpaulin coverings and oversized planters. Some plots had their own fence while others merged from one to the next. And even in November, when almost all the trees had given up and discarded their leafage in favour of a more skeletal look, there was green everywhere. Eric felt a small gasp of unexpected awe escape from above his Adam's apple.

'So, you've come then?'

Eric spun around.

The man's face was weather-beaten and wrinkled. He sported a ragged shock of white hair, and his vivid green eyes scowled almost to the point of closure. However, the man's most exceptional feature was his beard. Eric estimated, somewhat conservatively, that facial hair of that grandeur would have involved at least two decades of grooming and nurturing. He was unsure whether he was exceptionally impressed by this show of dedication or appalled by the lack of personal hygiene. The man glowered, narrowing his eyes even further.

'About time you got here,' he said.

CHAPTER 2

THE MAN OFFERED no more conversation. Stepping out of the shed, he shut the plywood door, clicked a padlock securely across it, and ambled into the maze of vegetation.

A few steps in he stopped, turned back to Eric, and growled, 'Are you coming, or what?'

Eric hurried to catch up.

Despite the age difference and sluggish speed set by his guide, Eric struggled to keep up. The old man trundled on, oblivious to the quagmire sinking beneath his feet. Eric picked his route on tiptoes. The trodden-down paths were no more solid than they'd been on the track outside, and more than once Eric lost his foot in a concealed mud pit.

On closer inspection, the effects of the cold weather were more apparent than he'd first thought. Most of the bushes had been reduced to spindly-twigged carcasses, and the grass which sprouted from the ground was wilted and yellow as it drooped over the soil. The musty scent of compost caught in his nostrils as the wetness continued to seep through his trousers.

He hugged himself and shivered as he walked. The temperature had dropped, and the lethargic speed was doing nothing to help ward off the cold. In front of him, the old man hunched as he hobbled on. Every now and then he'd stop to cough, giving Eric a few seconds to catch up.

'I didn't catch your name,' Eric said, hoping conversation would distract from the increasing chill and ruined garments.

'I didn't give it,' the man said, then proceeded to erupt into a coughing fit so violent his face glowed magenta.

'Are you okay?' Eric asked after a minute of coughing.

It was more of a lung-wrenching hack than a normal level cough, and Eric was concerned that the old man might drop down there and then. The last thing he wanted to do was perform mouth to mouth when faced with a beard like that. Besides, Eric wasn't exactly sure how to get back to the car without his guide. Fortunately, the man waved away Eric's offer of help.

'I'm old,' he said when the fit finally subsided. 'Bits of you stop working when you're old. You'd know that if you ever spent any time around old people.'

Eric's jaw tightened. He fixed it with the best smile he could muster.

'Is it much farther?' he said 'Only I need to be getting back. I've got lots —'

'Lots to do at the office,' the man finished for him. 'Aye, I know. Don't you worry. I'm not gonna keep you from your precious work. It's just up 'ere.'

Fairly certain he'd been insulted, and unsure as to why this old man grated on him so much, Eric followed him around one last left turn to a point where they could go no farther. They were on the edge of the allotment next to a thick hedge, behind which smoke rose from the chimneys of the pebble-dashed houses. Turning his attention to the plot in front of him, Eric blinked a few times. He took a step closer and blinked again. A small lump swelled in his throat.

Perfectly parallel lines sprang up from the dirt, all evenly separated and equal in size. At one end a dozen beanpoles, decidedly bare but perfectly balanced, waited patiently for spring to test their sturdiness. In the far corner stood a shed, newly painted in rust-red, with a veranda big enough for four and gingham curtains just visible through the glass. Unlike many of the other allotments, which were covered with cheap netting, or else left entirely bare, these bean poles and berry bushes had their own house built impeccably from chicken wire and two by fours. A sliding barn door provided an entrance at one end.

Each row of the allotment was labelled with a small plastic marker, which had the name of the vegetable printed in precise block letters, and even now, in the flurries of autumn, not a single blade of grass was out of place. With his heart in his throat, Eric stepped across one of the beds and placed his fingers against the wooden slats of the shed. A faint smell of paint hugged the air around it. He'd had no idea. All the times his father had spoken about the allotment, Eric had envisioned some grubby plot of land with a patch of potatoes and some green tomato plants wilting in the corner of a greenhouse. This was magnificent. Beautiful. He bent down to the ground and wrapped his hands around one of the plants.

'What the 'eck do you think you're doing?'

Eric jumped back, his moment with the vegetable severed.

'What do you mean?'

'Not this one. That one.'

The old man recommenced his coughing fit and after taking a minute to right himself pointed over Eric's shoulder. Confused and with his heart still racing from surprise, Eric turned to face the plot behind him. His heart sank.

This was everything he'd imagined and worse. Ten times worse, possibly a hundred times. In fact, Eric wasn't even sure that his imagination could've stretched far enough to conjure an image so heinous and abhorrent. Tangles of roots and leaves twisted upwards creating a two-foot blanket of nastiness that covered the entire ground. He could see nettles and thorns and things with jagged leaves that looked like they'd tear at your skin the instant you touched them. Insects, the like of which Eric had not come across since his childhood nightmares, with hairy legs and countless eyes, scurried around in the debris, while flies of various dimensions and wing formations hovered above what Eric could only assume was once a compost heap. There was a greenhouse, or he thought there was, hidden under a mass of browning vines at one end of the plot; and a water butt, tilted at an angle, filled with stagnant, green, and algae-ridden sludge. Rake ends, rusted and clearly tetanus risks, speared out from the undergrowth, and the overall aroma of the place was somewhere between an arboretum, a silage spreader, and a backed-up service station lavatory.

His pulse continued its uncertain staccato rhythm as Eric took a tentative step forward.

'What was that?' he said.

'What?'

'Something moved. In there.'

His guide shrugged. ''Spect it's rats. Nestin' in for winter.'

'Rats?' Eric stepped back.

'Probably.'

The man came and stood next to him. And stayed there.

It was a bizarre moment in which the silence rapidly went from contemplative, to slightly awkward, then downright uncomfortable. Had he been on his own, Eric would have probably picked up something near and thrown it into the rat's nest in front of him, or at least kicked something hard and with a substantial dash of profanities. But in the presence of a man who looked as close to joining his dad under the ground as any man he had met, Eric felt the need to withhold any of these possible outbursts. Besides, he was at a loss for words.

He didn't know why he was surprised. He knew his father had been a narrow-minded, egotistical bastard at the best of times, and it wasn't like he didn't have a spiteful side either; Eric had been on the wrong end of it enough times before. But still. Eric hadn't expected this.

'Perhaps if you'd come down last year,' the man said.

Eric raised a sceptical eyebrow and continued to stare at the refuse site in front of him.

'Harder work than people think, keeping an allotment. 'Specially at his age. With no help. And when his hands went —'

'When his hands went, yes I know.'

With a sharp intake of breath, Eric surveyed his legacy one last time before swivelling on his heel.

'Thank you for showing me the place,' he said, stretching out a hand to bid farewell. 'I'm sure I'll see you again,' he added.

'I'm sure you will. And subs are due on the third of January, so don't be late.'

'Subs?' Eric said.

'So technically, he's left me nothing,' Eric said. 'He secured a tenancy. What the hell does that mean, anyway?'

He was back at home, sitting on the sofa with a Thai take-away on his lap. Even in Sally, the drive home had been a torment. The car had been as flawless as ever – the growl of the engine, the hum of the wheels – but his insides roiled as he swerved around the bends and kept his foot on the accelerator. He wouldn't be surprised if a ticket came through the post in the next couple of days. Wouldn't that be the absolute cherry on the whole damn thing? Eric bit a prawn in two and swallowed it without chewing. What kind of man would do this to his son? What kind of parent would deliberately ensure that his child continued to suffer his miserable wrath even after he was dead and buried? And even if he'd left him a normal allotment, as opposed to the rat-infested, GHO admonished, cesspit of a plot he'd received, where exactly did he think Eric would find the time to go down to Burnham once a week with his work schedule?

Abi was already in bed by the time he got back. He had showered, crept in to kiss her goodnight, then traipsed back downstairs. Suzy had had the takeaway menu ready, along with a large gin and tonic, complete with ice and lemon.

'He left it to the church. The church. The house, the contents. Everything. When did he even go to church?'

'That's not fair. You know they were good to him when your mother died.'

Eric took a large swig of his drink.

'That was years ago. And what about mum's stuff? What about all her jewellery? Her engagement ring? That was meant to go to you. To Abi. Who the heck does he think he is?' He knocked back the rest of the gin then swapped his glass for his chopsticks and scooped up a mouthful of noodles.

Suzy scooched over to his end of the sofa and began to rub his shoulders.

'I'm sure he had his reasons,' she said.

Eric placed his takeaway on the ground and shifted forwards to make room.

'That I don't doubt.'

Suzy dug her thumbs into the top of Eric's spine and began to massage his back and neck. 'God, do I need this,' Eric said.

With her legs wrapped around him, Suzy kneaded her knuckles into his muscles and tried to work out some of the knots. She smelt of lemons, citrusy and fresh, and her hair tickled his skin as she worked. Eric sighed. Even Suzy's magic hands weren't working the way they normally did. He could feel a migraine coming on.

He and Suzy had bought their five-bedroom terraced in Islington nearly eleven years ago to the day, with the sale going through only two months before they'd married. She'd received a sizeable chunk of money as part of her divorce settlement, and Eric – having inherited his father's mindset for thrift and saving – also had a substantial contribution to add to the deposit. It had been in a miserable state back then, with leaking radiators, floorboards that sprang up if you trod on the wrong end, and a smell of cat piss that would disappear in the winter, only to come back even more noxious and pungent than you remembered in the spring.

It had taken three years of hard slog to get it into a liveable condition, and had it not been for the imminent arrival of Abi it would probably have taken even longer. Looking back on it now Eric missed those days. Life was easy as newlyweds. No big decisions except what colour tiles to use in the bathroom and how many plug sockets they needed on the landing.

Despite the occasional recurrence of the cat piss aroma, Eric still loved his house just as much, if not more than back then. He loved the location and the big bay windows and open fireplaces. He liked the low maintenance courtyard garden and the fact that the wide road meant there was almost always room to park the car out front. He loved the proximity to work and nice bars, for the odd occasion he got to go out for an evening. There was also the substantial appreciation in value over the last eleven years. Eric had worked hard to earn this house, and he was proud of it. At least that was one thing his father couldn't take away from him.

CHAPTER 3

A S EXPECTED, MONDAY saw the return of one of Eric's heinous and intolerable migraines. Had he not had two team meetings to run, along with a working lunch with Greg, plus after-work drinks with one of the chief executives of their latest partnering venture, he'd probably have considered working from home until lunch. As it was, he was on the tube at seven and sat in his office by seven twenty-five, trying desperately to evade the dagger-like stabbing behind his eyeballs.

It was a respectable office for someone of his age. Big windows – but not a river view – a solid oak desk, a mini-fridge, and a bookshelf crammed with books on *the art of business* which he had every intention of reading as soon as he got a spare minute. The carpet was vacuumed daily by a cleaner he never saw, and the space possessed an aroma of polished glass with undercurrents of mineral water and freshly pressed shirts. However, none of that helped with his migraine in the slightest.

In an attempt to lessen the pain – that felt like someone

was consistently firing a nail gun through his left temple only to have it ricocheted back off the right – Eric had worn his glasses. The narrow-rimmed, square-framed spectacles had the ability to transform him from a successful, attractive thirty-seven-year-old – albeit with a fairly weak chin and slightly receding hairline – to a geeky-looking seventeen-year-old, with an influx of unwanted memories to match.

Eric had worked for Hartley and Nelson since he finished university, and besides the CEOs, one of the senior associate directors, and Margery on the front desk, he'd been there longer than any other employee. For a long time, Eric had worn that fact as a badge of honour. Recently, however, it had become something he tended to withhold as opposed to reveal.

Eric had, throughout the years, looked at other jobs, applied for a few and even been offered a couple, but Hartley and Nelson had always been there with a backup offer, another promotion, one more step on the eternal ladder of leadership. He was comfortable, established, knew what he was doing, and most days could do the job in his sleep. People could rely on him.

His current position was Junior Associate Director, a title vague enough that more senior staff could still dump awkward accounts, clients, and tedious matters on him, but senior enough that he had his own office and spent an awful lot of his time running meetings and disseminating information. For the last two years, the business had been plagued with restructuring rumours. Some suggested abolishing all the Associate Directors in favour of regional ones. Others said they would be going down the sector route; educational works directors, public service works directors, and so on and so forth. Whichever route they picked, Eric wasn't fussed as long as it was a notch higher up the ladder. More money, more power, more respect.

A knock severed his thoughts.

'Come in,' Eric said.

The door swung open. The man who appeared behind it had hair so blonde it was near white, with piercing grey eyes and a watch around his wrist bigger than Eric's fist. He strode, hands on hips, to the centre of the room, before glancing at Eric and emitting a long, high-pitched hiss. 'All right, geezer, you look terrible. And rocking the Harry Potter look again I see.'

Eric pushed his glasses down to the end of his nose and rubbed his eyes.

'Migraine,' he said.

'Figured. Seriously mate. You need to take some time off. It's not good you being here. I mean, just looking at you's making me feel queasy. Honestly, I might. Here. In your office. I'm not kidding.'

He grabbed Eric's wastepaper basket from the floor and proceeded to make retching noises into it. Half a minute later, he dropped it back down on the ground, two feet from its original position.

When Greg had first arrived at the firm, Eric had been less than impressed. His constant need for attention, a penchant for saying things exactly as he saw them, and south London accent would put any aspiring soap actor to shame. He wore shirts and socks that Eric deemed more suitable for a night out in Soho than a respectable recruitment firm, and in his first year racked up more complaints with HR over inappropriate comments to the female staff than the rest of the company had in a decade. Two years down the line and Eric still wasn't particularly keen on the guy, but he was the closest thing he had to a work friend. Besides, with a tongue sharper than a sashimi chef's knife and an uncanny ability to slither out of any situation, Eric felt it wise to keep him onside. Still, Eric winced as Greg perched himself on the corner of his desk and began to rattle his pen pot.

'How did the stuff with your dad go? Dinner on you from now on?'

'Not quite that straightforward.'

'Nah, it never is. When my old man died, it was a right mess. Three ex-wives, twelve step-kids. He's the reason I got the snip at seventeen.' Greg pulled a pen out of the pot and lifted it towards his mouth. Eric plucked it back from between his fingers and dropped it down beside his computer.

'Was there something you wanted, Greg?'

'What?' Greg looked at his hand, seemingly confused as to where the pen had gone. 'Nah. Well, just thought I'd give you the 'eds up that the boss is doing his rounds. After next month's projections if you've got them?'

'I'm working on them now.'

'Dandy. Well, I better get on with mine. By the way, have you seen the new girl in HR?'

'No, I don't think so.'

'Oh, you'd know my son, you'd know. I mean, she's got knockers that'd take your eye —'

'Is that Jack heading to your office now?'

Eric did a mock peer over Greg's shoulder.

'Are you sure?'

'I think so, I mean I could be wrong, but ...'

Greg bolted for the door, scattering the pencils all over Eric's desk as he went. Eric sighed. How was it only eight o'clock?

Jack Nelson was a legend in Eric's eyes. Having co-founded the recruitment agency Hartley and Nelson at just twenty-eight, he'd gone on to establish a network of over 400 offices nationwide, owned properties in Europe, Asia, and America, and still ensured that every one of his six and a half thousand employees received a handwritten Christmas and birthday card every year. Rumour had it he spent the entire two weeks of his January vacation writing out all the cards for the upcoming twelve months and that you could tell the ones his wife, Jo, had written by how loopy the *J* was, but Eric had not bothered to investigate this detail. Even after all this time, Eric couldn't help but feel a rush of adrenaline whenever Jack spoke. The man was, after all, his hero.

That morning Jack Nelson glided into Eric's office wearing a royal blue suit offset with an emerald green tie. His hair was silver, but in a way that made it seem like going grey had been his choice. It wasn't just Eric who had a crush on him. 'Swoony' was the word that Suzy would most frequently use in reference to Eric's boss. 'Swoony and dashing.'

He had the airs and appearance of a man from a former generation. The type who knew the difference between a lounge suit and regular suit and undoubtedly owned several of each. His shoes were always polished, but his laces loose, yet they never came undone. He was truly a master of many arts.

Eric stood up as his boss entered the room.

'Jack,' he said.

'Eric.' Jack pushed the door closed in a considered and thoughtful manner, filling the air with tangs of Colombian coffee and genuine leather as he did. 'Got a minute?'

'Of course. Of course. Please, sit down. If it's those projections you want, I was just in the middle of emailing them to you now.'

Jack waved the comment away with his right hand as he pulled out a chair with his left.

'They can wait,' he said. 'Actually, I wanted to have a word with you about something.'

'A word? Sure. Yes. No problem. No problem at all.'

Eric felt the tie tighten around his neck, and a thin film of sweat permeated through the collar of his shirt. Jack didn't have words with people. Jack was a busy man. If you wanted to speak to Jack he had to make time for you; appointments were made weeks in advance. Unless it was something bad, some-thing *really* bad. A lump swelled at the top of Eric's throat as he threw a glance down at his phone. There were no reminders flashing wildly on the screen telling him that he'd missed some important deadline or event. Still, his pulse levelled a notch higher. He had a lunch meeting booked in for this Saturday, and a brunch for the one that followed, but there was nothing he was meant to have attended over the weekend, was there? No, of course not. He'd emailed Jack's PA two weeks ago and told her of the situation. Nonetheless, the lump in his throat persisted.

'Is there something wrong?' he said, trying hard to sound casual despite the ever-increasing constriction around his windpipe.

'Why don't you take a seat?' Jack said.

Bordering on hyperventilation, Eric lowered himself down into his chair. Jack followed suit in the chair opposite. He crossed his legs, then placed his hands on his lap.

An excruciating pause followed. The pummelling in Eric's chest escalated to such a level he believed he was about to vomit. The sweat around his collar had now reached dripping level and his migraine – fearing being upstaged in the pain department – doubled its intensity, causing the whole of Eric's vision to become fringed with a blue-white halo.

'So,' Jack said, nestling his hands deeper into his lap. 'I hear you've been having a bit of a time with it all at the minute?'

'I have?'

'With your father?' Jack said. 'I'm right in thinking he passed away last month, aren't I?'

Eric shook away the neurosis with a relieved sigh. 'Sorry, yes of course. Last month. It was a bit of a surprise. I mean, he was old but still. None of us were expecting it is what I mean.'

Jack nodded slowly as if absorbing every syllable that Eric had blabbered out.

'I was having a look through your file the other day,' he said. 'You know that you're entitled to five days compassionate leave a year?'

'I did know that, yes.'

'But you've not taken a day.'

'No, not yet.'

'Not ever. Well not in the last five years.'

Eric paused. Five years, was it really that long since his mum died? His chest ached. Five years ago, and yet he could still see the casket and smell the lilies as they rose in eddies around her pale skin. Abi had been two at the time, and Suzy had suggested they leave her in London with her godparents for the day. Eric had disagreed, insisting she'd be fine. The truth was he'd wanted them all there together, as if his mother could see one final display of his fatherhood. He'd wanted it to be perfect, that last moment with her, and he needed Abi there for that. Five minutes into the service, and after Abi's four hundredth 'Daddy', Suzy had taken her outside. Eric spent the rest of the service next to his father, trying to decide if he could slip out after reading the eulogy without anyone noticing.

'Look.' Jack's voice brought him back into the room. 'I know these times are never easy,' he said with a mastered look of professional compassion. 'And we all like to deal with things in our own ways, but you've got a lot of time racked up, holidays, sick days. No one would mind if you wanted to take a few weeks, longer even, and get your head around this. Spend some time with your girls.'

He rose from his chair. Eric followed suit.

'No one's saying you have to, of course. But the option's there if you want it.'

'Thank you, sir. I'll think about it.'

'I hope you do.' In two strides, Jack had reached the door and stopped. He twisted the handle, ready to leave, before turning back into the room for one last time. 'And you won't forget those projections, will you?' he said.

Eric did think about the offer for a whole fifteen minutes. That was when his email pinged, and his phone started ringing, and even the migraine had to play second fiddle to the chaos that ensued following the news that one of their clients – one of the largest chains of academy schools in the whole of the UK – was thinking of dropping them as their agency. Even Greg looked slightly panicked by the announcement. The whole office scurried as they rang number after number, trying to arrange meetings to resolve the issue. Eric buzzed through to his receptionist. He would be needing plenty of coffee this morning, could he prepare it for him? And would he ring Suzy when he got a chance? It didn't look like he was going to be home in time to take Abi to her ballet recital after all.

By the time Eric got home, a full body numbness had replaced his migraine. Upstairs, Abi was already in a bed. Her chest rose and fell as she murmured in her sleep, clutching a pair of pink, and slightly grubby, ballet pumps. Eric leaned down and kissed her forehead, absorbing the air around her with a deep inhale. Something about Abi's scent always reminded Eric of black-berries. Blackberries and candyfloss. Wondering if all children smelt that good, he slipped the ballet pumps out from her grip and placed them on the floor before switching off her light.

'Sleep tight, princess,' he said.

Downstairs, Suzy was curled on the sofa with a notepad and pencil in her hand and remnants of her takeaway on the coffee table. Her lips fluttered and wobbled as every inhale and exhale resonated in a snore. For a second, Eric considered taking out his phone and videoing her like this. They'd had more than one bickering match over whether she actually snored, and a video of this would put the matter to bed for good. However, his phone was in the kitchen and even that was too far to move right now. Hooking his elbows underneath her, Eric lifted his wife up, staggered up the staircase, and carried her into the bedroom. Pencil. That was Suzy's scent. Eau de graphite. He breathed it in and brushed an invisible hair behind her ear.

'Your dinner's in the oven,' she mumbled as he tucked her in.

'Don't worry,' he said. 'I'll find it.'

CHAPTER 4

I T HAD BEEN three weeks since Eric had sat in the
office of Eaves and Doyle, yet he'd still not had a chance
to take Sally out once. For the first two nights, she'd sat
on the road in front of the house, hidden under a dust cover,
barely an inch of her tyres visible to the world. But Eric had
panicked. There had been heavy rain that first night and he
wasn't entirely sure he'd wrapped her up properly. Every thirty
minutes he found himself jumping out of bed, opening the
curtains, and peering down to check if she still looked okay.
Sometimes a distant look wasn't enough to quench the fears,
and he'd be compelled to don his jacket and brave the freezing
cold and gale force winds. Then there was the impossibility of
transferring the insurance while she was out on the street. Add
to that the fact that Suzy had had to park the Audi a ten-
minute walk away in order to find a space. All in all, having
Sally at the house was a no-go. Fortunately, he called in a
favour with a friend to borrow his garage over in South Wood-
ford until he could think of a more permanent solution.

When they'd been at university together, Ralph had been

the playboy of playboys, never sleeping in the same bed twice, never sober long enough to remember where his own bed was. Eric had simultaneously looked up to and down on his comrade for his endless stamina, unlimited supply of chat-up lines, and unscrupulous demeanour. Fast forwards two decades, and Ralph now had three kids, a semi-detached house, and a golden Labrador retriever called Carson in reference to their favourite BBC period drama, a double bill of which was about as exciting as one of his Saturday nights got nowadays. With the youngest of the brood barely a month old, there was no risk of Ralph taking Sally out for a cheeky off-the-books spin without Eric; getting to have a shower was a luxury for him at the moment.

With Sally sorted, life went on as expected. At work, the academies were playing hardball with the company and still hadn't settled on a mutually conducive agreement despite everyone's best efforts. Eric hated dealing with companies like this. Hartley and Nelson were offering them a fair deal, and the company had more than enough money to pay for it, but they still had to take it down to the wire, skimping on every last penny they could. Eric had had to hand over his weekends to paperwork and emails and even had to slip out during Abi's school production of *Mamma Mia* to answer his phone. In fairness, the timing couldn't have been better; in Eric's opinion, a large proportion of children shouldn't be allowed within fifty feet of any raised platform on the off-chance they accidentally misconstrued it as a stage. Still, Suzy hadn't been best pleased by his sudden disappearance, although that was probably because she couldn't think of her own credible excuse to escape.

Apparently, the entire rendition of *Dancing Queen* had been sung a semitone-and-a-half flat and was accompanied by a boy on tambourine who appeared to burst into sporadic grand-mal seizures, and a girl on the recorder who not only gave the front row several burst eardrums but also a solid soaking of saliva to boot. Still, Abi had enjoyed taking part.

After nearly four weeks of toing and froing, endless emails, and a month's salary in double-shot, skimmed milk, no froth cappuccinos, today was the day they were finally settling on the agreements. The representatives from the academies were arriving at eleven and Eric had everything prepared. He sat in his chair and took a sip of his coffee, followed by a sniff. Something about it wasn't quite right; the milk perhaps? He took another sip. There was a near meltdown last year when one of the new receptionists thought everyone could do with a health kick and swapped the beans in the grinder for decaf. No one would be so stupid as to try that again. Eric took one more sip, decided he wasn't really in the mood for coffee, and parked the cup on the edge of his desk just as his phone began to ring.

He stared at the screen. While the caller was unknown, there was something decidedly familiar about the area code. He watched it ring for another second, trying to place it, and hovered his hand over the red button. Half a second later his thumb swiped down and across and opened the line to the unknown number.

'Eric Sibley here,' he said.

'Hello, Mr Sibley,' a male voice spoke. 'This is Christian Eaves here. I hope you're well.'

Eric blinked. Christian Eaves? Why was that name familiar? He pondered it for a moment. Down the end of the line, a throat cleared.

'Mr Sibley, are you still there? Like I said, It's Christian Eaves here. From Eaves and Doyle. The solicitors.'

Eric was struck by an image of cheap furniture and Blu-Tack, swiftly accompanied by an uncomfortable squirming in the pit of his stomach.

'Of course, Christian. What can I do for you?'

'Well, Mr Sibley. I was just seeing if everything is all right.'

'All right? Yes, well, busy, busy. But other than that —'

'Only I have it on good authority that you haven't visited the allotment since the day of our meeting?' He paused. Eric swallowed. 'I'm sure you remember that in order for the car to stay in your possession, you must ensure that the allotment is maintained on a weekly basis.'

Eric straightened his back and swallowed again, the squirming in his stomach intensified.

'Mr Sibley? Are you still there?'

'Sorry, pardon? Yes, yes I'm still here.'

'Mr Sibley –'

'Eric please.'

'Eric, then. I'm fairly certain I made the conditions of your father's will unambiguous. However, in case you don't remember the conditions, it is stated that if you do not tend to the allotment, the car shall be removed from your possession.'

'It has been a crazy month,' Eric began, then added enthusiastically, 'and I've been very ill. Very ill. Hospitalised in fact. Dengue fever.'

'Oh, well, I'm sorry to hear that. Obviously you're feeling better now?'

'Yes, fortunately, yes, much better,'

'Good. So, we can expect to see you at the allotment this weekend?'

'Well, I, I –'

'Brilliant. Because I would hate this to be anything more than a misunderstanding. And while you're on the line, Mr Sibley, there are a few more questions I need you to answer for me.'

'On good authority? On whose authority?' Eric seethed. 'I'll tell you whose authority. It's that damn miserable git with the plot next door. I could go seven days a week and the bastard would still say I hadn't been there once.' Eric was on his second gin and tonic of the evening and had no intention of slowing down. 'Twenty minutes he kept me on the phone. I'm surprised he didn't ask for our bloody wedding date. Bloody good job the academy people were late, or Jack would have had my balls. Thank God that went through.'

'He was only doing his job.'

'He was being bloody nosy. I had to give him Ralph's number too, just to corroborate information. I bet he was straight on the phone to him.' Eric took another large swig. 'You know what he thinks don't you? He thinks I've sold it. I bet that's what he thinks. Well, I bloody well should. It's my damn inheritance. I should sell it. I'm going to sell it.'

'No, you're not. It isn't yours to sell.'

Eric held his malignancy in and sighed heavily. Suzy took his empty glass and swapped it for a full one.

'Maybe I should give it up. Let the church have it. I mean it's just a car. After all, we can always go and buy another vintage DB4.'

Suzy gave him a withering look.

'I mean, we'd have to re-mortgage the house,' Eric said. 'And Abi would have to go to that school down the road where all the kids smell like baked beans and do their homework on used kitchen roll, but we'd get by.'

'You're not going to give it up,' Suzy said. 'We both know that.'

Eric thumbed the rim of his glass until it let out a deep, low hum. 'No,' he said. 'I guess not.'

'So, I guess we're all heading to Burnham this weekend?'

Twenty minutes later, Eric was sitting at his desk with Suzy peering over his shoulder. His laptop was open on the *Burn-ham-on-Crouch Village Website*, specifically the Classifieds. The page contained various lists and headings in colourful blues and greens with a serene picture of the River Crouch and sailing boats set as the background.

'I'm not sure this is what he meant,' Suzy said. 'I thought you said *you* had to maintain the allotment?'

Eric continued typing away in the little rectangular box. 'This is just a short-term solution to buy us a little time. Anyway, I'm maintaining it. I'll just be paying someone else to do the digging.'

'I'm not convinced.'

'Trust me. This will see us all a lot happier. Mr Eaves included.'

With a satisfied smile, Eric clicked enter.

'There. All done.'

Half a second later his succinctly worded advert appeared on *Burnham-on-Crouch Village Classifieds* page. "*Gardener wanted for allotment plot. Can grow anything. Will pay good money.*"

'Now all we have to do is wait for the applicants.'

To both his and Suzy's surprise, there were three messages waiting for them in their inbox when they awoke. One was from a lady named Nancy, who, in her own words, had a special connection to all things floral but a most profound bond with the blooms of the far east; orchids being her particular special-ity. She'd also attached a photograph of her window sill, the glass behind entirely obscured by the two dozen potted speci-mens of all shapes and colours.

'It looks like a funeral home. Or a hospice,' Eric said.

'Be kind,' Suzy replied. 'Besides, you said they could grow anything. Who are the other ones from?'

Eric clicked open. The second message was from a landscape gardening company. Eric considered the option. Expensive, yes, but at least the job would be done. Their website gleamed with displays of ornamental gardens, hand-crafted pergolas, and water features. Although extremely impressive, Eric thought that might be a little way off kilter and so continued to the last message. The final emailer was also a woman, by the name of Janice.

They wrote: 'RE: Allotment; Am an experienced gardener looking to extend my crops. Please contact me should you wish to know more of my credentials.'

'I like her,' Eric said instantly upon finishing. Suzy frowned.

'You don't know anything about her. She doesn't say anything.'

'Exactly. She doesn't ask any questions. She doesn't send creepy photos. She's perfect.'

'She might be old.'

'So?'

'You said the allotment was a state. A health hazard. You can't have an old woman working around in a rat's nest. Especially not now, not over the winter.'

'I'm only asking her to do a bit of weeding. And it's not like I've got her on a time frame. She can have months. She can have years. As long as it's getting better, not worse, then we're all winning. Besides, she doesn't sound old. How many old people use the internet?'

Suzy frowned again. 'I don't feel good about this,' she said.

'You're worrying about nothing,' Eric said, then turned back to the computer and began to type his reply.

CHAPTER 5

FORTUNATELY, JANICE DIDN'T seem the slightest bit put off by the current storms sweeping the UK. After agreeing on an hourly rate over email and arranging for her to start that week, Eric received another message from his newly employed gardener asking to confirm the allotment's site and plot. Until that point, he hadn't realised there was more than one allotment site in Burnham, and he didn't think that writing something along the lines of *vermin-infested cesspit in the corner next to miserable old git* as means of plot identification would greatly enamour her to the position. He decided to wait until lunch and have a rummage around in the files the solicitor had sent him.

Over the weekend, the office had been decorated in an attempt to inject a more Christmassy feel to their working environment. Silver and red decorations hung from the light fittings, tinsel was attached to all the window frames, and some dubiously placed mistletoe hung in large bunches outside the elevator door, in the stairwell up to the rooftop, and above the entrance to the ladies' toilets. Eric would hate to work in HR at any time, he thought, but Christmas must be the pits.

Through the glass windows, he spied Greg cosying up to one of the new graduate interns. She appeared to have a bit more spunk about her than a lot of them, with a nose piercing, a tattoo on her ankle, and a Christmas jumper sporting a knitted image of two fornicating reindeer. Eric desperately hoped she might give Greg a well-deserved rebuke for whatever misogynistic chat-up line he was currently using, but instead, she flicked her hair, covered her mouth, and let out a coy, little giggle. Eric went back to his work disappointed.

The remainder of the day was spent working through his mountainous to-do list, which – in the prioritisation of the academies contract – had managed to reach the length of a fully grown Burmese python with an overactive pituitary gland. He had an unsatisfyingly dry pastrami sandwich at his desk for lunch, four cups of coffee, three of which were stone cold by the time he got off the phone to drink them, and one bite of an exceedingly crumbly Ginger Nut biscuit. He dared not take a second bite after spewing crumbs everywhere in the first instance during his meeting with Jack. When he finally glanced at the clock on the corner of his computer, Eric did a double take. He quickly fired off a text to Suzy.

'Leaving in an hour,' he wrote, knowing full well he had three times that to go.

It was half-past eight when Eric finally decided to call it a day. The street lights had been glowing yellow for hours, and overly enthusiastic Christmas shoppers hurried about outside. Wrapped up in fur-hooded coats, colourful mittens, and waterproof boots, they scurried in and out of the cold, desperate to secure all the unnecessary bargains they could. Eric gripped the lid of his laptop, went to push it shut, then stopped.

'Bollocks,' he said.

It took him another ten minutes to find the documents from the solicitor. When he scrolled down, he found that not only was the site address and plot number given, there was also an A4 site map attached which gave a Google image of the entire allotment, on which his plot was clearly circled in red.

'It even looks like a disaster from space,' Eric said to himself.

Omitting any form of formalities or greetings, Eric fired off another email to Janice. Arcadia Road Allotment. Plot 54, he wrote, then attached the map for good measure.

When Eric arrived home, Suzy was in her study writing. He poked his head around the corner of the door and knocked lightly on the frame. She removed her headphones and swivelled around on her chair.

'You're late,' she said.

'I know, I'm sorry. Time just got away from me.' He ambled over and kissed her on the forehead.

'Have you eaten?' he said.

'I ate with Abi, but there's some quiche left for you in the oven and there's a bag of salad you can have with it in the fridge.' Eric considered the appeal of limp-leafed lettuce and rubbery egg pie.

'I'll get something delivered. Is Abi asleep?'

'Not sure. She should be, but she was still reading when I last went up there. You can go upstairs and check.'

Eric planted another peck on the top of Suzy's head then tiptoed upstairs and into Abi's room.

In daylight, Abi's bedroom was a multitude of pinks, from the princess duvet cover to the sparkly circus tent. A massif of soft toys sat beneath the window ledge. They had bought her toy cars to play with, diggers, and trucks, but she'd veered towards the dolls and tea sets. By the time Abi was five years old, they'd given up. When it came to clothes, she'd chosen her own for years now, and while occasionally she'd pick something a little left of the field – like her superhero dungarees or NYC baseball cap – most of the time it was the dresses that won.

The room was dark, save for a turtle-shaped night light that projected images of stars onto the ceiling above. Eric crept across to the bed and leant over his sleeping daughter. As frequently happened, Abi had fallen asleep with her head on a book, her hair splayed out across the pillow. As gently as he could, Eric reached over, lifted her head from the bed, and slipped the book out from beneath her. She stirred and moaned.

'Daddy?' she mumbled, rubbing her eyes.

'I'm here, pumpkin,' he said. 'Now go back to sleep. *Shh, shh*. Close your eyes.'

'I want to show my drawing. Can I show you the drawing I did?'

'In the morning, baby. Close your eyes and go back to sleep. I promise I'll look in the morning.'

She mumbled something more and then wriggled down deeper into the mattress. Eric swept her hair from across her face, exposing a mouse-like ear.

'Night night, my pumpkin,' he said.

Then he shut the door and headed back downstairs trying to decide whether Lebanese or Chinese was to be his takeaway of choice.

Eric opened his eyes only to shut them instantaneously. He winced, squinted, then blinked a few times, slowly allowing

them to adjust to the light. It was warmer than he'd anticipated, and the sun shone through the curtains and illuminated
the room with a whiteness that made it feel like spring. Eric
tried to recall the last time he remembered seeing a morning
that bright.

'Bollocks,' he said as he leapt from the bed.

He scrambled around on the floor, forcing his legs into
yesterday's trousers before grabbing the nearest shirt in the
wardrobe, and flying down the stairs.

Abi was sitting at the kitchen table creating dubious plaits
in her Barbie's hair while Suzy was buttering her toast. Eric
bouldered in, red and sweating, fumbling with his shirt
buttons.

'What the hell, Suze? What's the time? Why did you let me
oversleep?'

Suzy looked up from the butter knife.

'Do you want some breakfast?' she said.

'What? No. Why didn't you wake me?'

Hopping on one foot, Eric struggled with his socks which
refused to go on with the heel at the bottom. Suzy set a plate
in front of Abi, wafting the scent of the warm granary toast
under Eric's nose.

'You said you wanted to sleep,' Suzy said. She glided over
and attempted to brush down Eric's wayward bed-hair with her
hand. Eric flicked her away.

'When? When did I say that?'

'When your alarm went off. And again, when mine did. I
tried to wake you.'

'Well, you should have tried again.'

'I did, and you mumbled something about a half day.'

Eric gritted his teeth. 'When have I ever had a half day?'

'That's what you said,' Suzy insisted.

'Daddy, can I show you my picture now?' Abi said, looking

up from her Barbie and ignoring her breakfast. 'You said you'd look at my picture in the morning.'

'I can't right now, pumpkin,' Eric said, squeezing his feet into his shoes. 'Daddy's late. He's got to get to work.'

'But you said —'

'I'll look at it tonight, okay?'

'But, Daddy.'

'It'll only take two seconds, Eric. You can have a look.'

'Please, Daddy.'

'I don't have two seconds. I'm already an hour late.'

He swiped the piece of buttered toast from Abi's plate then bolted to the door, gripping the bread between his teeth as he picked up his keys, phone, and wallet on route.

'Love you,' Suzy and Abi shouted in unison, although Eric was already out the gate and across the road.

The office toilets were the first chance Eric had to check his appearance, and the discovery that he'd paired an orange tie with a pale green shirt was not a pleasant one. His breath tasted of last night's hummus and gin although after a deep dig in one of his desk drawers, he discovered not only a blue pinstripe tie but an unopened pack of Wrigley's mint gum. He hurriedly unwrapped two sticks and folded them into his mouth.

'You ready, big guy?' Greg appeared at his door. Today he was dressed in skinny, dark-purple denims and a shirt covered in tiny embroidered penguins. He had, however, donned a tie.

'Ready?' Eric said.

'For the dynamic duo. Hartley's in today.' He sat on the edge of Eric's desk and picked up a pack of Post-It notes from beside the computer monitor. 'I thought you had hard-ons about the guy? You, Hartley, Nelson. Isn't that where all the fun happens in your head?'

Eric frowned against the barrage of words.

'That's today?' he said, swallowing repeatedly. 'No. It can't be. Crap. How did I forget that?'

'Dunno, you're the dick who sent about a dozen email reminders last week.'

'Of course. Of course, I did.' Eric tried to regather some composure. He plucked the Post-Its out of Greg's hands. 'Of course it's today. Is he here already?'

'In Nelson's office. Probably wanking off over their bank balances.'

'Okay, great. We'll just give them another five minutes. I'll check everything's sorted, then we'll ask Margery to take them through to the boardroom.'

'Whatever you say.'

'Right. Can you just go and check that it's all set up in there? And remember no flowers in the room. He hates the smell of flowers.'

'Along with garlic, sunlight, and silver bullets apparently.'

Eric ushered Greg out of his office then pulled down the corner blind. With his back against the wall, he closed his eyes, took a few calming deep breaths, and found they made no difference whatsoever. 'Damn, damn, damn.' How could he have overslept? Half day, he hadn't been saying half day at all, it was bloody Hartley day. He kicked the base of his desk, stubbing his toe in the process. How could he have forgotten this was today?

Alistair Hartley was the more silent face of Hartley and Nelson. While he left the day to day running of the firm to Jack, Hartley was still well-known for his tempestuous outbursts or his sudden arrival by private jet from Geneva to cast his wily eye over his domain, demanding info on this account and that account, many of which had been closed for years. It was Hartley who was always threatening to restructure or reconfigure, or just shut up the place entirely. On more than one occasion he'd swept in unannounced, started making ludicrous demands, and fired people on the spot for no discernible reason. Fortunately for those staff, he had no idea who they were or what they did, and after few softening apologies from Jack, they were back at their desks, an amusing story – and probably a small cheque – in their pocket. If Eric were ever to make it to senior associate director, it was all down to getting Alistair Hartley on side during days like today. He took one more long breath which he expelled in a deep hiss. Then he strode out of his office and into the boardroom.

The meeting was the type where everyone, except the person talking, struggled to keep their eyes open. The lights were bright, the windows cracked open to allow a breeze, and an aroma of freshly ground Colombian coffee filled the air, but even that wasn't enough to stifle the yawns. Eric was no exception. Nelson and Hartley took alternate heads at the table while the three senior associate directors and the three junior associate directors – of which Eric and Greg were constituents – filled the seats between. Jack's PA, Graham, was sitting taking minutes while Hartley's entourage of four flitted in and out of the room, disturbing the presenters and completely oblivious to anything other than their lord and master.

One of the senior associate directors was pointing to a coloured bar graph with ambiguous axes and scaling when Eric's phone buzzed in his pocket. His muscles tightened. Fixing his eyes straight ahead and adding an extra nod and a smile, he slipped the phone out onto his lap, glanced to see the caller ID, then tapped the cancel button.

Ralph. Ralph only rang him to whinge. Or to muse and mull over his misspent youth. It was probably a fight with his wife, Sarah, or a hopefully hypothetical question about what to do if you'd got one of the kids trapped in the washing machine. He would call him back this evening; after all, kids were pretty sturdy nowadays. Eric slotted his phone back in his pocket. Thirty seconds later it rang again. Several pairs of eyes rolled in his direction.

'Sorry,' Eric mouthed, a visible heat flushing his cheeks. He cancelled the call again and went to switch the phone off, but as his thumb pressed down, a message pinged up on the screen.

Ring me now.

Eric's chest began beating with an irregular pulse and another two heads shot him unimpressed glares. Smiling widely at his colleagues, he offered a few more constructive nods towards the bar graph. Struggling to ignore what felt like the onset of fatal angina, he attempted to type a reply subtly under the table. Receiving a less than pleasant gesticulation from Greg, Eric reverted to his original plan and switched the phone off. He let out a small sigh of relief as he focused his attention back on the slideshow and the screen that was now showing two differently configured pie charts. One minute later, there was a knock at the door.

'Sorry to interrupt.' It was the intern with the tattoo. 'But there's a telephone call for Mr Sibley. A gentleman called Ralph.'

All eyes went straight to Eric, whose cheeks had transformed from light pink to fire-engine red. His angina progressed to possible heart-attack status. He cleared his throat then offered her his best smile.

'Thank you. If you could tell him I'll call him back when this meeting is over, that would be great.' Eric spoke in as even a tone as he could before turning back to the screen, fake grin firmly in place. The intern, however, did not move.

'What is it?' Hartley barked. 'You heard him, he'll ring the man back.'

The intern squirmed a little, then sucked on her top lip,

her gaze still focused on Eric. 'I think it's rather important,' she said.

'It's fine,' Eric insisted, 'I'll ring him back after.'

She hesitated, still unmoving, as she searched for the right words. 'I think you should ring him back now,' she said.

'For God's sake,' Hartley said. 'Is this a goddamn business we're running here or a call centre?'

'I'm sorry, sir,' Eric said. 'Perhaps I should just go and see what this is about.'

Eric looked at Jack, who gave him a small nod of approval. Keeping his head up – but with his insides feeling like a bag of jellyfish that were undergoing electroshock therapy inside his intestines – Eric pushed himself out of his chair and followed the intern out of the boardroom and into the corridor. It was little satisfaction to see that she, too, was fuchsia with embarrassment.

'Sorry,' she said and handed him the phone.

'Ralph?' Eric said down the line. 'What the hell is it?'

'I don't know what you've done,' Ralph said down the phone. 'But they say they're about to call the police. And I'm fairly certain they mean it.'

Eric left a message stressing an urgent family emergency with the intern – whose name turned out to be Emily – to pass to Jack when the meeting ended.

'Make sure he understands that this was an emergency. A real emergency,' Eric reiterated, as he snatched up his keys and wallet off his desk. 'You understand that? It was an emergency.'

'I get it,' Emily said. 'I hope everything's all right. Is there anything I can do to help?'

Eric didn't reply. He dashed for the elevator and slammed the call button repeatedly.

It was a toss-up between the tube or a cab. A tube would be quicker if all lines were running, but then he wouldn't be able to ring Ralph and find out what was going on. A cab would take longer, but then he might be able to placate the situation on the phone. As it was, he decided that time was of the essence and sprinted down the steps into the underground, swiping his Oyster card, and dashing down onto the platform without missing a step. With barely a bar of signal, he texted Ralph. *I'll be twenty minutes*, he typed. Then he got on the train and prayed.

CHAPTER 6

THREE MEN WERE standing outside the front of Ralph's five-bed, mock-Georgian semi when Eric finally arrived. Ralph, looking like a displaced member of the local am-dram society in a velvet smoking jacket and fleece slippers, was holding a mug in one hand and a baby in the other. Had it been another time Eric would have offered some quick-witted jab about fatherhood taking its toll, but at that precise moment his attention was rather preoccupied.

The other two gentlemen in the driveway were – if possible – even less sartorially skilled than Ralph. One, who was leaning against the drystone wall puffing on a cigarette, wore a fleece zip-up jacket – like the type commonly found in garden centres or animal shops – grey jogging bottoms, and a pair of steel-toe DMs. A set of heavy duty bolt-cutters rested on the wall by his knee, and he noted Eric's arrival with a long exhalation of smoke aimed directly towards him.

The final man, who was wearing a grey hoodie and ripped jeans – that Eric felt offered no serious protection from the current winter climate – was busy on the phone. He kept his mouth tight-lipped, occasionally emitting the odd, *umm, a-huh*, and *gotcha* until he caught sight of Eric. At which point he turned his back to him, covered the phone, and said something into the mouthpiece.

'What the hell is this?' Eric said to no one in particular.

His lungs were burning from panting in freezing air, and despite texting Greg four times to ask for an update on the morning's meeting, he had received no reply. Only Ralph acknowledged him, and from the manner in which he was bouncing the baby on his hip, he was far from happy.

'If you've got me mixed up in something dodgy, Eric —'

'I haven't. I swear.' Eric lifted his hands pleading innocence. 'This has got to be some misunderstanding.'

'I hope so for your sake. Sarah's only just forgiven you for setting light to her table runner last time you were over.'

'That was an accident,' Eric began, then stopped. People who used flammable table cloths to accent their tea-light centrepiece were never going to be people you could reason with.

'Look, give me two minutes and it'll be sorted. I promise.'

Eric stalked back across the drive to the man on the phone.

'It's for you,' the man said before Eric could speak, and thrust the phone towards him. Eric took the device and held it to his ear.

'Hello?' he said.

'Mr Sibley.' Eric recognised the voice immediately.

'What the hell is this? Who the hell do you think you are?'

'I can tell you're upset, Mr Sibley –'

'Damn right I'm upset.'

'But these people are acting under legal authority. They are *bailiffs*.' Mr Eaves emphasised the word just in case Eric wasn't sure what the gentlemen's roles were.

A rush of heat surged through his chest sending his pulse in an upwards soar.

'Well, you can tell them they've had a wasted morning harassing my friend. I'll see those two in a hearse before I see them in my car.'

His outburst was met by silence down the end of the line.

'Mr Sibley, I'm afraid my hands are tied in this matter. The terms of the agreement laid out in your father's will have been broken. As we discussed, only last week, you had to maintain the allotment —'

'I know. Jesus, it was one week ago. It's been seen to. It's *being* seen to.' Eric clenched the phone in his hand as he spoke.

Ralph had recently gone inside, and the two bailiffs were now standing suspiciously close to the garage. Eric breathed deeply and counted to ten in his head.

'I understand that I need to maintain the allotment,' Eric said, slowing down his words in an attempt to regain a little self-control. 'I have every intention of coming down this weekend.' He paused for yet another composure-maintaining breath. 'I can assure you, I'm doing everything in my power to make this situation work.'

There was another long silence. A light knocking travelled down the line. Eric could see Christian Eaves, cheap BIC biro in his hand, tapping it against his Ikea desk. *Tap tap tap. Tap tap tap.* The more Eric focused on it, the louder it got. *Tap tap tap. Tap tap tap.* Eric could feel his fist clench and unclench as he imagined reaching down the invisible phone line, grabbing the pen, and snapping it in two.

'Mr Sibley.' The silence finally broke. 'If it were merely a case of missing yet another week I could perhaps relent, but a more concerning issue of ... solicitation has come to my attention.'

'Solicitation?' The word exploded out of Eric's mouth.

Ralph – who had reappeared in corduroys and with cups of tea for the bailiffs – smirked. Eric's stomach knotted.

'Look —' he began, but the solicitor interrupted him.

'Mr Sibley ... Eric. I feel for you, I do. But I don't have the time for this and neither do you. The conditions have been broken, twice. The car is to be taken out of your possession.'

'No, wait. Please. There must be something. I need that car. I need it. Please.'

A heavy sigh reverberated down the line. Eric could hear his pulse drumming away in his ears. He held his breath.

'Mr Sibley. In case of these events, your father had placed some further documents in my keeping. If you could come down to the office, we could discuss —'

'Yes,' Eric bounced on the spot. 'Yes, when? I'll be there. I'll be down this weekend. Or Friday. I can do Friday.'

'It would have to be today.'

'What?' Eric stopped bouncing.

'You have to come down today. I'm afraid these issues have got to be resolved by the end of the day.'

'But I can't. My boss. The boss,' he stuttered. 'I have to go back to work today. I have to.'

'That's fine. I understand, Mr Sibley. I completely understand.' His voice was relaxed, compassionate. Eric's heart rate relaxed. 'Now if you could just hand the keys over to the two men with the bolt-cutters, we can all be on our way.'

Eric took Sally. It had taken another twenty minutes to persuade Eaves that he was going to drive straight to Burnham and have him call off the men with their bolt-cutters. Still, he wasn't going to leave the car unprotected. Eaves had informed Eric that any misdemeanours from this point – such as taking the car to another location – and he'd be forced to call the police and press charges. Despite Eaves' generally pleasant and somewhat wimpish demeanour, Eric was inclined to believe him.

It was gone one, and Sally had adopted a musty scent from the weeks she'd been cooped up. Eric braced against the cold and wound down the windows. A few miles into the journey, the traffic finally cleared. His shoulders sank into the leather seats and Sally's engine ran with a deep purr that swelled to a roar as Eric pushed his foot to the ground. Still, it was impossible to relax.

Even now, as he prepared to take the A12, it took all of Eric's willpower not to turn back towards the office. If he could at least offer his apologies in person, Hartley might be less inclined to remember him as the idiot who disrupted his last meeting of the year. And it would only add half-an-hour to the journey. At the same time, he reasoned, family emergencies – which was most definitely how this situation was classified – did not usually allow for time to pop into the office and offer explanations. He decided it was best to steer clear.

Layer after layer of grey clouds muted the sun's light, while an incessant wind hissed through the windows and scattered leaves across the road. Eric had become adept at ignoring the admiring waves and envious looks that other drivers gave the car at roundabouts and traffic lights. It was a skill he'd inherited from his father. During the old days, when his mother was still alive and he and his father would go out for afternoon trips, they would avidly avoid areas where wannabe car groupies may congregate, on account of protecting the asset. Antique auctions, craft markets, and garden centres were all out, as were open-air productions and National Trust attractions. Car shows, however, were one of the few places that George let up his blowhard snobbery, and he always attended one or two a year. Stops at service stations always meant separate trips to the toilet on these journeys though, so that one of them could stay and protect Sally from overly amorous admirers, particularly if they had children. And on the rare occasion that they decided to stop and get food, the establishment had to be in possession of a beer garden with a direct view over the carpark.

Eric made the eighty-minute journey without a break and arrived in Burnham at two forty-two, according to his watch. He drove along the High Street, past the Indian restaurant with a large *Under New Management* sign out front, and the fish and chip shop with a five-foot plastic cod hanging in the window. The light drizzle that had been pestering his windscreen for the last twenty minutes started to turn into something more substantial as he pulled into a space right beside the entrance to Eaves and Doyle solicitors. He got out of the car and came to an abrupt stop.

'This must be some kind of joke,' he said.

Eric tried the door just in case there was a mistake and the tacky *We Are Closed* sign, which looked more suitable for a downmarket salon than a solicitor's office, was merely the wrong way around. He pushed once at normal pressure then tried again with a little more force, then finally using the full weight of his knee behind him.

'You have to be kidding.' Eric moved around to the front window and peered inside. The door to Eaves' office was closed and the only light came from a blinking security camera tucked up in one corner.

Eric took out his phone and swiped across the screen. The first time it went to voicemail. The second time it was answered in one ring.

'Mr Sibley, I'm so sorry.'

'What the hell is this? You told me I had to come down

today. That was what you said. It had to be today. Those were your words.'

'Mr Sibley, I can only apologise. I'm afraid I had a family emergency.'

'Funny that,' Eric said, not seeing a funny side at all. 'So did I, that's why I had to sack off work, drive for an hour-and-a-half, and am currently standing outside your office in the pissing rain.' The rain had grown dramatically heavier in the two minutes since Eric had stepped outside of the car. Using his body to shield the leather from the downpour, he opened her door as little as he thought necessary to squeeze himself back inside, then placed his phone on his lap, clenched the wood of the steering wheel, and forced himself to breathe.

'If you can stay until tomorrow morning, I will be able to see you first thing.' Christian Eaves' voice rattled out of the phone.

'Tomorrow?' Eric snatched his phone back off his lap. 'I can't do tomorrow. I can't do today. You told me to come here now. I'm here now.'

'I understand. And I'm so sorry. But if you could just wait until morning. I'm afraid the situation is entirely out of my control.'

Eric ground his molars and looked at his watch. It was already five-past-three. If he headed back now, he'd hit rush hour traffic all the way from the M25 to home. If he was lucky, he'd be back for seven. His stomach roiled. The whole day was a disaster.

'Seven o'clock,' he said down the phone.

'Pardon?'

'I need you to be here by seven o'clock tomorrow morning. That's the latest I can do, then I have to get back to work.'

'Mr —'

'And don't you *Mr Sibley* me. You screwed this up, and

you're lucky I'm not on the phone to my lawyers now taking you for more than just my car.'

'Mr —'

'I will be here at seven o'clock. If you're not, I will be heading back to London, in *my* Aston Martin, and believe me, cheap Ikea furniture will be the least of your pathetic little firm's worries.'

There was silence down the line. Eric waited, jaw set.

'Seven should be fine,' the reply came, and although he couldn't see it, Eric was certain the words were said with a smirk.

CHAPTER 7

ERIC GOT A room at the Sailboat Inn. The rooms were chintzy and small and smelt of stale smoke and old people, and the pub downstairs had a menu selection consisting of salt and vinegar, cheese and onion, and prawn cocktail; but it was on High Street, opposite Eaves and Doyle. He rang Suzy straight away and ranted at her for twenty minutes before she left to collect Abi from school. For the next ninety minutes, he scanned through his emails, trying to get on top of what he'd missed.

Eric groaned. He had skimmed through twelve different documents, each containing at least a dozen graphs with next to no explanation as to what they supposedly showed. His eyes ached, his back throbbed, this whole thing was a mess. And through it all, his stomach growled. The packet of prawn cocktail crisps left empty on the nightstand had been satisfying, in a dirty and oh-so-wrong type of manner, but in no way warded off the hunger pangs that came from missing both breakfast and lunch. Hunger pangs that weren't helped by the wafts of fish and chips that somehow managed to traverse all the way across the road, rise to the second floor, and drift in through a window that barely opened an inch. Eric gave one last refresh of his emails before he rolled over and shut the lid on the computer. He was halfway to the toilet when there was a knock on the door.

'Who is it?' he said.

There was another knock.

'Hold on.' Eric zipped up his flies and dragged his heels along the two feet of carpet to the door. He cracked it open by an inch.

'Surprise!'

She stood in the hallway, a vision of green against the dirty magnolia walls. Pencil-lead aroma eddied around her, while beside her Abi was still in her school kilt, her white blouse creased under her heavy winter jacket.

'Daddy!' In an impressive display of springiness, Abi attempted to jump into her father's arms, kneeing him squarely in the testicles as she did so. Eric gasped.

'What are you doing here?' he said, dropping Abi on the bed and taking Suzy's bag from her before kissing her on the cheek and trying to ignore the pulsating burning in his nuts.

'We thought we'd surprise you. You sounded so miserable on the phone. So we got the train straight down after school.'

'You didn't have to do that.'

'We wanted to.'

Eric looked around the room and frowned. The majority of space was filled with the bed, but it wasn't that the bed was incredibly big, but rather the room incredibly small. There was a narrow wardrobe and a small chest of drawers with a television perched on top that looked like it had been made in the eighties. Abi was already bouncing on the bed trying to grasp at the cheap plastic chandelier on the ceiling. Eric grabbed his computer and tucked it away in the bottom drawer of the chest.

'Look, it's only for one night,' Suzy said. 'And I thought it would be good. Help end the day on a positive.'

Abi yelped as she hit the chandelier, then landed with a crack that sounded suspiciously like the bed frame giving way.

'Stop that, Abi. Get down off there.'

'Why don't we go out?' Suzy said. 'I thought we could grab some fish and chips and then drive around the houses and look at the Christmas decorations?'

'Fish and chips!' Abi shouted, now masterfully knocking the chandelier with every bounce.

Eric pulled her down onto the bed. 'Why don't you two go? I've still got a few things to see to.'

Suzy frowned. 'You need to eat,' she said. 'And we've come all this way to see you.'

'Well I didn't ask you to.'

The words echoed around in the air between them. Suzy pursed her lips and turned her attention to Abi. When she next spoke, it was in the tone that Eric feared the most.

'Why don't we run you a bath, darling?' she said. 'You're still all stinky from school. Then, when we're done, we're going to get fish and chips, and Daddy's going to drive us around in Granddad's car to see all the pretty Christmas lights. Won't that be lovely?' Eric clenched his fist and forced a smile which he quickly transferred from his wife to his daughter.

'Mum's right. Why don't you go into the bathroom and see how many spiders you can find?' he said. 'I found four when I was in there earlier, and at least one of them looked poisonous. I bet you can't find that one.'

'I bet I can,' said Abi and dashed away into the en suite.

'Look,' Suzy said, annoying Eric further by being the first one to speak. 'I'm sorry if we surprised you. I thought it would be nice. You haven't been home to speak to Abi in a week. She misses you. I figured this way we'd be able to spend a bit of time together somewhere away from home.'

'But she's got school tomorrow. We can't just pull her out whenever we fancy. Do you know how much that place costs?'

'Yes. I do. You seem to have forgotten that I pay half?'

An uncomfortable silence expanded between them. Eric's stomach rumbled audibly. He opened his mouth to speak then shut it again. The good old *Abi misses you* card, naturally she brought that one out. Didn't she think if they could afford for him to work less, he would? Did she think he actually enjoyed staring at a computer screen until his vision blurred?

Suzy had still not dropped her glare. Her hands were on her hips and her chin set forwards in a way that made Eric shudder.

'I need twenty minutes to go through my emails,' he said in a sulk. 'And we're not having fish and chips inside the car. They'll stink her out.'

'Perfect,' Suzy said, trying to conceal the twitch at the corner of her lips.

They ate their fish and chips on a tiny Formica table in the corner of the takeaway, sitting on fixed-position, round stools that Eric could barely slide past. Despite the stench of week-old oil, and the insipidness of their chef, the food was surprisingly good. While Abi and Suzy shared a portion of fish, Eric went for the battered sausage. After all, how much worse could it be than prawn cocktail crisps? And after deciding to embrace whatever damage had been done to his stomach, he ordered a side of mushy peas, curry sauce, a spring roll, and a bag of scraps.

'This is yummy,' Abi said, licking a week's recommended intake of salt off the back of her knuckles. 'Why don't we eat this every day?'

'Because we'd all be suffering from type two diabetes,' Eric said.

They concluded their meal with two Magnums and a strawberry Cornetto from Mick's corner shop before they wiped down their hands with some wet wipes then clambered into the car.

'Do you know, I think this is the first time we've all been in here together,' Suzy said as she checked Abi's makeshift seatbelt.

Eric glanced at the mirror. Abi had her nose pressed to the window.

'I'm sure it's not,' he said.

'It is.'

'Well, we'll try to do it more,' he said, at least half meaning it.

Eric had hated taking Abi for rides in the car when his father had been alive. George had thought nothing of flying down the lanes regardless of the speed limit with Abi, barely out of toddlerhood, screaming, 'Faster! Faster!' in the back. Any voicing of his concerns would brand Eric dull and institutionalised, or else see him accused of trying to suck the fun out of everything. Now, if he'd tried going at those speeds, it would have been another thing altogether. There was never any winning with his father.

'Daddy, Daddy! Look at those. Look at those. Stop! Stop, I want to see them!'

Abi pressed her face against the glass.

'Look! There's Father Christmas and Rudolph and a sleigh and a snowman and a palm tree and everything!' she said in one breath. 'Isn't it beautiful?'

'Why is there a palm tree?' Eric quizzed, pulling up outside the Burnham equivalent to the Vegas strip.

'Well Father Christmas has to go to hot countries too, doesn't he?' Abi reasoned.

'He does indeed, honey,' Suzy said.

While Eric considered the electricity implications of twenty thousand watts worth of fairy-lights, Abi continued to stare in wide-mouthed awe at the voltaic monstrosity.

'Can we do this to our house, Mummy? I want a reindeer on my roof.'

'Not a chance,' Eric said.

'Why not?'

'Because it's horrific —'

'Horrifically expensive.' Suzy cut into his response. 'Because it's horrifically expensive, darling.'

Abi sucked on her bottom lip pensively. For a minute she looked as if she might let the subject go.

'But we can use Granddad's money,' she said.

Eric and Suzy exchanged a look.

'What was that, sweetheart?' Suzy said.

'We can use Granddad's money. When Katie's granddad died, her mum got given all his money, so they could go skiing and to Disneyland, and then Katie's mum left her dad because she didn't need him anymore because she had all her grand-dad's money. We could use our granddad's money to buy deco-rations.'

Her big green eyes looked longingly at her parents, but it did nothing to calm Eric's rapidly boiling blood. Suzy reached out and squeezed his hand. He couldn't respond. His mouth had transformed to sandpaper and a writhing tightness corkscrewed through his gut.

'Right,' he said. 'I think we need to be heading back now. It's already well past your bedtime.'

'But we could use Granddad's money, couldn't we?' Abi said again.

'Maybe next year,' Suzy said.

At six forty-five Eric was standing outside Eaves and Doyle. Although the water at the Sailboat had been hot, the shower had possessed about the same amount of power as a salivating, expectorating camel. No amount of scrubbing had managed to remove the grimy, unwashed feeling that came from sleeping in cheap, guest-house bed sheets. Having risen early, Abi and Suzy were now taking a wander along the seawall in a vain attempt of seal spotting. The plan was for them to get the first train back, but it was still another hour before that left, so they had plenty of time to kill.

It was one of those crystal-blue days when the sky was so clear you could be misled into believing it was summer. Until, that was, you stepped outside and could no longer blink due to your tears freezing in their ducts. There was no breeze and no clouds, but an icy coldness hung in the air, crystallising everything it touched. With prior warning, Eric would have at least brought some form of jumper with him. As it was, he was open to the elements.

Eric blew on his fingers in an attempt to fight off the cold. Already his toes were numb, his ear lobes burning, and his jaw clattered so furiously he worried that he might crack a crown. Doubting his sense in arriving early, he scanned down the road, spotting Eaves on the other side of the High Street.

The solicitor was wrapped in a thick tweed coat, with a woolly bobble-hat, and scarf around his neck. While the coat appeared of decent quality, Eric noted that the hat and scarf looked like something left behind at the end of a charity table-top sale in aid of underprivileged otters.

'A bit nippy,' Eaves said, stretching out his hand to shake

Eric's. Eric accepted, but only after a notable delay. 'I'm ever so sorry, about yesterday,' he continued. 'I hope the Sailboat wasn't too awful for one night.'

'These things happen.'

'Indeed, they do.'

The solicitor, Eric observed, was making no attempt whatsoever to open the door and let them in. His hands were firmly by his side, entirely devoid of keys. Unless the door possessed some form of high-tech biometric lock that was invisible to the untrained eye, Eric decided keys were entirely necessary, if not crucial in the given situation.

'Shall we go inside?' Eric said, wiggling his toes to check for the onset of frostbite. Still, Eaves made no attempt to unlock the door or even make a move towards it.

'I thought you might like to get some breakfast,' he said. 'The Sailboat isn't known for its cuisine.'

'Pardon?'

'Well, it's a bit of an early start and all. And I can never think quite right until I've eaten. I thought we could head to The Shed?'

Eric blinked. All the brownie points Eaves had gained in arriving early disappeared.

'Sorry, you want breakfast?'

'It's the most important meal of the day.'

Eric blinked again. 'Can we just get this over with? I'm rather pressed for time.'

'Oh, of course. Of course you are.' Christian Eaves paused and bit down on his lip. 'Only it will take just as long here as it would there. The only difference being the fried eggs and bacon. And to be honest, it's a fair bit warmer in the Cabin than the office. You know what these old buildings are like. Gotta keep tabs on the electricity bills.'

'Well, I —'

'Don't worry, it's a great service. We'll have you fed and on the road in no time.'

Too dumbfounded to object, Eric followed the solicitor down the road and towards a small, wood-clad building on the seawall. Only in Burnham.

CHAPTER 8

I F NOTHING ELSE, Eaves had been right about the temperature. Within a minute of setting foot in the cafe, Eric's previously numbed toes and fingers tingled with pins and needles. He flexed his joints and tried to avert any oncoming thawing pains; the attempt failed miserably, and a burning sensation fired up through his palms. Shaking his hands about, he followed Eaves down a narrow passage and past a service counter.

The Cabin was a curious establishment with a multitude of little dining rooms all running off one main corridor. It possessed low ceilings with several well-placed beams that could easily have resulted in a mild concussion for anyone over five-foot ten; it smelt, if possible, even greasier than the previous night's eatery. This time, however, the smell of fats could be categorised into subtler bouquets of bacon, sausage, and black pudding.

'Griff,' said Eaves, greeting a man as he came out from the kitchen. 'The back room free?'

'It is for you. You having the usual?'

'Probably, but I'll take a menu, anyway.'

Griff gave one sheet of laminated paper to Eaves and one to Eric, who held it by the corner and tried to put as little surface area between his skin and the oily plastic as possible.

'It's good coffee too,' Eaves said, leading him down one set of steps into a little room in the corner. 'Proper stuff, none of that instant rubbish.'

The back room came as rather a surprise. With three long windows and a large conference table tucked against one of the long walls, there must have been seats stacked up for at least thirty people. The floor was wooden – laminate but still pleasant – and there were normal sized tables too, currently set out for three of four covers, with doily table-cloths and small vases holding plastic carnations. Eric took a seat on one of the wheel-back chairs and quickly gave the menu a once over. It was all the usual fare; full English, bacon butties, that type of thing, only they were given supposedly amusing names like the Fat Bastard or the Wimpy Git.

'The names were even worse when they first started, but they had to change them due to all the complaints,' Eaves told him.

'That does surprise me.'

After the previous evening's overindulgence, Eric settled on a Whiny Bitch egg white omelette, with a side of fried mushrooms, and an espresso. Eaves went for the Fat Bastard. Had they been friends, Eric would have been inclined to say something, but he managed to hold his tongue. Once their order had been taken and their coffees had arrived, Eaves finally deemed it time to start business. He shuffled around in his seat and placed his palms on the table.

'I really must apologise again for yesterday. And before I forget, I have to give you this.' He reached into his pocket, extracted his wallet, and pulled out three twenty-pound notes. 'For your room,' he said.

Eric hesitated. It wasn't in his nature to take money, but this man had cost him, not least for Sally's petrol to get down there.

'Thank you,' he said and took the money.

Underneath the tweed coat, the solicitor was wearing the same cheap suit as before, only this time he was tieless, and the top button of his shirt was undone.

'I'm going to be honest with you,' he said. 'Your father thought something like this might happen.'

'Of course he did. That's why he did this. So he could make the whole event as painful as possible.'

Eaves shook his head.

'No, I don't think that's the case.'

'You didn't know my father.'

'Well, actually —'

'The hell you did,' Eric stopped him before he could finish.

Eaves pressed his lips together then took a sip of his coffee. It was a long sip. Eric's muscles twinged with irritation at it.

'I'm sorry if I offended you,' Eaves said when he finished his sip.

'You didn't.'

'Good. Then, as I was saying. Your father had expected something like this to happen and in preparation put in a series of contingencies to ensure that you got to keep the car.'

'Except actually leaving me the car?'

'Yes, well I do see how that appears somewhat contradictory. Anyhow, the first condition was that you had to come straight down to Burnham when requested. And that you stay in Burnham when asked to do so.'

Eric took a moment to digest the words.

'You mean that all this hanging around, missing work, coming at the drop of a hat. That was all part of his game?'

'I wouldn't call it a game —'

'And everything yesterday, all the crap with the bailiffs, that was all part of it too?'

'I can assure you that the bailiffs were very real. Had you not come down to Burnham immediately, they would have taken your car.'

'This is ridiculous.' Eric slammed his fists on the table, bouncing the cutlery with a clatter.

'Whiny Bitch?' Griff appeared behind Eric and placed the plate down in front of him. Apparently oblivious to the tension encircling him, Griff continued on. 'Can I get you anything else? Ketchup? Brown sauce?'

'I'm fine, thank you,' Eric said through gritted teeth. Eaves also quickly shook his head, dismissing the restaurateur-cum-chef.

'While your father's methods may seem illogical to you, I'm only doing as I was instructed to do.'

'The fry up? This place. Is this all part of it too?' Eric said.

'No,' Eaves said. 'I just really fancied a cooked breakfast. My wife has me on an oat bran diet and it's about as enjoyable as munching on cardboard. This is all my doing.'

'Then you can pay for it.'

Eaves smiled. 'I was going to anyway,' he said.

The solicitor picked up his fork and speared a piece of sausage. Eric looked on longingly; his egg white omelette looked distinctly insipid by comparison. He took a mouthful and chewed, only to find that it tasted as good as an egg white omelette could. A few more mouthfuls down and Eaves reached around and into his coat.

'Your father wanted me to give you this. I haven't read it, and this is where my instructions end in regard to second chances. From now on, if you fail to abide by the agreement, I will be taking your car. There are no more do-overs.' He slid a small white envelope across the table, then stood up and retrieved his coat. 'I do hope everything turns out all right for you,' he said.

'What about the rest of your breakfast?' Eric said. 'You've barely touched it.'

Eaves shrugged. 'Damn oat bran. Can't eat more than a mouthful of anything now without, well, you know. Anyway. Take care of that car, Mr Sibley. And of yourself.'

With Eaves gone, Eric ordered another espresso. What he really wanted was a large portion of the black pudding and streaky bacon, but Eaves' last remark about the bran had made eating substantially less appealing. The envelope continued to lie flat in the centre of the table, and even when Eric had finished his second coffee, he decided to order himself a sparkling water, and then a portion of toast and jam. Anything to delay the inevitable. When his toast was done, his phone buzzed with a message from Suzy saying she and Abi were safely on the train. He stood up, took the envelope, slipped it into his pocket and left, leaving a tenner on the table to cover the extra food and drink.

Outside, the sun was doing an admirable job at battling the cold. Still, Eric kept out of the shade as he walked and managed to maintain a degree of warmth to his face. It was a shame he didn't like sailing. Days like today he could imagine himself out on the open sea, the sail flapping in the wind, Abi laughing as she joked around in her little orange life vest.

He ambled down as far as the yacht club, his mind focusing on nothing but the breeze and seagulls. When he reached the end of the path where the pavers disappeared into the grass, he turned around and retraced his steps back to the car.

It was only when he was tucked up in the bucket seats, the

warm leather moulding to his body, that Eric took out the neatly typed letter and began to read.

To My Only Son, Eric,

Eric paused. At least this meant there wasn't about to be some long confession about a life of bigamy and seventeen other children spread between John O'Groats and Land's End. After wasting a moment dwelling on the possibility of endless siblings, he came back to the letter.

To My Only Son, Eric,

I can only imagine your disappointment. No doubt you have disowned me and cursed my name many times since receiving news of your inheritance, but the fact that you're here, now, reading this letter, proves that there is hope for you and for me.

It may surprise you, but I've tried to express myself to you in person, both before your mother's passing and since, but believe me when I say stubbornness and pride are hard to relinquish after all these years and now, with less time left than I would have hoped for, I've given up trying to teach this old dog new tricks. At my age, more than ever, time is better spent rejoicing in what you can do, not dwelling on what you can't.

Somewhere along the line, I lost sight of what mattered in this life. I put the emphasis on what I could achieve instead of focusing on what I had achieved and as such ignored the most important gifts I already had. Though, worse than my failings as a husband and father is the fact that I've passed these failings on to you, my son. My deluded ideas of success and wealth. My misguided ideas of what life should be like. I've made you place value on things that are worthless and seen you cast aside and neglect those that are most precious.

This is not a lecture. I'm far too old to lecture and you're far too old to listen. And I'm not asking you to do this for me, I'm asking you to do this for your mother, for your wife, for your daughter, but most of all for you. You may not see it now, but what I have left you is worth more than money, more than the house.

Eric turned the paper over and searched for a conclusion; some final farewell or at least a signature to prove that that sans serif typescript was his father's own composition, but there was none. He flipped the paper back again, read once more through the words, then folded the letter back into the envelope. A heavy weight had descended on his chest.

'Screw you,' he said and threw the letter onto the passenger seat.

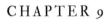

CHAPTER 9

ERIC HAD HAD every intention of driving straight back to London. Suzy had messaged to say she'd be getting off at Woodham and going to visit her sister Lydia, which on the plus side meant that the house would be empty for him to have a shower and get himself sorted before going into work; on a less positive note, it meant they were seeing Lydia. Eric deleted the first reply he wrote and instead sent a diplomatic *Have fun*. Now, not only was Abi missing school, she was being indoctrinated into Lydia's *all of life is brilliant which is why we've made you a dreamcatcher out of twigs and cat fur for Christmas* mindset. Perfect.

The day had maintained a powder-blue skyscape, and the salt breeze brought with it a tang of earthiness from the marshlands. Eric focused on the feel of Sally as he tried to block out all the other conversations going on inside his head. It was only when he'd been driving for over a minute that he realised he was heading in completely the wrong direction.

'Sod it,' he said as he passed some familiar pebble-dashed houses. A minute later he was parked up outside Arcadia Road.

Unlike his previous visit, the ground was rock solid, and a sharp frost gripped the bushes and grasses. Eric pulled his sleeves down over his hands then folded his arms as he tried to protect them from the cold. The pinboard was still in place on the shed, this time with a few extra notices and three sealed envelopes each addressed with a lot number. Eric gave them the once over and moved on.

Full of confidence he marched onward, down the exact path he'd previously taken with his elderly guide. The place felt more familiar than expected; he remembered a couple of the more ornate fences and well-maintained plots, and several of the raised beds jerked his memory too. After a couple of minutes, he reached a large blue water butt that he distinctly recalled from before and turned left by it. Two minutes later he saw another and turned left again.

'Must have done that too soon,' he said to no one in particular.

It took eight blue water butts and triple that in number of turns before Eric admitted what he'd known six butts earlier. He was lost. Every other plot, it appeared, had a tall, blue water butt. Every fourth lot had a yellow shed, and he could have sworn that a particular scarecrow, with a green shell-suit jacket on, was moving around just to wind him up. Eric became decidedly concerned that he might never manage to find his way out again, let alone find his abhorrent excuse for an allotment.

'Can I help you, deary, you look a little lost?'

Eric spun on the spot, muttering to himself as he moved.

The offer of help came from a small woman who appeared to have been plucked straight from the pages of a Beatrix Potter tale. She wore a thick khaki duffle coat with brown trousers, brown ankle boots, and a tartan headscarf that was wrapped around her chin in a manner that made her eyes look larger than a barn owl's. She hunched over slightly as she hobbled forwards while balancing a pair of thin-rimmed spectacles on the end of her nose, enhancing her overall owl-like demeanour.

'I'm looking for plot fifty-two,' Eric said.

'Fifty-two.' Her eyes popped, magnified to preposterous proportions behind her glasses. 'Oh.'

The little woman stayed rooted to the spot. After a minute, Eric considered the possibility that she might have frozen when her throat emitted something between a squeak and a cough.

'Sorry? I didn't quite catch that,' he said.

She squeaked again. Eric leant in closer.

'I'm Janice,' she said.

'Janice?' Eric frowned. He pursed his lips, then inhaled an exceptionally long intake of air.

For the next five minutes, Janice showered Eric in apologies. Apparently, she'd passed her news about the extra allotment to her neighbour Geoffrey, who had then told his wife. She, in turn, had conveyed the information to her sister-in-law, whose neighbour from across the road was friends with one of the committee members and was also the nephew of Christian Eaves.

'I'm terribly sorry for having caused such a problem. I wouldn't have offered to help otherwise.'

'Really, it's fine,' Eric said.

'You see it's such a long waiting time here —'

'Honestly. Please, don't mention it.'

'Unless you inherit one, or you're on the list —'

'I'm rather short on time —'

'If there's anything I can do.'

'Yes. Yes, there is one thing.' Eric's tone stopped her gabble mid-flow. Janice's eyes bugged beneath her spectacles. 'You could show me where plot fifty-two is.'

The apologies continued, even as Eric followed Janice weaving between the rows.

'I'm not as quick as I used to be,' she said over her shoulder. 'Bunions. Damn things. Lucky my hands and knees are still on side. It's just up here though, you were almost there.'

In less than a minute, Eric recognised where he was. In front of him sat the perfectly manicured allotment and rust-red shed with veranda he'd been so keen to claim. Next to it sat his own disgusting septic tank of a plot, complete with festering, algae-filled, blue water butt and dilapidated greenhouse.

'Well, this is you,' she said. 'How lovely for you. No doubt you'll have this spick and span in no time. And lucky you, having the plot next to the Kettlewells. Wonderful couple. Temperamental at times, but wond ... oh look. Speak of the devil.'

Norman Kettlewell glowered at Eric with his cat-green eyes before commencing yet another coughing fit.

'It was all a misunderstanding,' Eric said before the accusations began.

'Aye, you can say that again. Trying to get a pensioner to do your work for you. Bloody big misunderstanding.'

'That wasn't what I was —'

'Well if you've come to say farewell, you can consider it said —'

'That's enough, Norman. The man has said his apologies, now it's time to move on.'

A woman, Eric could only assume was Norman's wife, was doing the talking, after which Norman erupted into a coughing fit. While Eric considered that the fit could indeed have been genuine, it could also have been an opportunity to stop his wife berating him. Half a minute later when he was still going, and his eyes streamed, Eric conceded that it was most probably genuine.

'Cynthia,' she said, stretching her hand to Eric, which he promptly took and shook. Then to her husband, she said, 'Why don't you go and sit in the shed for a minute. Catch your breath?'

Doubled over to the knees, Norman shook his head, but when he went to voice his objection, he could barely breathe.

'Shed. Now,' Cynthia said.

This time, Norman moved.

With Norman and his bronchial malaise shut away in his shed, Eric found himself at the mercy of the two elderly women. The pair were polar opposites to look at. Cynthia, with her mane of dyed burgundy hair and plum colour lipstick, looked like she'd be more at home in a 1950s cocktail bar than an allotment, as opposed to Janice, who Eric wholeheartedly believed lived in a hollowed-out tree with nothing but a log fire and mice dressed in waistcoats for company. Both, however, had the ability to talk nonstop over one another, without a second to digest or breathe. Perhaps it comes with age, Eric thought as they continued to prattle away. Maybe you reach a point where you become worried that your conversations are numbered and therefore try to squeeze as many words as possible into each one, regardless of the situation or how many people are present.

'It was an impressive plot this time last year,' Cynthia said. 'Your father was a very good gardener. Very good. Had an impressive crop of runner beans, from what I remember.'

'And his gooseberries,' Janice overlapped. 'Don't forget his gooseberries.'

'I hadn't forgotten his gooseberries, I was just mentioning his runner beans.'

'Well, anyone can grow runner beans. They don't take any skill at all. If you want to acknowledge someone's gardening skills, you don't praise their runner beans.'

'I'm sure they were equally impressive,' Eric said diplomatically.

Cynthia smiled knowingly. 'He said that about you. Never liked an argument. Always a peacekeeper. How's little Abi doing? I have to say we miss the updates. She was just starting swimming lessons last we heard.'

Something tugged beneath Eric's sternum. Abi had started swimming lessons over a year ago. She'd already got her one-hundred-metre badge and moved up from the tadpole to the turtle group. He was almost certain he'd spoken to his father several times since then but racking his mind, he couldn't think when or what they would have spoken about.

'She's doing well. Spending the day with her mother,' he said.

'Oh, has she not got school?'

'Teacher training day,' Eric lied.

There was a brief pause during which he felt the eyes of the old women scrutinise him at an uncomfortable depth.

'Are you planning on doing any work today?' Cynthia said. 'I only ask because Norman's got a spare pair of gloves and wellies in the shed if you need them. You won't want to be getting those nice shoes of yours covered in mud.'

Eric raised his hands apologetically. 'Unfortunately, I have to be getting back to London to see the girls. I should have already left. I only dropped in to have a quick recce.'

Both women looked notably disappointed.

'Already?' said Janice. 'Such a shame, you've hardly got here.'

'I'm sure he'll be back soon enough,' said Cynthia. 'And then you can bore him with tales of your bunions like you do the rest of us.' She reached out her hand. 'Have a safe journey back. And I'm so sorry about your father.'

'Thank you.'

His phone buzzed with an email, and though he ignored the message he glanced at the time, surprised to find that it was already gone ten.

'Thank you for all your help,' he said, bidding the ladies farewell before he dug his heel into the ground and began to walk away.

'Where do you think you're going?'

Eric stopped. He didn't need to turn around to know Norman's face was going to be sporting a glare and grimace. What he didn't know, was how he'd managed to install such a lingering bee in this old man's bonnet. Slowly he turned around, fastening his teeth into a perfectly aligned smile.

'I'm sorry,' Eric said. 'I didn't want to disturb you. Anyway, I'm off now.'

Norman's torso leant out of his red shed door. A second later his legs caught up, and he limped the few steps across the empty vegetable beds.

'Eric was just going back to London,' Janice said. 'Abi's got a teacher training day.'

'Mid-December?'

'Private school,' he lied.

Norman locked his eyes on him and a cold shudder ran the length of Eric's spine. His eyes were impressively green, Eric thought, although he may have found them more impressive if it didn't feel like they were trying to bore a hole straight through his eye sockets into the centre of his cerebellum in order to render him entirely extinct.

'Aren't you forgetting something?' Norman said, his gaze unmoving.

Eric cleared his throat awkwardly. 'I don't believe so.'

'You don't say? What about that old inheritance of yours? What about that contract?'

'Norman.' Cynthia struck her husband on the arm. 'Don't be so rude.'

'Rude. I ain't the one that's being rude. He's the one who's done nothing. Nearly two months now he's left that patch to go to waste.'

'Norman, this is not the time.'

'It's exactly the time. You know how long the waiting list on one of these plots is? Do you?' He wagged his finger in Eric's direction. Eric stuttered.

'I ... Well, not exactly, but I've heard it's quite substantial.'

'Eight years. Did you hear that? Eight years people have to wait for a plot like this to come around, and you're there letting the whole thing go to spoil. Your father did more work with his zimmer frame than you've done since you got the place. Christ, this is worse than the bloody mole fiasco.'

Eric bit his tongue, hard. Diplomacy, he told himself. Be diplomatic. After all, two years could be a long time if this continued. He took a deep breath in through his nose.

'Mr ... Mr Kettlewell, isn't it? Norman. I really am sorry about the state of things. I am. And I will get around to sorting it. But right now, I have to get home.' Norman harrumphed again. Eric ignored him. 'I'm so grateful for your understanding over all this mess. I can assure you I will be back in the new year to get the whole place sorted. Hopefully, we will be able to start afresh.'

Finishing with his best salesman smile, Eric reached out a hand. Cynthia and Janice were beaming, Janice so much so that her bespectacled face now looked bizarrely reminiscent of an elderly praying mantis. Norman, however, did not move a whisker.

'Well,' Eric said, retrieving his hand, and placing it back

beside his leg. 'Ladies, it was lovely to meet you. Norman, nice to see you again.' For the second time, he braced himself and moved to leave.

'Weekly maintenance.'

'Pardon?' Eric turned back.

'Weekly maintenance,' Norman growled, still statuesque on the same spot. 'That's what you've got to do right? That's what your father said. Every week, down here making this place better. That's if you want to keep that car.'

Eric sniffed and raised his chest.

'Mr Kettlewell, the legalities of my father's will are entirely confidential —'

'Bollocks to that. Who do you think typed out all his letters when his hands went?'

'Norman.' Cynthia's voice was different this time, wary, threatening.

'Well, who does he think he is? Confidential my arse. His father was a good man. A good man. But I know men like you. I know what you're about. Your father might have thought there was something worth saving, but you money grabbing types are all the same, and we don't want you here.'

'Norman, that's enough.'

'Tell me then, twice he's trotted down here in his fancy-pants suits and pointy shoes and not lifted a bloody finger. Not once. And d'you know how many times he's mentioned his father? Not once. Not a single bloody word. No sir, you can please and thank you all you want, but your smarmy manners don't mean nowt to me. Either you do the work, or I'll see that you're gone. And that pretty little car you value so much goes too.'

Eric found himself momentarily dumbfounded by a man who was essentially a life-sized garden gnome.

'I ... I ... well I'll have you know ...' he began, but within a second his stuttering astonishment was gone. In its place was something hot and angry that had his back teeth grinding together with more pressure than an industrial Delonghi espresso maker.

'You want me to do some gardening?' he said. 'Now?'

'At last, the boy understands.'

'Oh, I understand. I really do,' Eric said. 'You want me to tidy up. Now. Today.' Eric could feel the adrenaline taking hold. 'Today, when, as it happens, I found out that I drove seventy-five miles and missed what could be one of the most important meetings of my career because my father wanted to ... to what? Save me?' He paced the length of the plot. 'I can assure you, Mr Kettlewell, I do not need saving. Not even a bit. And if I did, my father is the last person I would go to. The very, very last. And here's another thing. You did not know my father. Not the father I had. Because if you did, if you knew even an inch of him, you wouldn't have the gall to stand there in front of me and tell me he was a good man. I knew my father, and I knew exactly what he was.' He stopped pacing and placed one hand on his hip and the other on the swampish water butt. 'But if you want me to do some maintenance, then that I can do. In fact, that would be my pleasure.'

With his glare still locked on Norman, Eric sidestepped along the grass, where he placed both hands firmly against the slime-covered plastic of the water butt. 'This maintenance enough for you?' he said. With one giant shove, he sent the whole thing toppling. Water sloshed over the side, cascading into giant streams of green-smelling gunk that spread across the ground in front of him. It stank as it spread, oozing out in all directions.

'I think it looks better already,' Eric said and with a satisfied smirk marched back to his car without getting lost once.

CHAPTER 10

ERIC COULD SMELL the algae on him all the way to London. He had cleaned off his shoes and washed his hands and was certain he hadn't transferred any of the pungent slime into the car, but the smell remained all the same. *I may smell like this forever*, Eric thought. Once I was Eric; now, Algae Man. He was delirious, he had to be.

After the final incident with the water butt, Eric accepted there was no possibility of him going straight into work now, not even to apologise. The email that buzzed earlier had been from Jack, telling him to take as much time as he needed, which was a nice sentiment, but utterly pointless. What he needed was the time back; a time accumulator to restore the hours wasted on his father's pointless pilgrimage.

The letter had fallen into the footwell of the passenger's seat, where it fluttered about demanding Eric's attention. His father wanted him to fail, Eric thought. He could see it now. The whole thing was merely a fantastic way of alleviating a selfish old man's guilt at wanting to leave his son nothing but miserable memories. This way George died the good one, the one who gave his son a chance. It was Eric who was branded the villain. It was a smart plan. Only it wasn't going to work. Not this time. Eric was determined.

The lunchtime traffic was its usual abomination, and by the time he reached home, Eric regretted his choice of a Whiny Bitch breakfast even more than he had in the morning. Still, he refused to allow himself to eat until he'd fully eradicated the stench of algae and rotten vegetables from his skin. He dropped his shoes on the porch, threw his clothes directly into the washing machine – switching it on to the intensive clean setting – then sprinted up into the shower where he double-scrubbed everything from his ankles to his fingernails. On the second scrub, he chose to use Suzy's expensive pink gel over his more subtly scented man-wash; even jasmine and wild lavender was better than he currently smelt. Properly clean for the first time in two days, Eric sauntered back downstairs and gathered a selection of cold cuts from the fridge to munch on while he tackled his emails.

Nothing stood out as urgent, besides the minutes of yesterday's meeting that – so the email read – would be discussed at another meeting next week. Meetings to discuss meetings. What a fantastic use of time. Eric was still studying the screen in front of him, trying to prioritise his seemingly endless to-do list, when another email, in the middle of the page caught his eye. His throat tightened. After hovering the cursor over the message for a solid fifteen seconds, he clicked open.

'Sorry about today. His bark's much worse than his bite. I hope he didn't upset you too much. Have a long rest over Christmas and we'll all start over in the new year. It was lovely to meet you. Cynthia.'

A softening sensation momentarily floated through his stomach before it instantaneously hardened.

'You think I'm going to fall for that,' Eric said and shut the lid with a sizeable force.

Suzy and Abi were back at three. While Suzy drifted in serenely and delicately pecked her husband on the cheek, Abi was bouncing off the walls.

'They've got nine rabbits. Nine! Can we have one, Daddy? Can we? Uncle Tom thought they were both girls and if they don't find the babies homes, he says they're going to eat them. Can we have one, Daddy, pleeeease? We can't let him eat them.'

'I thought Uncle Tom had an excess of experience in mammalian genitalia,' Eric said. Suzy shot him a glare. 'No, we can't, Abi,' he said. 'Rabbits are vermin. They're not pets. They're tailless rats.'

'That's what you say about hamsters.'

'The same is true.'

'What about gerbils? They've got tails.'

Sensing the need for a distraction from the rabbit topic, Eric nodded to the canvas bag in Suzy's hands. 'What's that?' he said.

'Leftovers. Lyd made a lasagne for lunch.'

'Is it edible?'

'It's yummy!' Abi said, jumping up and once again kneeing Eric in the testicles.

'Abs, honey, can you go put the lasagne in the fridge? Then go check the computer and see if the teachers have emailed you any work.'

'The teachers email you?' Eric said.

Abi raised an eyebrow. 'What do you expect them to do, text me?' Then, shaking her head at the idiocy of the older generation, she disappeared into the kitchen.

'So,' Suzy said, kicking off her shoes and moving into the sitting room. 'What did he say?'

Eric slumped down into the armchair opposite, then reached into his pocket and withdrew the letter.

'See for yourself.'

Once Suzy had finished the letter, she folded it neatly and placed it back in its envelope before leaning back into the sofa, her lower lip disappearing under her teeth.

'And that's not the worst of it,' Eric said.

'No?'

'No, the worst part is that this whole rigmarole was part of his plan. Me missing work, me spending the night down there. It's all some twisted game that he's mapped out for me from beyond the grave. He's probably got years' worth of stuff ready to torment me with. Decades even.'

'What else did the solicitor say?'

Eric shrugged. 'Not much. Apparently, this is the last chance I'll get. Either it's maintain the allotment or give the car back. Oh yes, my day just keeps getting better and better.'

Suzy stayed silent, which was her typical response when she had something she desperately wanted to say but suspected that Eric's views would differ from hers quite substantially. After a couple of minutes, she levered herself out of the chair and left Eric to his laptop. The rest of the evening went in a blur, except for the lasagne which stood out as an unexpected highlight of the day.

'Perhaps you should come across to see them next time,' Suzy said.

'It wasn't that nice,' Eric replied.

With Monday and Tuesday lost, Eric's feet barely touched the ground for the remaining three days of the week. He attempted to gain information from Greg about whether Hartley had given any hints about creating a new senior associate director position, but evidently Greg had lost focus after Eric left the meeting, apparently on account of glimpsing indications of more intimate tattoos on the red-headed intern.

Jack popped his head through the glass door several times. 'Alistair was impressed with the contract you put together for the Fortune account. Very impressed,' he said. Eric gave an internal sigh of relief. At least he hadn't made an entirely horrific impression.

Ralph, on the other hand, hadn't been best pleased to see Eric return with the car.

His arrival at the house had coincided exactly with dinner-time for the three wildlings, and as such all conversations transpired over clatterings of cutlery, flying yoghurt, and dubious lyrics to well-known pop songs.

'It's called *Uptown Funk*,' Ralph said, as his eldest belted out his own, less censored version. 'Funk, son. Funk.'

'Are you sure?'

'Yes, quite sure.'

'So, it's *Up town* —'

'Funk you up. Yes, definitely funk you up.'

'Huh, who knew?'

The child — Joshua? Jonas? — went back to painting eyebrows on his sister with various condiments and desserts, leaving Eric and Ralph to continue their conversation.

'I don't know,' Ralph said. 'Sah went mad over the thing with the bailiffs. I missed the baby's nap time. It put her out for days. You have no idea what it's like with three. They have to nap. They have to.'

'It won't happen again. I swear. It was all a misunderstanding. And I'm trying to sort out something more permanent for the car. I just need another couple of months. Three max.'

'Two max,' Ralph said. Eric agreed and sprinted out the door before Ralph changed his mind and Eric was roped into helping with bath-time and bedtime. There was only so far his friendship could stretch where Ralph's children were concerned.

It wasn't until Friday evening that Eric finally managed to find time to have a meal with Suzy. The takeaway was already dished up when he dragged himself through the front door at nine fifteen.

'Abi already in bed?' he said.

'She tried to stay up.' Suzy handed him a plate. 'But she's knackered. You know what the last day of term is like. All Christmas parties and sugar crashes.'

'Today's the last day of term? God, how did that happen?'

'I have no idea.'

They carried the plates through to the living room and balanced them on their knees to eat.

'What time do you want to leave tomorrow?' Suzy asked after a mouthful of chow mien.

Eric looked blankly at his wife.

'Tomorrow, Lyds. You do remember it's Christmas next week, don't you?'

'Of course I do.'

'And what do we always do the weekend before Christmas?'

Eric let out a long, drawn-out groan. 'But you saw her on Tuesday? Surely that counts?'

'We saw her, Abs and I. You didn't. Besides, we didn't take gifts. And it's tradition. So yes, we're going.'

'But what about the allotment?'

'What about it?'

'I have to go.'

'You went on Tuesday. And the email from Cynthia said she'd see you in the new year. I don't think anyone's expecting you to go in over Christmas. I know it said every week, but there have to be some reasonable concessions.'

A guttural moan rose from the base of Eric's throat as he bit into a prawn spring roll. He waited until he'd chewed and swallowed before he spoke.

'I know what their plan is, and I'm not falling for it. No, I need to go this weekend. I have to.' He mulled the issue over during another mouthful of spring roll. 'Could we not just go to your sister's in the morning? I can leave after breakfast and pick you and Abi up on the way home? That way I've only lost half-an-hour or so.'

'You have to stay longer than that,' Suzy said. 'Besides, I've told her we're coming for lunch.'

'Well ring her and ask her if we can come earlier. Blame me. She always likes it when you blame things on me.' Suzy didn't look convinced. 'She'll be the hero. She'll love it. We'll just have to say how grateful we are a hundred and fifty times. And there's a foot rub in it for you,' Eric added for good measure.

Suzy exhaled loudly. She was still frowning, but her pout had diminished slightly. Eric sidled up beside her and nuzzled into her shoulder.

'You're my angel,' he said.

'I'll ask, that's all. But if she can't change, then you're still coming.'

'Tell her I'm happy to have turkey for breakfast if that helps.'

Lydia was fine about changing from lunch to brunch, so by eight thirty the next morning the three of them were piled in the Audi, the backseat a menagerie of silver-and-gold-wrapped gifts. The car reeked of plastic and frivolously spent money. Eric hadn't bothered asking Suzy about taking Sally. She wasn't keen on Abi going above thirty miles an hour in her, and Eric was on too much of a mission to have to think about things like speed limits. Besides, as well as the fact it had been pouring with rain all night and showed no signs of stopping, he needed the boot space.

The winter sky was fully in place, and along the street faint remnants of smoke twisted up from the chimney stacks. Had it not been for the cars, electricity pylons, and lampposts, they could have been in Victorian London. Eric breathed in the smell of wood fires and long nights. According to his phone, it was dry in Burnham and had been all week. He'd believe that when he saw it.

Abi was already glued to her iPad as they drove along the A12, and Suzy rambled on about the latest freelance pieces she'd been asked to write. Eric's mind was elsewhere. Time management. That was all this business with the allotment came down to, decent time management. And decent time management was something Eric was exceptionally good at.

They reached Chelmsford in good time, but rather than taking the route down to Woodham, Eric steered the car left towards the town centre.

'Where are you heading?' Suzy asked. 'I said we'd be there at nine thirty, it's already ten to.'

'Don't worry,' Eric said. 'It'll take five minutes. Promise.'

CHAPTER 11

ERIC CONSIDERED POPPING into a town centre the last weekend before Christmas and expecting a quick turnaround about as likely as turning up at a vegan festival in a pair of crocodile skin loafers and sheepskin jacket and expecting to be invited to share a tofu burger. Still, he grinned to himself smugly as he veered away from the dozens of tail-lights, all vying for a handful of empty parking spaces by the town centre, and headed over to the other side of town. They continued through two industrial estates and past a handful of new car showrooms before taking a left at two consecutive mini-roundabouts and drawing up at a prime spot directly in front of Tools4U. He reversed in, cut the engine, and turned to Suzy.

'Do I even want to know?' she said.

'I'll be fifteen minutes, tops,' Eric replied. 'There's a garden centre up the other end of the road. Why don't you take Abi to have a look around? I bet they have animals. They always have animals at garden centres.'

Suzy raised her eyebrows and sucked on her top teeth

before turning to Abi and motioning that she could undo her seatbelt.

'Fifteen minutes tops,' she said to Eric, and then back to Abi added, 'come on, let's go look at the guinea pigs.'

'Remember to tell them you want to buy something,' Eric called, as they crossed the road ahead of him. 'They only let you stroke the things if they think you're actually going to buy one.'

Suzy offered him a dismissive wave and headed off towards a large green building. Eric went straight to the bright blue doors.

The chrome-accented foyer of Tools4U smelt of metal and manliness. Having done his research online, Eric had identified four tool hire companies in Chelmsford. Two of them were big chains, and the third was shut until the new year. While the big chains offered all sorts of promotions, like double deals and accidental insurance, free pickup and drop off, Tools4U had come out top in Eric's mind, partly because of its location on the outskirts of town and partly because the website featured only photos of tools. This was opposed to the chain stores' websites, which contained hundreds of images of overly smiley people man-handling machinery in carefully curated poses that ensured a perfectly even mix of gender, ethnicity, and age was gained in every shot.

Eric stepped inside. It was surprising how primal and arousing the petrol and woodchip aromas were. The shelves, stocked twelve feet high, exuded a sense of power with their gleaming metal engines and masculine words like *horsepower* and *throttle* written in bold. Even the roof was manly with its thick metal girders and exposed ventilation systems. After two minutes perusing, he remembered the time constraint and headed to the service desk at the back.

It took three forceful coughs before the freckled youth

behind the counter raised his head from the computer screen. Although he met Eric's gaze with a smile, Eric felt it was definitely an enforced customer-service smile as opposed to a genuine, pleased-to-see-him smile. Eric reciprocated nonetheless. The youth in question looked a little over eighteen, with cinnamon red hair, cut into a John Lennon style mop-top, and a blanketing of ginger freckles. Despite the weather, he was wearing a memorabilia T-shirt of a band which Eric thought sounded familiar – if for no other reason than its distinct assonance to a venereal disease – and had a single headphone jammed into one of his ears.

'Hello,' Eric said. 'I need to get a chainsaw.'

The boy plucked the headphone out of his ear and stashed it in his pocket. He leant forwards over the counter, locking eyes with Eric.

'Sure,' he said.

'Excellent.'

'Is there any type of chainsaw you had in mind?'

'Yes,' Eric said, straightening his back, and feeling most authoritative. 'I think I need something with a decent HP. Preferably with low vibration, spark arrest muffler, and decompression valve.'

The corners of the young man's mouth twitched.

'Wow, you do sound like you know what you want.'

'Basically, I want whatever's best. And I don't mean to be rude, but I'm in a bit of a rush.'

The youth's twitching lips pressed tighter together.

'Okay, I get that,' he said.

He stood up and came around to the front of the counter at an infuriatingly leisurely pace. From the shelves beneath, he selected a thin looking brochure, which he placed in front of Eric.

'What kind of work are you doing, exactly? I mean, are you

thinking of felling an entire woodland, or just chopping down a few saplings? If you have a look in the catalogue here, you can see there's a range of different models depending on —'

Eric waved him quiet.

'Yes, I read all that online. What I'm after is the 550XP. It did say you had it in stock. If you could grab me one and get the paperwork sorted that would be fantastic.'

The youth took a step back.

'Sir,' he said with a slight hint of trepidation. 'If you don't mind me asking, how often do you use chainsaws?'

'Why, does that affect the price?'

'No, of course —'

'Then why are you asking? I told you want I wanted. I also told you that I'm in rather a rush, and I'd hate to have to waste the weekend before Christmas ringing up your customer service department in order to lodge a complaint.'

The young man's nostrils flared in and out, and a glimmer of something unpleasant squirmed behind Eric's belly button as he puffed his chest out farther still. He hated acting like a prick, but some people were just born time wasters. He met lads like this all the time. Give them the slightest hint of power and they leapt forty metres above their station. He had read up on every specification and chainsaw know-how list the internet had to offer. There was certainly nothing this jumped up little pot-head could tell him that he hadn't already read on Google.

The youth finally dropped his gaze and went back behind his desk.

'Of course, sir, I'll get someone out back to prepare the XP for you now. There are just a few bits of paperwork that need reading and signing. I hope that's okay? Unless you'd like a demonstration on the machine first?'

'That won't be necessary,' Eric said.

'I thought as much,' the redhead said, then he offered Eric an even faker smile than he had when he first arrived.

It was another twenty minutes before Eric left the shop. There had been an unending stream of papers to sign – insurance waivers, credit card details, deposit refund criteria – before he could leave. By the time he'd squeezed the chainsaw bag into the boot and clambered into the driver's seat, they were well behind schedule. Suzy had an extreme version of *the look* on her face. A thick crease had formed between her eyebrows, and her chin set in a position that told Eric his best hope was to drive fast. He kept his mouth shut and at 10.00 AM, thirty minutes late, they pulled into Tom and Lydia's driveway.

The contents of the hanging baskets hung by the porch were dead and decaying, although their rather morbid presence was offset slightly by the oversized wreath that covered the upper half of the front door. There was a family of reindeer – or possibly rhinos – on the ground by the front step, obviously homemade with their jagged, sawn edges, protruding nails, and stuck on googly eyes. It reminded Eric of a family of creatures from a Tim Burton animation, only infinitely more sinister.

'Suze! Abi! Come in, come in.'

At forty-two, Suzy's sister, Lydia was every bit the aging hippy, with braids in her hair, denim skirt, tie-dye leggings, and homemade Christmas pudding jumper.

'Eric,' Tom stretched out a hand. 'Good to see you. Good to see you.'

Tom was one of those unfortunate men who had started going bald before he'd even finished puberty and by twenty-two had had a head smoother than an Olympic swimmer's swim cap. He too was wearing a Christmas jumper, though his exhibited a three-dimensional face of Father Christmas which sported a cascade of white threads for his hair and beard. Poor Tom. Eric couldn't help but think the world was mocking him.

'Come in, come in,' Lydia continued to beckon. 'I was just about to call you and see if you'd got lost.'

'Sorry,' Suzy said. 'Eric had a few errands to run.' Lydia reached out and accepted their coats as they peeled them off their backs. The house was warm with a hot, radiator-fuelled heat and filled with smells of fresh baking and farmyards. Outside, a cockerel crowed multiple times. How no one in the estate complained about the noise was a mystery to Eric.

'Hugo and Ellery are outside, Abi. The chickens got loose again, so it's a bit of mayhem out there. I bet they'd love your help.' Then glancing at Abi's feet, added, 'There are spare wellies in the utility.' Abi looked at her mum for permission.

'Can I?'

'Just make sure you wash your hands properly before you eat.'

'I always do,' she said, then vanished out through the back of the house.

Now inside, Eric realised the outside of the house had got away lightly with only a wreath and demented deer family by way of decoration. From where he stood in the hallway, it appeared as though every inch of the three-bed semi had been plastered in tinsel, fake snow, or else some other homemade Christmas monstrosity. Paper snowflakes – the type he'd briefly tried to make with Abi some years before when she stabbed herself accidentally in the thigh with the scissors – were strung on the bannisters, while salt-dough stars and pipe cleaner angels hung off the lamps. Tissue-paper Father Christmases and six-inch high elves were staggered along the carpets leading the way to a six-foot Christmas tree while half a dozen wilting poinsettias were set along the staircase.

'Well,' Lydia said. 'Food will be another fifteen minutes. It's frittata, I hope that's okay? I'd planned on doing a full roast, but of course, with you coming earlier than expected ...'

'Frittata sounds lovely,' Eric said diplomatically, then to Tom, who was pouring a bright orange, reduced-alcohol Buck's Fizz, added. 'Not too much for me though. I'm afraid I've got to head off after food.'

'Lyds was telling me,' Tom said, handing him a full glass. 'What a mess.'

'You don't know the half of it.'

'But we don't need to talk about any of that right now,' Suzy said. 'Tell me, how did the boys' nativity go yesterday?'

'Oh, it was fantastic,' Lydia gushed.

'Fantastic,' Tom agreed. 'Without a doubt, the best *X-Men* nativity I've ever seen.'

The frittata was palatable, bordering on tasty. It could have been enjoyable were it not for Tom and Lydia's insistence on mentioning their own eggs every twenty seconds. Eric estimated that he could have bought his father's house back off the church had he been offered a menial ten pence for each time they were commented on. Dessert was alcohol-free Christmas pudding, which they ate obligingly, and was followed by present giving which took place around the tree directly afterwards.

The four adults, three children, and their Old English Sheepdog, Broccoli, crammed into the tiny room. The parents took up positions on the sofas, leaving the children scrambling around the coffee table trying to find a patch of carpet not covered in spray-painted pine cones or clumps of matted fur. The room smelt like a dog-friendly arboretum, or rather what an arboretum would smell like if the only trees it contained were pines and the dogs that walked there stank implausibly of sulphur and Pedigree Chum.

The tradition of meeting at Lydia's for Christmas had

started over a decade before. Suzy and Lydia's parents had long been part of the cruise ship scene, and only once since Suzy and Eric had met had they visited over the Christmas period. That year Eric had insisted they all go out for lunch.

'We have plenty of room at ours,' Suzy had said.

'I'm well aware,' Eric replied.

Nowadays Eric didn't get involved in Christmas preparations. Especially not gift purchases, even when the direct family were concerned. A few years ago, Suzy had asked him for a bread maker for her birthday. He had had every intention of getting her one, but when he got to the store he was swayed by a self-driving vacuum that scurried around the house sweeping up dust as it went. He thought it was fantastic and comparable in present terms. Apparently not. Since the incident, his credit card had been the only requirement of Eric during festive and holiday seasons.

That afternoon, Suzy, who had done all the shopping weeks in advance, watched as her purchases were opened to an appreciative chorus of *oohs* and *ahhs*; an organic llama wool crocheted scarf for Lydia along with a pair of silver earrings apparently from Abi, a Leatherman multi-tool for Tom, and a set of build-it-yourself motorised dinosaur kits for the boys. By contrast, Eric and Suzy received the standard bottle of homemade elderflower wine, this year accompanied by a set of psychedelic homemade clay coasters.

'We thought the colour scheme would go perfectly in your house,' Lydia said.

'Definitely,' Suzy said.

Eric wondered where exactly in their house fluorescent pink, vomit green, and turd brown all mingled into one.

Having opened the remainder of the presents, all eyes were on Abi as she tore at a small parcel of crinkled – and blatantly recycled – Christmas paper. She ripped off the Sellotape, cast the rubbish aside, and pulled out what appeared to be a yellow knitted condom with wings.

Eric's jaw hung loose as he attempted to fathom the gift.

'Will you use it?' Lydia said to a wide-eyed, mystified Abi.

The silence was palpable. Even Tom appeared to be having a hard time keeping a straight face at the disturbingly fashioned gift.

'That's lovely!' Suzy said finally, rescuing the situation by the skin of her teeth.

'What is it?' Abi said. Using her fingertips, she pinched the atrocity, stretching the fabric lengthways, then along its girth. Eric wanted to vomit.

'It's an egg cosy,' Lydia said. 'For your boiled eggs. So that they stay warm. Look, it's a little chick, there are its eyes and beak. Ellery made it himself.'

Lydia rotated the condom around, showing that it did indeed have eyes, big scary psychotic eyes that would no doubt appear in Eric's nightmares for years to come. A second silence followed. Lydia and Ellery's smiles stayed frozen on their faces, their foreheads crinkled in expectation. Eric's own pulse took a speedier pace as he stared at Suzy, who in turn had her eyes locked on Abi, willing her to say the right thing. Abi held the object in her fingertips, out at arm's length, and turned it over in her hands.

'I don't think I like eggs,' she said.

Eric decided then would be as good a time as any to leave.

CHAPTER 12

T HE INTERNET HAD indeed lied about the lack of rain in Burnham. As Eric approached the town, the puddles grew wider and deeper, and sprayed up and under the wheel arches with a deep, sloshing whirr. The sky had a true winter feel about it, desolately vast and almost violet in colour. The bare-branched trees that lined the winding roads gave the impression that he was driving towards the end of the world, not merely the end of western civilisation and culture as he knew it. The Audi's heater blasted steel-smelling hot air out into the car, keeping his fingers warm and his windscreen clear; another definite advantage with not having brought Sally.

Eric was surprised to find the allotment a veritable hive of activity. Several figures huddled over their little beds or else pottered amongst the bushes. Amidst those brandishing rakes and trowels and other forms of multi-spiked-instruments was the wood-dwelling owlet, Janice, who was crouched close to the ground in a manner that would have left Eric's thirty-seven-year-old knees wincing at the strain. Eric searched for another route to his plot but didn't know the way well enough. He had no choice but to head straight on.

Deliberately avoiding any sideways glances, Eric strode past her as fast as he could, his eyes forwards, and the chainsaw bag – which weighed heavy as it perched on his left shoulder – shielding his face from her view. There was no way she could spot him; not with the bag covering him and the fact she was facing the other direction. Still, he daren't look in her direction. He was well past the end of her neighbouring patch when a shrill voice cut the through the relative peace.

'Woohoo, Eric?' Eric stopped, then immediately regretted the decision.

'You should have kept walking,' he said to himself. Forcing his lips up into a toothy smile, he inched himself around to face her, the chainsaw wobbling precariously as he did.

'Janice,' he said. 'I didn't notice you there.'

'Oh, I'm so glad you came back,' she said, hobbling across the grass towards him. 'I was a bit worried last time. You know, what with Norman being the way he was.'

'It's all fine.'

'Norman will be Norman. Some days I don't know how she puts up with it, I really don't. But then he has a good heart. A very good heart.' Her eyes lit up. 'You should come and meet everyone else. There's lots of us out today.'

'I've seen.'

'We're all trying to make the most of the mild weather before the frost comes back, you see. You can't do much in frost, not when the ground gets as hard as it does, but that rain last night loosened it all up. I'll tell you what, it's a good time to dig your runner trenches. It's a good time to check your compost heap, too. Now listen, people think compost makes itself, but it doesn't. At least not good compost. Good compost requires —'

'Sorry,' Eric interrupted. 'I don't mean to seem rude, only I haven't got much time today.' He nodded to the chainsaw, now resting against his knee. 'I've only got this for a couple of hours. Perhaps I can meet everyone else the next time I'm down?'

'I'll hold you to that. And I've got the memory of a fox.'

'I'm sure you have,' Eric said, hitching the chainsaw back onto his shoulder and wondering exactly how good a memory the average fox had.

The decision to knock over the water butt had not been a wise one. The branches and debris were now covered in a thick, congealed green slime that, while adding a splash of colour to the vastly brown terrain, filled the surrounding area with a redolent musk not dissimilar to that that you'd find in a hippopotamus' sleeping chamber.

Eric touched a patch of the slime then withdrew his hand rapidly. He wiped the gunk onto the back of his trousers. His eyes travelled across the length and breadth of the plot, a weight building in his stomach. Where the heck did he start?

Rather than deliberating over which end of the patch was more disastrous than the other, Eric decided to unpack the chainsaw on the premise that he'd work out what to attack with it once he'd figured out how to get the thing going. A nervous tingle of adrenaline spread up from somewhere around his bladder as he unzipped the bag. He hadn't appreciated how new it was in the shop. Nor the size. The metal blade glinted in the winter light as Eric brushed his hand across the chain. Sandblasted and perfectly smooth.

Eric whipped his hand away, blushing at the inappropriate tenderness he'd just shared with a 3.7 horsepower piece of hardware. He checked over his shoulder and, after deciding no one was the least bit interested in his mechanophilic tendencies, began to tackle the job at hand.

After unpacking the item in question, Eric skimmed through the instruction booklet. He double read the safety issues, oil filling information, and instructions on how to start the engine. He had already read up on cutting angles and correct grip positions on the internet at home but decided it wouldn't hurt to have another quick read through on those too. Using the labelled image on the back page, he identified all the main features – from the chain sprocket cover to the back-handle guard – on the actual specimen. After twenty minutes, a hesitant petrol fill, and his back already aching from being leant over for so long, Eric was ready to start.

Holding it again resulted in yet another influx of adrenaline. He was going to enjoy this, Eric thought to himself. Really enjoy it. He knelt, checked the chain break, and slipped off the cover, before pressing the decompression valve. Standing upright, he secured the saw with his foot. His pulse rose an extra notch. Was this the right type of ground? Or was it too soft? Would he be better off moving it over to one of the patios to start? Choking back the fears, Eric grabbed the cord for a pull start. Was it far enough away from his body? What about kick back? Chainsaws like this all gave kick back, didn't they? It was no good. Eric let go and stepped away. His hands were quivering, and his legs trembled, his earlier confidence all but gone.

'Man up,' he said out loud.

'You can do it,' a voice called back from somewhere behind him.

Eric spun around and saw a man on crutches, with a very wide grin, waving at him. He hurriedly looked back away.

With a lump still lodged in his throat, Eric secured the chainsaw yet again. This time he didn't wait for any of the doubts to start creeping in. He took one deep breath, held it in, and yanked. There was half a second of silence, in which the air trembled as he held it in his lungs and the taste of iron ran thick under his tongue, before the engine spluttered, then coughed, then roared into life. Eric's heart leapt. It was like being a child again, not that he ever got to play with chainsaws as a child, but still, his whole body felt electrified with energy.

'Throttle, throttle,' he reminded himself and pushed down and out before placing it, still running, on the ground.

Aware of the deadly machinery at his toes, Eric stepped away from the running power tool to resurvey the land in question. With so much to be done, and no one place seeming any better than the another, he picked up the chainsaw and began the assault exactly where he stood.

It was exhilarating. Every slice felt like a weight from his past had been cut from his shoulders. *Thwack.* That branch was the time his father told him he wasn't allowed to audition for the school musical. *Thud.* That one was for the time Eric had to cut his honeymoon short because his father thought he was having a heart-attack. *Thump.* That one was for the time he left him a worthless little patch of weeds as his inheritance.

Eric cut the engine, placed the saw back on the ground, and stepped away to deliberate his next move. Sweat slid down his forehead and into his eyes. He wiped it away with the back of his hand. He liked the chainsaw. He really liked it. He liked the feel of it in his hands, the weight of it in his biceps, and the release as it cut through the debris. He liked the sound, the smell. He liked it all apart from starting the bloody thing; that still terrified him. Still, after a five-minute rest, he stripped off his jumper, tied it around his waist, restarted it, and carried on.

After fifteen minutes, the bushes had been truly decimated. Blueberry, gooseberry, whatever they had been in the previous spring months, they were now nothing more than a broken pile of twigs shrouded in a veil of dust. Eric took another pause and surveyed his handiwork. Predominant aromas of petrol and sawdust knotted the air, and a bubble of pride rose through his gut. It was looking good. Really good. Well, almost all of it was.

With its broken glass and metal framing, Eric had naturally avoided the greenhouse area in his chainsaw-wielding juncture. Unfortunately, now that so much of the rest had been flattened, its obtrusiveness stood out like a Marilyn Manson wannabe at a rendition of Stravinsky's *The Firebird*. Eric kept the engine running as he perused. Its low, growling patter was just loud enough to drown out the ever-increasing chattering from the other allotments. More and more faces peered over the tops of their perennials, having grown interested in his goings-on. He placed the chainsaw on the ground and strode into the rubble, kicking aside the smaller twigs and stones and tossing a long, sawn-off branch, and metal girder to the side. Eric was not a man who left a job half done, and this was no exception. There had to be a way to tackle the greenhouse today. There had to be. He flicked a piece of glass with his foot.

The problem was all the fragments. There were so many little pieces of glass that the only way he'd be able to clear the patch was to pick them all up by hand. There were big bits too though. Huge sheets, the size of a coffee table, jagged and cracked, jutted out of the earth. Even if he did manage to pull those out, Eric wasn't entirely sure he knew what to do with them afterwards. Still, he glanced at his watch. He was meant to pick Suzy up in forty minutes in order to get back to the tool hire place before it closed for its Christmas break. If he drove fast, that still left him with twenty more minutes to work. Crouching down, he began to pick up the glass.

He had done a good job of averting the locals thus far, although he suspected his previous outburst with the water butt, combined with wildly waving a chainsaw, had had something to do with the matter. Now that he was on his hands and knees, however, he appeared to be an easy target.

'Big job you've done there, laddy.'

The man who spoke had crow-like eyes and a long, ratty nose.

'Still got a way to go,' Eric said without lifting his head.

'Aye. You want to be careful. 'S broken glass in there.'

Eric didn't respond. He continued to remove fragments from the mulching soil.

'Big saw you got going there. You know it's –'

'Sorry,' Eric said. 'I don't mean to be rude, only I'm short on time. Is there anything in particular I can help you with?'

The man opened his mouth then shut it again. Without so much as a nod, Eric's head went back down into the weeds. A minute or so later a throat cleared behind him. Eric gritted his teeth and ignored it. He had finally managed to wrap his fingers around two smooth edges of a large sheet of glass and was wiggling it against the binding stems and roots. Letting go of it now would cause the thing to slip back out of his grasp and probably smash into a thousand pieces. The voice coughed again.

'Hey there, laddy —'

'Could you hold on a second?' The sweat was beading on Eric's fingertips. He could feel the glass inching out of his grip. 'I'm kind of occupied.'

'I can see that. It's only —'

'Just one minute, okay? If you can give me one minute?'

'I thought you might —'

'Can you just hold on one bloody second?'

Eric stepped back as he spoke. His fingers squeezed at the sheet, emitting a high-pitched squeak. One inch more, that was all he had to move it, one inch more to free it from all the vines and creepers and finally render this place usable. With the most forceful tug he could manage, his elbows sprang back and for less than a heartbeat, the massive pane balanced in his dampening grasp. Then, as if in slow motion, the whole thing tilted, wobbled, and fell with a sickening crash to the ground.

'For the love of...' Eric kicked the ground, his soft-toed boot landing squarely on the point of a shard of broken glass. 'Argh!' he yelled as a searing pain bolted from his big toe all the way up his leg. It was blinding, horrific. Every nerve end from his toe to his calf was on fire as he hopped around while a stream of expletives left his mouth.

'Now, hold on a minute, laddy —'

'Bloody, buggering —'

'Look here, you might —'

'*What?* What do you want?'

Eric could feel the wetness of blood pooling at the end of his shoe. A smell of ash and burning was muddling in his senses. His head began to swim. He turned to the man with the ratty nose.

'What is it? What do you want?'

The man's jaw momentarily slackened. His gaze lowered onto Eric's bleeding toe before returning to meet his eyes.

'I thought you might want to know that your chainsaw's on fire,' he said.

CHAPTER 13

T O GIVE TOM his due, he managed to keep up the small talk all the way to A&E. Even in the allotment, when Eric was draped over his shoulder, whimpering and wincing with every step as he left a trail of blood from the plot to the car, Tom had managed to maintain a positive demeanour.

'Don't think you've severed an artery,' he said. 'There's lots more blood when you sever an artery.'

Humiliation was an understatement. As Eric limped out, glass shard still protruding from his toe cap, it seemed that every Burnham resident over the age of sixty-five had come out to watch the event. Leading the crowd was, of course, Norman, who had, of course, appeared in time to see the smoke pouring out of the chainsaw. The day was a fail in every way possible. A&E was rammed, full of inebriated adults, children who had swallowed Christmas tree baubles, and doctors and nurses who looked so stressed that they should have been admitted themselves.

He lost the shoe. It could have been a lot worse, but still, seeing the insole ripped mercilessly from the leather upper of his two-hundred-pound outdoor shoes was never going to be a nice event. The doctor on his case wasn't going to pull the glass out without assessing the damage underneath first, so with a delicate hand, he cut around the sole, then the sock. Needless to say, once he'd done that, he pulled the glass straight out anyway. Later, Eric wondered whether Tom would inform Lydia of her brother-in-law's pitiful screaming, though, at the time, he could barely even think through the pain. Four stitches and a bucket load of shame. It could have been worse, but it really didn't feel like it.

It was dark by the time they left the hospital. Not early evening dark, or just as the moon rises dark, but stars in the sky, all curtains drawn, very close to midnight dark. The tool hire place closed at six and didn't reopen again until the new year. Eric didn't even care. All that mattered was his throbbing toe and battered ego. Besides, Tom had looked over the chainsaw and decided it was most likely just an issue with the oil. An easy fix. Eric would probably only have to pay for the late return, he said. Eric didn't have the energy to respond.

While his foot felt like it had been dunked in a vat of concentrated sulphuric acid and his head was fuzzy, furry, and altogether rather confused from the painkillers, Suzy was beyond half-cut from an exceptionally extended brunch and a teetotal sister who insisted on topping up her glass the entire time. Given that the trains had stopped running, and no one was fit to drive, there was no choice but to stay the night at Tom and Lydia's. Abi camped down in the boys' room, under a makeshift tepee Lydia had fashioned out of bed sheets and old broom handles, while Suzy and Eric got the spare room. The batik patchwork quilt that covered their bed was embroidered with tiny mirrors and golden thread, and smelt of sheep and ayurvedic nonsense.

'Lydia got this when she first went to India,' Suzy said as she hoisted Eric's leg up and onto the bed.

'I don't think she's washed it since,' Eric replied.

He wriggled himself under the sheet, grimacing against the pain of his foot. Through the walls, he could hear the cousins giggling.

'I'm sorry you've had an awful day,' Suzy said. 'I hate seeing you like this. You know it really isn't worth all this stress.'

'Don't say it,' Eric cut her off before she could continue. 'I'm not getting rid of her. Certainly not after today. There is no way that man gets to win.'

'But what is he winning? Your dad is dead, Eric. There are no more competitions.'

'That's what you think.'

'Well if that's the case, what's wrong with you just letting him win? What are you gaining from all this? We hardly see you as it is. The last thing I want is Abi not seeing her father for the next two years because he's too busy at work and down the allotment.'

'That's not going to happen,' he said.

'Hmm,' was all Suzy said in response.

Christmas, and the days that bookend it, were a washout. For six days it rained constantly; hard, vertical pillars of water that turned windows opaque and made travelling anywhere a suicide risk. The sky remained an indolent grey, bleak, dull, and without imagination; Eric reflected the sentiment to a tee. The office shutdown over Christmas made it impossible to get on top of things the way he would have liked. Still, he lay on the sofa, foot propped up with a mountain of cushions, and fired off emails, waiting in vain for responses and silently seething as each half hour passed without so much as an out-of-office reply. Even Jack Nelson took two days to get back to him, and told him not to worry, they would sort out any issues in the new year.

Christmas Day was pleasant enough. Abi was pleased with her presents, which had nothing to do with him. All the same, it made a fuzzy ball of sentiment blossom as he observed the unabashed glee with which she ran into their bedroom, stocking in hand, leapt on their beds, and tore at the paper. From Suzy, Eric got a gin tasting course, twenty types of gin in one afternoon; it sounded ideal. From Abi, he received a mug. The image on said mug resembled something that a goat having an epileptic fit with a paintbrush between its teeth would create if said goat were particularly skilled at painting eyeballs and ears.

'Do you like it, Daddy?' Abi said. 'It's abstract art. We're doing abstract art at school and this is what you look like. See, you're even wearing a tie.'

'It's wonderful, baby,' Eric said, taking the mug in hand. 'Remind me how much we're paying for this school again?' he said to Suzy.

The first day the sun made an appearance was the 28th December. In Eric's mind, the gap between Boxing Day and New Year's Eve was some form of time vortex. The wrapping paper and leftovers had long been discarded and forgotten, yet it was still a sizeable period until the inevitable new year. You could guarantee, during that five-day-long black hole, that nobody you spoke to had any idea what actual day of the week it was, and as soon as the twenty-seventh arrived, no one had any plans either. In Eric's mind the working week would be much better preserved should New Year be shuffled a few days earlier.

Suzy opened the curtains, causing Eric to squint at the sudden onslaught of light. She then redeemed herself slightly by handing him a cup of tea.

'How's the foot?' she asked as she proceeded to remove the duvet and begin prodding at his dressing. 'It looks much better. I don't think it'll even leave much of a scar.'

'I have to be honest, I was worried about that. Big toe scars can be quite stereotyping. People might start to think I belong to a gang or something.'

'Fine. Be like that. So, have you got anything planned for today?'

'Only to catch up on a bit of work —'

'Good. Because we're going out.'

Eric shuffled himself into a more upright position. 'Did you have anywhere in mind?'

'Funny you should ask,' Suzy said.

Eric tried to make her see sense. While Suzy was right from one perspective – if he was going to keep up with this whole escapade then he really couldn't take a weekend off no matter how much he wanted to – she had no real idea what the actual situation entailed.

'It's not safe for Abi,' Eric said for the third time. 'God knows what's lurking about in there. She could catch rabies. For all I know, I already have.'

'You're being dramatic.'

'Besides. I can only just stand. And you expect me to go digging about in six inches of mud?'

'No, I expect you and Abi to sit at the sides and play cards while I dig about in six inches of mud.'

'Wow, that sounds exciting.'

Suzy's *look* followed.

The thin rays of sun that cast every other plot in the allotment with a narrow glimmer of optimism could do nothing to disguise the dismal landscape that stood before them. A smell of bonfires drifted in from beyond the hedgerows, bringing up memories of crematoriums and ashes. Maybe burning it would be a solution, Eric pondered.

'It looks a lot better than it did,' he insisted. 'I wish I had some photos to show you. It really does look much, much better. Loads better. Heaps and heaps.' But his voice couldn't hide his disappointment.

'See,' he said after another minute's silence. 'I told you it was a stupid idea coming here.'

It did look better than last time. All the bushes and dead plants had been cut back to nothing and one side of the green-house had been all but cleared of saw-toothed broken glass. That it looked better was not in question. Whether it would ever look anything more than a health inspector's wet dream, was.

'Just tell me what to do and I'll do it,' Suzy said and pulled on her gardening gloves. 'The sooner we get started, the sooner we'll get it done.'

'I really don't think there's anything you can do,' Eric said, then he stopped talking; he was wise enough to know when he was beaten.

Eric had spied some green gardening bins. They were way back under the notice board at the entrance, so while he and Abi folded out their picnic chairs and divided the cards ready for an epic game of Top Trumps, Suzy headed back to the gate to collect one of the four-feet containers.

'I can help,' Eric said several times as he watched Suzy crouched over what had once been a tomato sack, pulling out another handful of weeds and refuse.

'It's fine,' Suzy said. 'I like it. It's therapeutic.' One by one, she shovelled forkfuls of debris out of the ground and into the bin. Eric sat in his chair, leg extended, admiring his wife gliding between the detritus, attempting to make a little sense out of the chaos.

'Make sure you stick the fork in first,' Eric said. 'Don't just put your hands in. There are rats in there.'

'Can we have one, Daddy?' Abi piped up. 'Harry Nini at school has a pet rat. Can we have a pet rat too?'

'No. Now beat this. Silvertip Shark. Maximum depth, eight hundred metres.'

She went back to studying her cards.

Eric wasn't sure why they'd had a gardening fork hidden in the depths of their utility room cupboards in their London home, but watching Suzy attempt to move the weeds with its skewed prongs and bent handle confirmed his thoughts that they would need to buy better tools. More money being spent without a penny in return.

It was a little under an hour later – when Abi pulled out the Top Trumps Disney Princess cards – that Eric called a halt to the work.

'You should stop,' he said. 'You've done loads.'

'Just another ten minutes.'

'Really, hun, we should head back. Besides, I don't feel right just sitting here watching you and Abi's bored stiff.'

'Rubbish. You're still having fun aren't you, sweetheart?'

'Nuh,' Abi said non-committedly. 'Dad's really rubbish. He only says what's on the cards. It's way more fun playing with you.'

'Fine.' Suzy wiped the sweat from her forehead, leaving a slight smear of dirt in its wake. She stepped back to observe her handiwork. 'To be honest, I'm surprised at how little I've got done. I thought I'd cleared far more.'

'What are you on about? I can see at least thirty centimetres there with no weeds on it at all.'

She swiped for her husband, but Eric caught her hand and kissed it.

'You've done amazingly,' Eric insisted. 'There's always going to be loads to do. We could come down every day for a month and the place would still look like a bomb site.'

'Eric.'

'Sorry.' He hoisted himself up to standing and limped over to the plot. 'I mean it will still look a mosquito breeding-ground cesspool. But you've done an amazing job. Thank you.'

'And it wasn't that bad having us down here with you?'

'I guess not.'

From his newly elevated standing position, Eric gazed past his wife and surveyed the plot behind her. He was reasonably sure he could see where she'd been working.

CHAPTER 14

NEW YEAR'S DAY brought an inevitable headache, aching muscles, and a mouth that tasted of dry slippers and flaccid mushrooms. It was unfortunate that it was the same day of their next planned trip to Burnham.

They had gone to their neighbours, Ben and Belinda, whom they saw on average three times a year: the inaugural summer BBQ, held sometime between May and July; Ben and Belinda's joint birthday, which Eric knew for certain was either in September or October, or perhaps November; and New Year's Eve. His social ties with these long-term friends were in fact so tenuous that when Eric had bumped into Belinda down the Indian takeaway the week before Christmas, it had taken him a solid two minutes to fit a name to the face. She just didn't look right without a sparkly scarf around her neck, white wine spritzer in her hand, and party blower buzzing in an ungainly manner from between her lips. The combination of drink and painkillers resulted in a considerably later start to the day than Eric had anticipated.

It was a damp day, with a hazy drizzle that fogged up the windows and caused frequent, involuntary shivers when he glanced outside and caught sight of the sky. The pain in Eric's foot had lessened to a dull throb which, provided he avoided sudden movements, or particularly trenchant surfaces – Abi's Lego Princess starship being one of the most recurring offenders – remained moderately pain-free. The leftover alcohol in his system was no doubt helping the situation too.

Suzy had picked up three pairs of gardening gloves in the post-Christmas sales, which she was keen to put to the test. Hers and Eric's were both sturdily made, with thick faux leather grips on the fingers and palms, and a suede cuff which covered a good four-inches above the wrist line. Abi's were much more impressive, with floral linings, fancy stitch work around all the seams, and appliquéd ducks on the top.

Abi had loved them in the shop. Now, however, she'd decided they were too babyish.

'Why can't I have the same as you and Mummy?' she said.

'Mummy and I wanted the same ones as you have,' Eric said. 'Only they didn't do them in our size.'

'I'll look like a kid wearing these,' she said and skulked off to her room, slamming each door in the interim behind her.

Abi's vile mood continued throughout the car journey. The music on every radio station was "crap," the heater was either too hot or too cold or not blowing out enough air or blowing out too much air. Her seat belt was too tight, her iPad didn't have enough battery, and Suzy's driving was making her feel sick.

'I can't spend two hours with her in the allotment being like this,' Eric said to Suzy, not even bothering to hush his voice. 'I want to throttle her already.'

'She's just out of her routine. Why don't we go get some breakfast somewhere first?'

Eric suspected that a large majority of the clientele at the Cabin were there with the aim of relieving their hangovers from the previous night, and for a minute he worried they may struggle to get a seat, but when Griff spied him at the door he beckoned him over. They hurried inside, where he found them a table at the back next to a window. Still not feeling brave enough to face a complete Fat Bastard, Eric opted for a Greedy Git, although given that Suzy pilfered half his bacon, black pudding, and one of the sausages, he once again wished he'd ordered up. Abi's meal was, unsurprisingly, wrong.

'I didn't think the beans would be on the bread,' she whined. 'You know I don't like it when the beans touch the bread.'

Steeling himself against the tension building in his muscles, Eric called Griff over for a re-order, this time specifying that the beans be in an entirely separate container placed on the other side of the plate to the toast.

'Why don't you head off?' Suzy said. 'We can walk down when we've finished here.'

'It's quite a walk.'

'It's fine. It'll give missy here a chance to walk off that chip on her shoulder.'

'Are you sure?' Eric wasn't convinced.

'Positive.'

Eric got up from the table and went to settle the bill. He glanced at the scrap of paper, noting that Abi's first breakfast was missing.

'We'll pay for all of it,' Eric said.

'It's fine,' Griff insisted. 'I've got three of my own. Grown up now mind, but they could be little terrors when they wanted to. It's no problem.'

'If you're sure?' Eric said, then feeling guilty placed the remaining balance in the little jam jar labelled tips.

Eric was surprised how quickly he forgot about the drizzle. As he entered through the gates, he grabbed one of the green bins and motioned briefly but politely to Janice, indicating the bin as his reason for not being able to stop. The dampness from sweat and the dampness from the rain were soon indistinguishable as he continued from where they'd let off the previous weekend. Perhaps it was the lessened pressure of not having Suzy or Abi with him there, or perhaps the lack of time constraints, but the work seemed easier today. He found a rhythm, fork, swing, dump, fork, swing, dump, and even his foot wasn't hurting enough to distract him.

'Carrot cake?'

Cynthia's flame-red hair was currently hidden beneath the blue hood of her wax jacket. Extended towards Eric was a long tube of crumpled aluminium foil, the insides of which contained a rather orange looking carrot cake.

'I baked it this morning. It's not my best, but it's better than my worst.'

'Oh, well, um. It looks lovely,' Eric said.

'Take a piece,'

'Actually, I've only just had breakfast.'

'Then take a piece for later. Or take some home for the family. I hear you had them up here helping a couple of weeks back?'

As she spoke she was pulling out several slices, sealing them in a ziplock bag which had appeared from her pocket, and handing them to Eric. A quick sniff caused a slight rumble beneath his belly button.

'Thank you.' He took the package of cake, which appeared to be almost three-quarters of the loaf. 'Yes, they just came up to help for an hour or so.'

'And your foot? How's that holding up? You've got to be so careful ...' She stopped mid-flow and frowned. 'I'm sorry. I'm doing that old lady thing, aren't I? Asking you lots of questions and not giving you any time to respond.'

'It's fine.'

'No, I should let you get on. You've got lots to be going on with.' She turned as if to leave, then paused. There was something about the way she stopped, as if suspended mid-animation, that made Eric wait.

'I know you don't really know me,' she said, turning back. 'And I know you and Norman didn't get off on quite the right foot. But I was wondering if perhaps in the next few weeks, if the weather gets a bit better, you might, you might ...'

'Yes?'

'I know it's a lot to ask. I do really. But I was hoping you might be able to take him out in that car of yours?' There was a childlike quiver to her lips when she spoke, and something about her eyes tugged at a place in Eric's chest cavity. 'He used to go out with your dad quite frequently, you see. And I know he misses it. At our age, something like that ... it would mean a lot to him, that's what I'm trying to say. But not if it's any trouble, of course. I don't want to inconvenience you.'

The tug in Eric's chest had built to a point where it now affected his throat as well, and when he spoke the words came out far more hoarse and croaky than he'd expected.

'Well, it's really not very good taking her out in weather like this —'

'Of course, I completely understand. Forget I asked. Forget I asked.'

'But I'm sure in the spring when it's not quite so wet.'

The old woman's face bloomed into a smile, squashing her wrinkles into even deeper crevices.

'Thank you,' she said. 'It would mean the world to him. To us both.'

With a sudden awareness of heat rising to his cheeks, Eric

busied himself with the topsoil. He could sense Cynthia still standing there, watching him, but he kept his head down, for fear she might burst into tears or worse still, try to hug him. A few seconds later she spoke again.

'Well enjoy the carrot cake. And I do hope I get to meet the family next time they're around.'

Eric paused, considered his next sentence, and said it anyway.

'If you can hang on a few minutes, you can meet them now,' he said. 'And they can you thank you in person for the carrot cake.'

'I don't want to interfere with your family time,' she said. 'Besides, I ought to dash. I need to be home for when Norman gets back.' With that she scurried away around the back of her potting shed and down the path, stopping to offer a final wave before she disappeared out of view.

It was another forty minutes before Abi and Suzy arrived. The drizzle had subsided into a wet, muggy mist that soaked into the earth and made everything smell like a cheap pub side-salad. Abi looked to be in a better mood, in the sense that she was no longer throwing random screaming fits, but still had a scowl reminiscent of a cat who had just spent three hours with its tail caught in the tube of a vacuum cleaner. Oblivious to the ongoing cold spell and onset of winter, she'd somehow managed to find a strawberry ice lolly, which she repeatedly licked, shuddered, then licked again. Neither the rain nor the brain freeze could deter her from her sub-zero treat.

'You've got a fair bit done,' Suzy said, coming up behind him, and placing her hands on the small of his back. 'It's getting there. It's definitely getting there. Another three or four weeks and you'll have most of it cleared.'

'Yeah, if I can get it all sorted by the beginning of March I'll be pleased.'

'Any idea what you're going to do with the greenhouse?'

Eric cast a disapproving eye over the rusting monstrosity.

'I guess the tip. But I'm not going to think about that now.' He turned his attention over to Abi. 'Right,' he said. 'Time for you to get your hands dirty.' He rolled up his sleeves in a mockery of hard work then kicked up his good heel and dug a line in the dirt. 'I need you to pull up all the plants on this side of the line,' he said. 'But you're not to go over this line. Okay? There's still glass and junk and God knows what other crap in there.'

'Language,' Suzy chided.

'Gotcha. Mustn't go over the line. Lots of crap,' Abi paraphrased, proceeding to lick her ice lolly, and showing no signs of moving. Eric smiled at his wife.

Suzy slipped on her gloves and tied her hair back in a ponytail. A sweet gust of nostalgia swept through Eric. There was something about the way her hands ran through her hair that reminded him of the way she was when they first met. Determined, focused. Not that she wasn't still, he just didn't get to see it so often anymore.

Eric couldn't help but steal glances at his wife. Nothing was ever too much trouble for Suzy, no task too big, no problem unsolvable. She took everything in her stride. Her first husband was a dick, that was for sure, but it was a fact for which Eric would be eternally grateful. If he hadn't been, he and Suzy wouldn't be where they were now.

Aware of the need to refocus on the job in hand, he cast her one more wistful gaze before bending down and attacking his weed problem. Eric was knee high in nettles, grabbing them from as close to the roots as possible when Suzy stopped.

'Oh, I forgot, this was on the notice board for you.' She stood up and pulled a thin white envelope out of her pocket. Eric's name was typed on a sticky label that was stuck on the front. In the top corner, a green stamp consisting of a crossed fork and shovel had been unevenly inked. Eric took it from her.

'Thanks. Where did you say it was?'

'Pinned up on the notice board by the bins.'

Eric shrugged. 'It's probably just something about the tenancy. I forgot I had to pay it this month.' He ran his finger under the seal and ripped the envelope open. Inside was a single sheet of A4 paper, the same stamp on the corner beside some unfamiliar address.

Heat rose up through his belly, accompanied by a definite acceleration in heart rate. It was only a short letter – two and a third lines long, with a couple of extra bullet points beneath – but by the time Eric had reached the final words his fists were balled, his pulse pounding, and his eyes bulged so wide they looked to be making an escape bid from their sockets.

'What is it?' Suzy said.

'They have to be sodding joking.'

CHAPTER 15

ERIC RANG CHRISTIAN Eaves. It took six attempts to get through. Each of the previous tries he stayed on the line – the sawtooth tone cutting through his eardrum – until it went to voicemail. It didn't deter him. While Suzy drove, and Abi slept, Eric kept on ringing.

Finally, he picked up.

'Can they do this?' Eric said when he'd explained the situation in microscopic detail. 'Surely they can't do this, can they?'

Christian Eaves was silent down the end of the phone. The sound of smacking lips echoed several times before he eventually spoke.

'Mr Sibley, I don't mean to sound rude, but firstly, today is New Year's Day which, like most people, I am spending with my family. Secondly, why exactly have you come to me with this problem?'

'Who else am I meant to go to?'

'This sounds like something to be sorted out within the committee. At this point in time, it's not a legal issue.'

'But if they can do this. If they *do* do this, I'll lose the car, won't I? That's what you're saying right? I'll lose the car?'

'If it comes to that. Then yes, but, Mr Sibley, this still might all be some misunderstanding —'

'After all the work I've put in.'

'I'm sorry, Mr Sibley.'

'F-ing bastards.' Eric slammed his fist against the dashboard. Suzy shot him a glare. 'She's asleep,' Eric mouthed, then noticed that Abi was very much awake and staring at her father, her mouth opened in a gawp. Eric took a few deep breaths, mouthed an apology to his daughter, and put the phone back up to his ear.

'Okay, so there has to be some way around this. Something I can do? I've been down at that *flipping* allotment every weekend for the last month and I've got some moderately impressive scars to prove it. Surely that has to count for something?'

Christian Eaves sighed. The vibrations fizzled down the line.

'I really wish that was enough,' he said. 'But unfortunately, you can't maintain the allotment if you no longer possess the tenancy to it.'

'Well thanks for nothing,' Eric said and hung up the phone.

Suzy was staring at the road, pretending to concentrate, with her cheeks sucked in, and hands gripping the steering wheel. Eric considered the fact he should probably apologise for his language but decided against it. He was an adult. If he wanted to swear in front of his daughter, he should be able to do so without being made to feel like he'd personally drowned a dozen day-old Labrador puppies. He sank back into the seat, closed his eyes, and breathed in loudly through his nostrils. Fifteen seconds later his eyes sprang open, he retrieved his phone from his pocket, and with his thumb tapping at a record speed, began to type on the screen.

'What are you doing?' Suzy said in a monotone voice he knew was intended to feign disinterest.

'Looking for something,' he said.

'For what?'

Eric stopped staring at his screen and turned to her. 'Christian Eaves said this was a committee decision. Not a legal one. So, I'm trying to find out who's on the committee. That way I can appeal to their better judgement. Or find out if it's a misunderstanding. Or at least offer them some kind of bribe.' He said the last line with a slightly jovial lilt although truthfully neither he nor Suzy was entirely sure if he was joking.

'Maybe it was meant for your father?' Suzy said. 'Maybe they've been holding onto it since last year?'

Eric shook his head. 'It's addressed to Eric Sibley, not Mr Sibley. And besides, it's dated last week. I mean, Unsatisfactory Cultivation. What does that even mean? What do they expect me to be cultivating? It's bloody winter for crying out loud. And seven days. What kind of notice is that? Surely I can't be the only person with an allotment there who has an actual job. Actual working commitments. They're a bunch of nasty, small-minded, bigoted coffin-dodgers the bloody lot of them.'

'What's a coffin-dodger?' Abi asked from the back.

'Your dad,' Suzy replied. 'If he doesn't start watching his language.'

Eric muttered something quietly under his breath, though judging by Suzy's instantaneous glare he didn't mutter it quietly enough.

The village website wasn't cut out for mobile use, and after ten minutes of trying to find contact details, Eric decided to abandon the task until he was home and on his laptop. In the meanwhile, he checked his work emails. His inbox had filled over the day. Apparently, the academy chain had been so impressed with Eric's handling of their account they'd asked the company to manage another three of their outlets, once again in the education field. Eric's stomach fluttered. Hartley had hinted about restructuring the junior and senior associate directors from regions to focus groups for over a year now. If that were to happen, he'd have to be a definite shoo-in for the education position now. At least that was one bit of good news. Perhaps if he got the position, he could buy another Aston Martin and be rid of the whole fiasco.

At home, Suzy ushered Abi straight into the downstairs shower, rather than allowing her to traipse up the stairs with her mud-covered jeans and ice-cream-sticky fingers. Eric wasn't entirely sure how she'd got so much mud on her, as the closest he saw her get to the actual allotment patch was when she was trying to work out if snails could hang upside down on nettle leaves.

Steam drifted into the room as Eric fired up the computer. He would shower later; now there were more important things at hand.

The allotment committee page was part of the same Burnham-onCrouch website where he'd advertised for help. Eric had initially thought identifying who to contact would be a quick process, but it turned out there were an awful lot of committees going on in Burnham.

There was a carnival committee, a horticultural committee, and the waterways committee. St Mary's Parish Choir committee and The St Mary's Recorder Club committee shared a joint page, as did the summer, autumn and winter festival committees. There was the Burnham organists committee, the Burnham fisheries committee, the Burnham am-dram committee, not to mention the local vegetarian, vegan, and freegan community pages. There was the school council, the food and clothes banks volunteer pages. The Burnham for building, the Burnham against building, the Burnham quilters, twitters, and philatelist pages as well as a whole three extra pages of groups and assemblies that Eric didn't read through because he'd already found what he was looking for. The Burnham-on Crouch Arcadia Road Allotment Committee. Eric clicked on the link. The page took a second to load. The second it did his throat clamped shut.

The banner across the top of the page was a picture. Eric recognised the setting as outside the town hall although the car parking spaces had been completely overhauled in place of tables and marquees and tents. In the centre, a group of people stood beneath a hand-painted sign that read Burnham Allotments and was decorated with childish drawings of fruit and vegetables. In the centre of the group was a man sitting on a chair. On his lap, a pile of what looked like courgettes and runner beans. Eric almost didn't recognise him, with the flat cap and smile. But there was no mistaking the narrow eyes and sticky-out ears.

'Dad,' Eric said.

Eric was certain that the sudden onset of emotion was caused more by surprise than actual distress, and in less than a minute he'd sniffed back any tears and was once again focused on the task at hand. He scrolled down, paying as little attention as possible to the photos of the harvest festival and autumn fair until he reached the committee members. It appeared a fair glut of people were involved in the running of an allotment. As well as the normal roles you'd expect from any committee – Secretary, Treasurer, Deputy chair, etcetera – there were also more particular roles, such as Trading Manager,

Fair Growth Manager, and Pesticide Control Manager. Eric was unsurprised to see both Janice and Cynthia's name on the board of committee members, although at that precise moment there was only one name that mattered.

Eric's fingers flexed then clenched. His nostrils flared. *Chairman*, the page read. *Norman Kettlewell*.

'That miserable old —'

'Eric ...'

'You know why he's doing this don't you? Bitterness. That's why. Spiteful, old-man bitterness. Well if they think they can bully me out, they've got another think coming.'

'Perhaps if you just talk to him.'

'You can't talk to people like that, Suzy, you can't. They don't listen. No, these people need action. And so much for not being a legal case. I've got a legal case. He said he didn't want me having the car. The second time I spoke to him he said that. Probably thinks he's next in line or some stupid crap like that.'

'You need to calm down.'

'And his wife. What a conniving old wench.'

'Eric —'

'No, I mean it. You know what she asked me this morning? She asked me if I would take him out in Sally some time. She actually had the audacity to ask me, when all the time she's plotting this behind my back.'

'Perhaps she didn't know.'

'Of course she knew. And she gave us cake.' Eric stopped. 'Where is it? Where's the cake? You're not eating it. It's probably poisoned. They probably thought they could get rid of me that way.'

Suzy placed her hands firmly on her hips.

'You're being irrational. You know what you sound like, don't you? You sound like an absolute loon.'

'Where's the cake?'

'Abi and I already ate it in the car.'

'When?'

'When you were busy screaming down the phone at the poor solicitor. And look, we're not dead. Not even a little.'

Eric harrumphed.

'Look,' Suzy said. 'Look at yourself.' She took hold of his hands. 'Think of it this way. If what your father really wanted was to drive you mad, like you keep insisting, then it's working. And I thought you said you weren't going to let him win?'

Eric pouted, sucked on his bottom lip, and tried to wriggle out of her grip like a chided toddler.

'As far as I can see, you have two options,' Suzy said. 'You can take a week's holiday, go down to Burnham, and get the place sorted. You said yourself you've got weeks and weeks stacked up. That's option one. Otherwise, you can ring Mr Eaves and tell him that you no longer want to keep the car. I don't care either way. But this,' she moved her hand indicating Eric as a whole. 'These outbursts. They've got to stop. Poor Abi thinks you're having a nervous breakdown. And I'm not entirely sure she's wrong.'

Eric dug his toes into the carpet.

'Fine,' he muttered to his feet.

'Pardon?'

'I said fine. I'll do it. I'll take the holiday. I'll go down to Burnham.'

'Good,' said Suzy. She reached up on tiptoes and kissed the top of his head. From the bathroom, Abi yelled, and Suzy went to her aid.

'If Norman Kettlewell wants my plot acceptably cultivated, he can have it acceptably cultivated,' Eric said. Then he sat at the computer and got to work.

CHAPTER 16

ARRANGEMENTS COULD ONLY be made for the following Thursday. It wasn't ideal, but it was manageable and in turn, meant that Eric could get a lot more real work done than he'd envisioned. He felt slightly bad, lying to Suzy when he left dressed in his jeans and Barbour jacket, his polished black brogues squashed inside his briefcase each morning, but he was doing it for her too. This method meant Eric wouldn't get stressed about missing work, nor would he have to miss out on seeing Abi over the weekend. It was ideal for everyone, really.

He kept a spare suit and a couple of shirts at work, which he changed into in the men's toilets. Although they were from last year and a little snug around the midriff, they looked perfectly suitable for the morning team meetings and staff briefings he had to run. Greg made one or two digs about the tensile strength of buttons, but then Eric refused to take clothing remarks from a man who still wore Velcro fastening shoes. Being at work also meant Eric was able to cover for Jack and take one of the head honcho clients out for lunch, earning him some serious brownie points in the process.

As an excuse for not taking the car each day, Eric concocted a reason about weekday parking charges in Burnham. He also downloaded a birdsong clip to his computer, which he played quietly in the background whenever Suzy rang, and arrived home rubbing his calves and whinging about how much his back ached and knees throbbed. On Tuesday when he had to stay late for an emergency meeting on the restructuring of the Southeast clinics he rang Suzy and told her the trains were delayed – debris on the tracks – which she bought without hesitation. That was the advantage of being a husband that never usually lied; Suzy always assumed he was telling the truth.

On Thursday morning, the alarm buzzed its way into his dream. Eric yawned, stretched a little, then remembering what day it was, bounded from the bed in a similar manner to that which Abi had done on Christmas Day. By the time Suzy had showered and dressed, Eric was on his second cup of coffee and neither his hands nor his feet could make contact with the same surface for more than a nanosecond before finding somewhere else to be.

'What's wrong with you today?'

'Nothing,' Eric said as he bounced from one side of the kitchen to the other. 'Just excited that's all. The allotment's coming on really well. Really, really well.'

'That's brilliant.' She took the cup of coffee from between his shaking hands and kissed him on the lips. 'I'd love to see some photos. Can you remember to take some today please?'

'Definitely.' He glanced at his watch. 'I'd better get going, actually. I was going to take the car down today.'

'Sally?'

'No, the Audi. Sally needs a proper check over before I

take her out in this weather. Maybe next weekend though we could all go for a drive? If it's not too cold.'

'That sounds like a wonderful idea. You know, if someone had told me six months ago that you'd be taking a week out of the office to go down and work on your dad's old allotment, I would have thought they'd lost the plot. I'm so proud of you, you know.'

Eric's stomach squirmed as he avoided his wife's gaze.

'Well have a nice day,' he said. 'And tell Abi I love her lots.'

'Will do.'

It was a perfect day for driving, and a few miles onto the A12 Eric regretted his decision not to take Sally after all. It was windy enough that the leaves danced around on the tarmac daring you to chase them, but not windy enough to affect the drive. The sky was cerulean, with white clouds dappling the skyscape. It was only the seventh of January, but it could have been May the air was so mild. *If all the year goes this well,* Eric thought, *I'll be laughing.*

He had rung the company before leaving home. One of their representatives would be at the allotment at ten with a few bits of paper for Eric to sign. Then he'd be good to go. Unfortunately, their representative needed to do several more drop-offs that morning so wouldn't be able to stay and help.

'Would that be a problem?' the man down the phone line asked.

'Not at all,' Eric replied. Everything was going to plan.

He drove into Burnham, down the High Street, and was heading to park in what he now considered his spot, when he encountered a snag in the form of a three axle, semi-articulated, thirty-tonne truck – although none of those features he knew until the ginger-haired, freckle-faced pubescent told him this.

'I thought you worked at Tools 'R' Us?' Eric said.

'*Tools4U*, and I do,' the boy said in response to Eric's question. 'You ordered from one of our third parties. It's all our gear. Just means it costs you more, that's all.'

'Brilliant,' Eric said.

'Actually, you're lucky. We wouldn't have been able to loan you it. Not after the mess you caused with that chainsaw. Have you never heard of bar oil?'

Ignoring his remark, Eric wandered over towards the cab and surveyed the lorry. There was absolutely no way it was going to get any closer to the allotment. Eric was amazed he'd got it that far.

'And you drove this thing? On your own?' Eric said, still searching for the sign of some other member of staff.

'Got my HGV licence four days after my eighteenth birthday.'

'Which was when exactly?'

The boy didn't reply.

'Look,' he said. 'I've backed it up this far. I'll get it down the ramp for you and I'll talk you through the controls, which you may or may not listen to. After that, I've got to go.'

'That's fine.'

The boy frowned. 'I know there's no point in me asking you this. But have you ever used one of these before?'

Eric laughed. It was a deep manly laugh that was meant to give the impression of maturity and knowledge, but on reflection realised it made him sound like one of the villains from a *Scooby Doo* cartoon.

'Of course,' he said.

The boy rolled his eyes. 'Well, let's get this stuff signed and we'll get her unloaded.'

It was a two-and-a-half tonne, zero-tail-swing, mini digger with two tracking speeds, glass-enclosed cab, and a smell of petrol that got the testosterone flowing faster than a *Game of*

Thrones mini-marathon. Its miniature caterpillar tracks and pygmy sized bucket reminded Eric of the type of toy you'd have at the seaside as a child, assuming you had the coolest and most irresponsible parents in history.

The boy, whose name Eric had now learnt to be Lewis, gave a brief demonstration, showing Eric where each of the controls were and how small an increment of movement was required.

'It's the opposite of cooking,' Lewis said. 'You can always take more out, but you can't put it back in. Same thing with speed. Just take it slow. Really, really slow.'

'Trust me, I will be going very, very slowly. Snail's pace. Arthritic snail's pace,' Eric said. 'As long as I'm done by nightfall, I'll be happy.'

'Well, I'll be picking it up at four, so you'll need to be done by then.'

'Fine, by four then. Either way. I will be fine.'

The boy pulled out his phone and checked the time. 'Are you sure you're okay? I mean, this flat bit here'll be easy, it's once you get onto those little paths, it gets harder. You've got a full tank of fuel, there's no way you'll use all that. I'd hang on a bit, see you down the lane, only I've got to get this next one delivered for eleven.'

'I'll be fine.'

'I can drive it down to the entrance if you want?'

'Lewis.' Eric stretched out his hand. 'Thank you for all your help. I will see you at four o'clock, and I have your number should any extreme emergencies pop up.'

'I'd rather they didn't.' He gave one more sceptical sigh towards the digger. Eric slapped him on the back.

'Fine,' Lewis said. 'I'll be off. Enjoy.'

Eric had to admit he was more than a little impressed

watching Lewis maneuverer the thirty-tonne truck back onto the road and out through the estate.

'And this is where the fun begins,' he said.

Eric had, understandably, watched several YouTube videos on how to control a mini excavator since concocting his plan, and was reassured by the number of hillbillies that managed to manipulate the machinery with careless ease. If they, with their obvious lack of education and limited grasp of grammar, could do it, he most certainly could. Hopping up into the cab and squeezing himself around the controls, a horde of butterflies swarmed behind his belly button. As a stroke of luck, the allotment appeared empty for once, although he suspected it wouldn't stay that way for long. The last thing he wanted was for one particular naysayer to turn up and start interrogating him before he even started.

The engine was quieter than he'd expected, nothing like the high-octane thrum of the chainsaw. More a low, underworld growl. Eric snuggled into his seat, checked behind for any oncoming traffic, then pushed the lever forwards. Slowly and smoothly the excavator followed the route.

With his cheeks aching from grinning, he pushed the lever further forwards and trundled down the track towards the allotments. Of course it was easy; it was driving. Eric was good at driving. He was great in fact. Eric continued to bolster his own ego as he rolled on before glancing at the bare hedges beside him. His stomach fell. Despite his enthusiastic outlook, he was inching forwards slower than a sloth with muscular dystrophy. Still, better to take things slow and steady, he reminded himself. Slow and steady wins the race.

'Sod this,' he said two seconds later, changing his mind.

His thumb twitched towards the two-speed yellow button. How fast was fast, really? After all, if he carried on at this pace he wouldn't even reach the gate by four, let alone do the allotment. And it wasn't like he found it hard. He had perfect control. Eric hit the second speed.

Eric lurched backwards as the tracks clicked into the higher pace. A millisecond later he was back in control. The breeze whipped around the back of his neck as the trees moved past him. His boyish grin returned. This was better. Now he could get some real work done. He angled himself to make the entry to the allotment and glided between the gates like a pro. He would see if he could get a video of this on the way back; maybe Lewis could take one if he had the time. He probably wouldn't show it to Suzy though. No, he wouldn't show it to Suzy, but he may let Abi have a quick peek before bed tonight if she promised not to tell her mother.

Eric was past the entrance and squeezing himself between the first two plots. He had planned his route already, following an in-depth examination of Google Earth along with a few mental calculations. He knew which right and left turns would get him there with the least possible hassle and which paths were too narrow for him to try. The final route he'd decided on may not have been the shortest, but it avoided any nasty turns or bulbous polytunnels. Mentally he recalled his next action.

The excavator was sinking slightly. It was no more than expected, but still enough to churn up what little grass there was beneath the tracks. Eric had studied the allotment's terms and agreements where it was clearly written that this size and type of machinery was allowed. Still, he wanted to do as little damage as possible. Momentarily forgetting about the sinking, he started preparing for his next turn. Turning was always going to be the hardest part. No matter how many YouTube videos he watched, he knew there was no replacement for the real thing. Eric fixated on the T junction and in less than a minute was upon it.

The pulsing in his pressure points deepened and an unfamiliar tension built around his neck as he switched down the speed, held his breath, and turned. Beneath him, the tracks switched course.

It was a perfect turn. Flawless in every manner. Eric fist punched the air. He was the master of all things mini and excavatorous. With a small whoop of delight, he hit back up on the two-speed and continued down the path. That was when he saw it.

It hadn't been on Google Earth, of that he was positive. By the whiteness of the metal and the transparency of the glass, it could have even gone up since Christmas. A generous present, or sale splurge perhaps? Where it had come from didn't matter, what mattered was that it was there. A beautiful, shiny greenhouse jutted out into the path straight in front of him. Eric glanced over his shoulder.

There was no way back. The greenhouse sat parallel to an old blue shed and turning around might cause the arm to hit one of the structures. Reversing wasn't an option either. He had already churned up the ground so much he could end up getting stuck.

Eric stopped the engine and got out. Using his arms and eyes he assessed the size of the gap. Several times he paced back and forth, arms open at the width of the digger. After his third check, he sighed with relief. He could make it. The excavator could make it. Slow, calm, precise movements, and he'd be completely fine. Eric climbed back into the cab, took a few steadying breaths, then, when he sensed he was as calm as he was going to get given the situation, restarted the engine.

Low speed, that was for sure. The front of the tracks slid between the gap and sandwiched perfectly between the shed and the greenhouse. A second later and the whole digger was enclosed. Sweat trickled down behind his ears. One slight movement of the pedal, or the arm, or the bucket, was all it would take for the greenhouse to come tumbling down. He pushed forwards a millimetre at a time. Every second, a second closer to the end. Soon there was barely a foot to go, before his whole body flooded with relief as the bucket emerged out the other side, then the arm, then the tracks. Eric wiped the sweat from the back of his neck and took a moment. It was only two more turns now to his allotment, this right one, then another left. Only two turns to go.

As he angled the tracks to finish the turn, something beneath him jolted. It was a small jolt, like a piece of earth shifting or a track clicking into place. Eric ignored it and moved forwards. The next jolt was substantially more significant. He glanced over his shoulder. The soil beneath the back of the track was waterlogged and causing the digger to slip. Eric pushed the lever forwards and urged the machine on. It refused to budge. He tried again, thrusting his own weight forwards too in the hope that that would help. It didn't. He could feel his pulse rising, the moisture evaporating from the back of his throat. He needed more power behind him. That was his only option. Closing his eyes and muttering a quick non-denominational prayer, he flicked the two-speed switch up and pushed on the pedal.

CHAPTER 17

I T TOOK A total of nine men, three women, and seven flasks of tea to get the excavator upright and out from of the rubble. It was a mess. Splinters of the blue wooden shed lay spread among the serrated edges of greenhouse glass. Within the destruction were seedlings, twisted tools, gardening gloves, and what only minutes earlier had been an antique radio, but was now nothing more than a bouncing mass of coils and wires.

The noise alone had been enough to generate a crowd. They arrived seconds after the crash; those who could came running; the rest hobbled behind.

'Help me,' Eric called. His head lolled downwards, a trickle of blood running down his forehead. 'My bloody trousers are caught.' People wrenched and tugged, pulling from every direction as they tried to dislodge him from between the levers. For a brief second, Eric believed that this was it, the end. He was going to die there, stuck on his side, trapped in the cabin of a mini excavator, until, with a hard yank, someone tore the seams of his jeans, finally freeing him. With his heart pounding, blood in his mouth, and Mickey Mouse boxers that Abi had bought him on display, Eric crawled out the wreckage.

'Well you've made a right mess there,' someone said. Eric couldn't disagree.

He had had to call Lewis and agree to pay a two-hundred-pound "tip" for the service. Even then they had to call upon the help of the local coast guard volunteers as well as those allotment owners who were able to bend their backs without it taking them forty-five minutes to straighten up – of which Eric was surprised to find quite a few. Still, he didn't think he could have wedged the digger in at a more awkward angle if someone had paid him. Griff had appeared with the flasks of tea and bacon butties, and although Eric wasn't entirely sure who had called him, he was eternally grateful. The sweet liquid flooded through his veins and only when Eric removed the mug from his lips did he see how much he was shaking.

'You're lucky,' Griff said. 'You could have caused some real damage. To yourself I mean.'

It was the bucket that had caused the most damage, coming down squarely through the roof of the shed. The contents had spilt their innards out onto the path, catching in the digger's tracks and twisting into the chain-links. Eric hadn't come out of it unscathed. There were several superficial gashes on his arms and legs and an egg-shaped welt ballooning on his thigh. The whole of his left side radiated as if he'd gone ten rounds in a bullring.

'What a mess,' Janice was shaking her owly head. 'What a mess.'

'I'll pay for the damage,' Eric kept saying. 'I just don't understand what happened.'

'Stupidity is what happened.' Eric turned his head to see Norman standing at the back of the crowd, tight-lipped, and scowling. 'Stupidity and arrogance.'

Eric pretended he didn't hear and carried on trying to piece back together the fragments and wires of the broken radio.

As luck – good or bad he wasn't sure – would have it, the owners of both the shed and the greenhouse happened to be away in Europe. One was visiting his children and grandchildren in Belgium while the other was on an over-sixties singles' event in Amsterdam. Eric left his details with Janice, who promised she'd pass them on. He didn't doubt it for a moment.

It was 4.00 PM by the time he left Burnham, and the sun was already slinking off behind the clouds. Eric's stomach growled. Beside the cup of tea Griff had brought him, he'd had nothing to eat or drink all day, and the effects of low blood-sugar combined with general fatigue and shock were showing. He texted Suzy and suggested they get a takeaway from down by the station and took her lack of reply as agreement. His phone had countless messages and emails, many of which were from the office, but with his head thumping and stomach getting angrier by the second, he decided it would be best to deal with them all later.

He kept to the slow lane as he drove, letting other cars and lorries whip past. The bruises on his leg had started to colour with an impressive blend of purple hues. After the day's events, getting home in one piece was his current priority.

Abi's bedroom light shone down onto the street below. Eric could make out her silhouette, prancing behind the curtains. His chest expanded. At least he was home to see her before she went to bed. That was something. He clicked the key in the door and embraced the rush of warm air. It was like hitting a wall of sheer exhaustion. His jaw clicked loudly into a yawn, his eyelids sagged, millimetres from closing, and everything ached.

'Suze, honey. I'm home,' he said, limping his way down the hall.

'In here,' she said from the kitchen.

Suzy was sitting at the dining room table in half-light. A thin white film had built on her cup of tea. The curtains were drawn, the radio was silent, and the only sounds came from the whirring of the dishwasher and the occasional burst of singing from Abi upstairs.

'What a day,' Eric said, whipping off his jumper and slinging it over the back of the chair. 'I could do with a drink.'

Suzy met his gaze. Her expression was neutral, passive. 'There's tonic in the fridge,' she said and ended her sentence there.

Eric hesitated, partly to see if she was going to make one – somehow a gin and tonic always tasted better when she made it for him – partly because something was nipping at his gut. It was the type of gnawing that occurred when he'd forgotten something important, like an anniversary or to leave money as a proxy for the tooth fairy. Something felt out of place. He glanced around the room. There was nothing different, nothing out of order. No doubt it was his mind playing tricks on him from all the stresses of the day. When Suzy didn't say anything else, Eric went to the fridge and hunted out the limes and tonic water himself. He poured his glass and sat down opposite her.

'Sorry, you didn't want one too, did you?' he said.

Suzy shook her head. 'I'm fine.'

A short silence ensued. Eric took a sip of his drink. It hit the back of the throat in exactly the right place.

'Wow, I needed that,' he said.

With a deliberately exaggerated movement, he brushed his fingers across the cut above his eyebrow and winced. If Suzy saw, she didn't say anything. He did it again to the same effect. A mild heat of indignation bloomed around his midriff. It was unlike Suzy not to question him about his day, particularly when he looked like he'd been in a mud-slinging contest with a sumo wrestler and a cactus. No doubt she'd feel terrible about it later when they went to bed and she saw what a state his legs and side were in.

'So, how's your day been?' he asked.

'What about yours? How did you get on?'

Eric's eyes rolled. 'To be honest. Pretty damn horrific.'

'Oh,' Suzy said impassively. 'That's a shame. You said the last three days had been productive. What happened? Did you not manage to get as much done as you thought?'

Eric observed his wife. She hadn't moved an inch since he had arrived. Her hands were still folded neatly on her lap. Her tea untouched.

'I ran into a few small snags,' Eric said. 'Well. A few huge snags. Took a bit of a tumble too.' He pointed to the cut on his head.

'Looks nasty,' she said, her voice devoid of any form of concern or sympathy.

Eric pursed his lips, unsure of how to respond.

'But the allotment's still looking good?' Suzy said. 'I mean, one bad day's work after three good days. It still must be a huge improvement?'

'Well ...' Eric's sentence drifted off.

'Have you got any photos for me to see today? Abi would like to see them too. She's been telling all her teachers at school how her daddy's given up work to be a gardener for the week.'

Eric's eyes darted around the room. His mouth and throat had become inexplicably dry, and a large lump was forcing its way up his oesophagus.

'So, the unsatisfactory cultivation order, you think that'll be overthrown now? Now that you've done all this work?'

'Well, I don't know. I mean there was an awful lot to —'

He cut himself short as his eyes finally laid claim to his sense of uneasiness. The lump in his throat evaporated to leave a feeling of nausea that spread from the soles of his feet and upwards.

'What's that for?' he said, nodding towards the object by Suzy's feet.

It was only small, but big enough. Big enough to hold a week's clothes, perhaps two.

'I've just packed a few things,' she said. 'Abi and I are going away for a while.'

'What do you mean?' Eric said. 'Where? Why?' A trickle of sweat meandered down his back. He held his wife's gaze, but it was hard. His hands were shaking, his legs were trembling. His whole body quivered where he stood.

'Jack Nelson rang,' she said. 'He couldn't find the folder with the artwork in for the college accounts, I think he said it was?' Eric nodded. Tears brimmed in his eyes. One escaped and slipped down his cheek. 'He wanted to know if you'd taken it with you when you left work yesterday, but he couldn't get through to you on your phone. I said I'd ask you when you got back. He also wanted to thank you for taking that client out to lunch on Tuesday? He said you were quite the star.'

Suzy rose from her chair. Her lips were quivering, but she maintained a poise and posture that cut straight between Eric's ribs. She picked up the suitcase, walked past him, and placed it by the front door. Then she started up the stairs to collect Abi.

'I really thought you were different,' she said.

CHAPTER 18

I T WAS TWO excruciating days before Suzy spoke to him. Eric had spoken to Abi of course – Suzy facilitated a video call to him once in the morning and once before bed – but the phone was handed to and taken from her without so much as a 'Hello, you lying arsehole,' from Suzy herself.

Eric was in pieces. Had she at least called him out on his bull, it could have given him something to yell back at. A chance to put his side across. But there was nothing. Complete radio silence. Thursday night, after they left, he ran himself a bath, after which he collapsed on the bed. He was too tired to argue, too tired to explain why his lies weren't that big of a detail, too tired to kick up the fight she deserved and make her stay.

Friday night he convinced himself it was nothing unusual, that it was no different to when Suzy went away on her book tours, as more often than not she took Abi with her then too. He stayed late at work then brought extra papers home, which he spread over the dining room table in an attempt to disguise the gaping vacuum. When he was done looking at them, he put on manly films with unnecessary quantities of blood and guts that Suzy would have never let him watch if she were home too.

But when week melted into the weekend, and the prospect of an unadulterated full day out in Sally was scuppered by ice and salted roads, the lies to himself got harder to maintain.

It was Saturday evening when they finally spoke. The house now smelt of amalgamated takeaways – oil-soaked paper bags, boxes, cartons, and little Tupperware tubs lay strewn across the kitchen worktop – and the stuffiness that occurs from having the heating on for too long without opening any windows.

'We're going crabbing on Tuesday,' Abi said through the little screen on his phone. 'And Uncle Tom says if we catch any really big ones we can take them home and eat them.'

'Tuesday? Are you planning on staying there next week too? What about school?' A burning sensation pricked his eyes.

A pixelated Abi shrugged. 'I've gotta go now, Dad. Aunt Lydia's making meatballs for tea, and they've got cheese in the middle and everything.'

'Cheesy meatballs, you wouldn't want to miss those, would you? Love you.'

'You too.'

'And I miss you. And your mum too. Tell your mum I miss her, won't you?' But Abi was already off screen. He was about to hit the hang-up button when Suzy came into view. Her eyes were off screen, most likely waiting to check when Abi was out of view and earshot. After a minute passed, she faced Eric through the computer and offered a sad half-smile. A flaming great fissure tore open in his chest.

'How are you?' she asked.

Eric sighed. 'Miserable. When are you coming home?'

There was a long pause. A few times Suzy opened her mouth as if to speak, then closed it again. Eric could feel his eyes welling up.

'I know,' he said. 'I know what I did was wrong, and I shouldn't have lied about where I was —'

'You wore different clothes, Eric,' Suzy silenced him as she spoke. 'You left the house, pretending you were going somewhere else. What kind of person goes to that length to cover a lie unless they've got something serious that needs hiding?'

'I told you. I was at work. I was just at work.'

'And when you were late back? On Tuesday when you were late back, you said it was because there was a tree on one of the lines or something? Where were you then?'

'I was at a meeting. I swear.'

'But how do I know you're telling the truth? This could easily just be another lie to cover all the other ones.'

'I'm telling you the truth, Suze, I promise. I wouldn't lie to you about something like this, I wouldn't.'

Suzy sighed and rubbed her temples. Her eyes were red-rimmed; she looked a decade older. As Eric waited for her to speak, she steepled her hands on the desk in front of her and rested her forehead against her thumbs so all Eric could see was the top of her head. He continued to wait. Three minutes passed before she looked up again.

'I don't know what to do,' she said. 'I don't know what I'm supposed to do right now.'

'Come home,' Eric said. 'Please. That's what you're supposed to do. Come home.'

She shook her head. 'I've been through this, Eric. I've done a marriage where all I get is lies. I'm not doing that to myself again. And I'm certainly not doing it to Abi.'

'This is not the same,' Eric was waving his hands at the phone. 'I messed up. I really messed up and I get that. I get why you're upset, I really do. And I know it's all my fault. But please, please don't do this. I will never lie to you again. I swear. I swear.'

In an elegant sweep, Suzy wiped away the tears that slid down her cheek. Eric sniffed his back down his throat in a much less demure manner.

'Will you at least keep speaking to me? I can't stand it when we don't speak. Please? Tomorrow night, or whenever. Whenever you want, can we talk again?'

Suzy's bottom lip disappeared under her top teeth.

'We'll see,' she said and Eric's stomach fell. Whenever he said *we'll see* to Abi, they all knew what it meant.

Suzy let him speak to her the next night. It was a somewhat strained conversation to start with. In the background, Eric could hear Abi and the boys shrieking as they ran up and down the stairs. Twice Suzy went off screen to ask them to be quiet. The third time she told them, even Eric was scared.

'So, what are you going to do?' Suzy said.

It had taken thirty minutes of tense small talk but finally, Eric reached a place where he felt he could tell her about the Burnham misdemeanour. By the end of the tale, there was even a small smile on her lips, although Eric was fairly certain it was revelling at his injuries and humiliation as opposed to actual happiness.

'I don't know,' he said. 'The owners were away last week, but apparently, they get back this weekend. I guess I'll end up paying out. Do people have allotment insurance?'

'Even if they do, I suspect digger-wielding maniac attacks aren't covered,' she said. Eric smiled, and for the first time, it was reciprocated. A smaller glimmer of hope flickered.

'So,' he said. 'Any more ideas about when you're coming home?'

Suzy's face immediately hardened. 'Don't push me on this,

Eric,' she said, stamping out his little glimmer. 'Right now, I don't even know if I am.'

'But what about Abi, her school? You have to think about Abi.' Then Suzy gave him the glare that told him he definitely should have stopped at the smile.

With his spirits newly dampened, Eric poured himself a gin only to open the fridge and find it entirely devoid of tonic.

'Bollocks,' he said. There was no tonic in the pantry either, although thanks to a spark of inspiration, Eric remembered that they'd shoved a few bottles of spirits and mixers in the cupboard under the stairs before Christmas when the wine racks and surface tops could no longer handle the overspill. He was in luck. He clunked a couple of ice cubes into his glass and took a long indulgent draw.

With nothing on the television, Eric flicked up his laptop and perused the potential new client list Jack had sent around at the beginning of the week. There were some big names on there. A couple of education luminaries to boot. If Eric could land one more of those it would really seal the deal, should the restructure come about. After tidying up a few odds and ends in various documents, he returned to his emails.

His inbox had gained three new additions since he'd last checked, and only one was work-related. He braced himself and clicked the first message, titled *Garden Green House*.

Eric scanned the message. It was short, curt – probably deservedly so – but reasonable in its requests. Allotment insurance was apparently a costly and rather futile experience, and as such the owner, a P. Hamilton, had requested Eric replace the destroyed greenhouse with a similar model. P. Hamilton had also included a link to a webpage showing such a greenhouse on sale for two hundred and nineteen pounds. They had stipulated however, that should Eric be considering any more excavator expeditions, then they would much prefer the toughened glass model, which would set Eric back a further hundred and twelve pounds. Three hundred pounds, give or take. It was a fair enough, Eric reasoned. P. Hamilton had also requested that Eric sort the issue as soon as possible, as they would like to get on with sowing their Bunton's showstoppers in order to gain a good head start on their competitors before competition season began.

'Another weekend in Burnham it is then,' Eric muttered to himself.

With the expectation of another two hundred pounds quickly fleeing his pockets, he clicked on the second email, which was more dramatically titled, *Ravaged Garden Shed*.

Once again, the email began most civilly and stated yet again the problems with getting insurance for allotments and the wish that Eric merely paid the cost of the destroyed items. That was where the good news ended. After quoting Eric an astronomical six hundred and fifty pounds for the replacement shed, the email then included an itemised list of all the objects – once again with web links – that were apparently destroyed at the time of Eric's rampage. The list included: a pair of Japanese secateurs for forty pounds, a digging fork for ninety pounds, eighty pounds for a Bulldog rubber rake and forty-nine pounds for a digging spade. There was also a one hundred and thirty-four-pound wheelbarrow, a forty-pound hedge trimmer, eight pounds fifty for a pressure sprayer and ninety-nine pounds ninety-eight for a Hoselock twenty metre auto-rewind hose, plus accessories. This did not include incidentals, such as seed trays, bulbs, fertiliser, and bug pellets among other things, for which the writer requested an extra two hundred and fifty pounds. Finally, was his vintage Roberts Radio, which was now no longer produced, although a similar model could be picked up, Eric was informed, at any good John Lewis or department store for around a hundred quid.

Eric sat back in his seat and tried to comprehend what he'd just read. A rough estimate brought him to fifteen hundred pounds. Fifteen hundred. Eric downed the rest of his drink and thumped the glass back onto the desk. Who did this person think they were? Fifteen hundred pounds, plus the other greenhouse? This was a month's school fees for Abi and a bit to spare. His tummy muscles tightened, strained, then a minute later flopped out in resignation. There was only one person to blame for the whole fiasco and that was, most irritatingly, himself. After refilling his gin with a double measure, he fired off two responsive emails, both agreeing to pay the stated cost. After which he downed the remainder of his drink and dug out the menu for the Indian around the corner.

It was a pinging email that woke him in the morning. The house was hot, stiflingly so, and condensation ran in streams down the windows and puddled on the sills. Eric had never got the hang of the central heating timer, and adjusting it accordingly was one of Suzy's jobs. As he'd gone to bed the night before, he'd switched up the thermostat in the hope of lessening the chill of an empty bed. It had definitely done that. His skin was clammy, and his hair stuck to the pillow in a way that only usually occurred in summer months or after nights of heavy drinking. He peeled himself out of the duvet and took a sip from the glass of water on his nightstand. 10.00 AM, the clock read. Eric blinked and checked it again. He couldn't remember the last time he'd slept like that. Not that he felt refreshed.

His phone pinged again and coaxed him over from the bed. He flicked on the screen noting the little inbox icon at the bottom. Seventeen new messages had come through since he went to bed. Eric did his second double take of the morning. That number of emails on a Saturday night could only mean an absolute work catastrophe. Or news, important news. He gulped. Perhaps it was about the restructuring. Perhaps Jack had finally caved to Hartley and was giving it the go ahead. With his heart racing, he clicked on the inbox icon.

CHAPTER 19

'I T'S LUDICROUS, THAT'S what it is.'

Eric was on the computer speaking to Suzy. Abi was outside at Lydia's apparently catching newts in the pond, although he strongly suspected the only kind of life present in Tom and Lydia's pond was a particularly virulent strain of E-coli. The kitchen was in a marginally better state, with Eric having collected up all the used takeaway boxes that morning, although the sink was now filled with moulding teacups and a scent of fermenting milk.

'Listen to this one.'

He read off his phone as he spoke. '*Dear Mr Sibley ... blah, blah, blah ... wait a sec ... oh, here it is. Your haphazard driving last Thursday caused not only irrevocable damage to my perineal, —*' I'm fairly sure she means perennials here but anyway, '*— it also near obliterated my prize-winning damson tree. I've estimated the cost of replacing this at two thousand pounds*.'

'That sounds a bit steep.'

'A bit steep? I was nowhere near her bloody damson tree.

And I was most certainly not near her perineal. Haphazard driving? My driving was perfect.'

'Until you crashed.'

'Yes. But up until that point I didn't hit a thing. Not one.'

'Well, if you're sure ...'

Eric's nostrils flared.

'Sure? Of course, I'm bloody sure. There are messages here saying that I ran over someone's compost heap. They want me to pay for replacement worms. And that I massacred their black currant bushes. One says I deliberately beheaded his scarecrow. I mean, it's obscene. Half of them have threatened to sue me if I don't pay up within a month.'

'Can they do that?'

'Of course not. It's preposterous.'

'Then perhaps you need to get a lawyer involved?'

'And how much is that going to cost us?'

Eric huffed and slumped back onto the bed. Suzy was lying on the sheep-scented batik quilt in her slobby clothes; they consisted of his old tracksuit bottoms and a vest top with a frayed hoody over the top. If only he could hold her, nuzzle down into her shoulder, he might feel just a tiny bit better.

'Please come home,' he said. 'I miss you. I need you. I'm a wreck without you.'

Suzy leant away from the screen.

'We'll talk about it later,' she said. 'I need to go now. I said I'd watch the kids.'

'Have a good day then.'

'You too. And try not to stress about it. And don't respond while you're angry. I'm sure it'll sort itself out.'

'I hope you're right.'

'I usually am.'

Suzy's more forgiving attitude made Eric feel a little more

optimistic about the future, and taking her advice, he decided not to respond to any of the emails there and then. Instead, he chose to busy himself tidying. On the slim chance that Suzy decided to come home without warning, a bathroom that smelt of four-day-old underpants and a kitchen fridge that looked like it belonged to a bunch of excessively frivolous students may just be the things to send her away again. After tidying he went upstairs and changed into his running gear. The rest of the day was going to be spent doing useful, productive things, Eric decided. After all, a clear head was what he needed to deal with the situation.

Unfortunately, the next week did not allow him a clear head at all. Abi had apparently got involved in some scouting expedition with the boys, which Eric took as a sign to say they had no intention of returning home anytime soon. At work, Jack had been called away on a family crisis and one of the senior associate directors was stuck in the Maldives due to a volcanic ash cloud somewhere over Indonesia. Eric flitted from one telephone call to another while Greg yo-yoed back and forth to different meetings with various VIPs. Wednesday already felt like Friday, and the thought of another two days like the three just past made Eric's legs heavy with dread. It was Friday night before he finally got to address the issue of the allotments once again, having done an admirable job of ignoring the deluge of emails that had continued to flood his inbox since the beginning of the week.

'I told them I'd see them all tomorrow morning,' Eric said to Suzy as he scooped a chopstick full of noodles into his mouth.

It was gone eleven, and the fact that Suzy had stayed up late so that they could talk, he read as either extremely positive or else terrifyingly negative.

'Are you going to manage that? To speak to them all I mean?' she said. 'I thought there were loads of them?'

'There are, but I'm hoping most of them won't get their messages until it's too late. I only sent it fifteen minutes ago.' Suzy didn't look convinced.

'So what time are you going to meet them? And what are you going to tell them?'

'Well, I've got to sort out this bloody greenhouse too, although I might wait until the rest of the stuff is done. I was going to get there about ten?'

'And you're going to tell them what?'

Eric paused. He had had less time to dwell on the matter than he would have liked, but he had a vague idea. He puffed out his chest as he spoke,

'I'm going to tell them that every incident will need to be verified by my lawyer and should the incidents turn out to be bogus, not only will they be expected to reimburse my costs, but I will take legal action in reference to libel and slander. That should stop them.'

Suzy frowned. 'Is that a good idea?'

'I don't see why not? And I can't think of a better one, can you?'

She tilted her head in a half-shake, half-shrug.

'It just seems very negative, that's all. You've already got this order for unsatisfactory cultivation. Now you want to upset them further by threatening to sue them?'

'They threatened to sue me first.'

Suzy raised an eyebrow. 'Well, that's a great response.'

Eric pondered the thought for a second.

'I'm certain it's the best way. The only way,' he said.

'Well, there you go then.' She smiled. It was only a small one, but it glinted in her eyes and sent Eric's stomach into butterflies.

'What time are you planning on leaving then? Only Abi will want to speak to you in the morning I suspect.' Her noncha-

lant tone brought the sting of the separation sharply back to
the forefront of his mind.

'I don't know. I was planning on leaving about nine.'

'Okay. I'll make sure she calls you before then.'

'I love you,' he said.

'I know,' Suzy replied.

Eric drove Sally to Burnham. It wasn't the most sensible idea,
with bad weather pestering regions all around the coast, but
for all he knew Christian Eaves was at the allotment ready to
strip him of his keys and tear from him the last hand-hold to
his family life. As such, Eric was determined to get in one last
decent drive. Abi had been up at the crack of dawn, so Suzy let
her call him at just gone seven. Eric could feel the tears
building behind his eyes as she rang off without so much as an
I miss you. They had only been gone a little over a week, yet it
felt like she'd grown up months in that time. His heart ached
and burned with the stupidity of it all.

It was while brushing his teeth that Eric decided he'd go
and see them the next day. Suzy had said she wanted space, and
he'd given her that. But now he wanted to talk. In person.
Enough was enough, he wanted his family back. With a
substantial amount of force, he spat the toothpaste into the
sink, rinsed the bowl, then fetched his driving gloves from the
back of his top drawer.

Steering clear of the dual carriageways, Eric took every
back road he could. He raced down the narrow, twisting, tree-
lined lanes. He soared past a glorious fifteenth-century church
and drank in the lingering views of the river. His wheels
hugged corners time and time again while his lungs bathed in

the adrenaline of it all. This was living; this was what it was about.

Passing through a village even smaller than Burnham, he slowed to take a small cobbled bridge and caught sight of a bevvy of swans circling in the water. The place was idyllic. Three cottages sat on the riverside, one with a *For Sale* sign out in front of it. *Abi would love it here*, Eric thought. She could fish in the river, climb trees. His chest tightened as he tried but failed to swallow the image back down.

He glanced at his watch to distract himself and was surprised to see it was already twenty to ten. If it was to be his last drive, he thought, at least it had been a good one.

Fifteen minutes later, Eric drove through Burnham High Street at less than twenty miles an hour in an attempt to peer into the window of Eaves and Doyle as he passed. It didn't look like anyone was there, which could have been because it was a Saturday and most solicitors were closed on Saturdays, or, it could have been because Christian Eaves was already waiting for him at the allotment.

He had hoped that the drive would relieve some of the tension he was experiencing over today's confrontations. However, as he plodded down the track towards the metal gates – his back and shoulders as rigid as one of Norman's anally aligned beanpoles – he realised that this was not the case. A few metres in front of the allotment entrance he stopped.

His pulse was pounding against his ribs and a film of sweat glazed his palms. As well as the possibility of some very unpleasant conversations and loss of his most beloved possession, this sudden spike in blood pressure – Eric realised to his own astonishment – also came with the realisation he may be losing the allotment too. The infernal patch of dirt had been nothing more than a protruding thorn in his side for two months now and utterly consuming in every way possible. Without the car and the allotment, not only would he have vast amounts of excess time on his hands, but his topics of conversation would be dramatically reduced. Perhaps it was a good thing, he said internally, then corrected himself out loud.

'It would definitely be a good thing.' Eric let out the air from his lungs in one deep sigh.

That was when he heard them. He had just finished his mini self-motivational pep talk when a sudden expulsion of laughter came from somewhere beyond the gates. He bit down. Laughter. Full belly-wobbling laughter. It sounded like a whole group of them, men and women. The nefarious little titters of blue-rinsed grandmas flew through the air like needles to his eardrums.

Eric froze, livid. His pulse took on a new, more violent pacing. They had planned this whole thing together, the lot of them. A plot to rinse him dry. Well, he'd see how well that turned out for them. They weren't going to get a penny from him. Not one. Not even P. Hamilton and his or her obliterated greenhouse and certainly not the damn Roberts Radio.

With his fists clenched and blood pounding, Eric marched through the gates and across the allotment. The mob had their back to him, all tweed coats and wax jackets, and as he approached Eric cleared his throat in a loud and not even slightly polite manner. A man with several piercings in his ears turned around.

'Ahh, look, here he is now,' he said.

The rest of the crowd began to turn. There were nearly twenty of them in total, all of them grinning, teeth on show, ready to devour Eric alongside their Tangtastics and Survivor peas. Eric gulped but held his ground.

'Nice of you to turn up,' one of them said.

'Well, now that I'm here, we can get started.' Eric

addressed the crowd with his hands on his hips. He wasn't going to dilly-dally about with niceties.

'So, you are aware,' he said, 'I've read every one of your emails and I've found them to be —'

'Daddy, Daddy!'

Eric stopped. He squinted. Through a gap in the throng, a little figure was squeezing its way through to the front.

'Daddy, look what we made!'

His knees went. Turning it into a deliberate gesture Eric knelt on the floor and stretched out his arms.

'Daddy, guess what we've been doing? Guess what? Guess what?'

Eric failed to suck back the tears as they breached his lower eyelids.

'What is it, pumpkin?' he said, pulling his daughter into his chest and hugging her so hard he thought he might crush her. 'What have you been doing?'

She wriggled out of his grip and back onto the grass where she skipped over to a large box on the ground.

'We've been baking. Mummy and me. We've done loads and loads of baking.'

Suzy stood in the centre of the crowd. Her hair hung loosely about her shoulders and a large tin weighed down her hands. It could have been a decade ago, the way his heart skipped and stalled at the sight of her.

'It's true,' she said, holding Eric's gaze with nothing more than the movement of her lips. 'We have done a lot of baking.'

CHAPTER 20

TO ERIC, IT felt like summer, or how summer would feel if it was so cold it turned the tips of your ears blue and your breath fogged each time you spoke. Suzy glided between the allotment owners, handing out squares of freshly baked brownies and blondies. Abi offered a tray of curiously decorated cupcakes while asking each person how old they were and if they owned any chickens because her cousins had chickens and for the last week she'd collected the eggs.

Suzy, Eric noticed, began guiding one of the owners in his direction. It wasn't someone he recognised; a tall blonde lady, only about his age, with her hair held back by a green bandana.

'Eric, this is Penelope. Penelope Hamilton,' Suzy said, then added, 'P. Hamilton,' when Eric still drew a blank.

'P. Hamil– oh yes.' Eric's eyes widened, his brain finally engaged. 'Of course. P. Hamilton. Penelope. I'm so, so sorry. I mean, I can't describe how terrible I feel. Of course, your greenhouse. I will reimburse you immediately. Get the new one ordered today.'

Penelope gesticulated in a similar vein to the queen. 'Please call me Penny. And don't fuss. It's not a problem. Accidents happen to the best of us. Your wonderful wife here was just telling me what a tough time you've been having with it. Running back and forth between here and London. And of course, losing your father.'

'Well ... umm. I suppose it's been an interesting start to the year.'

'Well, anything I can do to help. And really, don't think twice about the digger incident. Water under the bridge already.'

Bewildered, Eric drifted from one person to the next and found the conversations eerily similar. Even Mrs Maddock with her damaged prize-winning damsons was ardent to discuss her change of heart.

'There was a big storm you see, that night. So, when I got there, and my tree was broken I thought it must have been you with your digger. But thinking back on it now, I think it must have been the storm, as you were right over the other side of the allotment.'

'Well, I did think —'

'To be honest, I'm not sure how I could have thought it was your digger. Think it was the trauma you see. Shellshock, they call it.'

It was remarkable how many situations could suddenly be explained by the raging storm that had apparently attacked Burnham allotment a week last Thursday. Particularly remarkable given that he could see no evidence of this mini- typhoon whatsoever.

'What did you say to them?' Eric asked when he finally managed to get Suzy away from the endlessly babbling bean growers. 'What did you tell them?'

'Only the truth. That you'd been finding balancing the

allotment with work tricky. And you really want to do your father justice as you know the place meant so much to him.'

'That's it?'

'That's it. Well, I might have thrown in a few lines about Abi's school struggling with her ADHD and offered to do a reading at next month's book club.'

Eric studied his daughter. She was currently balancing on one foot, using half a bean pole as a sword while smearing green butter icing across her cheeks as war paint.

'Abi doesn't have ADHD,' Eric said.

'Does she not?'

An hour later and the new greenhouse had been ordered and paid for and a more reasonably priced shed selected from the B&Q website. The shed owner, a stubbled and greying Richard, had decided since his initial email that several of his tools were still in fine working order. He also explained that he'd found his gardening gloves in his coat pocket, discovered that he'd lent his hose to one of his neighbours and confessed, rather sheepishly that his electric strimmer hadn't worked for several years. After sitting down and tallying up the total, Eric agreed to pay him five hundred pounds. He suspected he'd have settled lower, but he wanted to make sure there was enough in the kitty for the Roberts Radio; he'd hinted enough, and he probably deserved it for the mess.

By midday, all business was dealt with and Abi was higher on sugar than Willy Wonka after a trip in the Great Glass Elevator. The crowd had dispersed completely, either to their respective plots and greenhouses or else home for lunch and a nap. Eric yawned. His head thrummed with numbers and names, but his shoulders felt like a fifty-kilo dumbell had been lifted from them.

'So,' he said to Suzy, while Abi licked the crumbs from the bottom of one of the cake tins. 'What now?'

'Now? You take us back to Lydia's.' The weight on Eric's shoulders landed back with a wallop.

'Really?' he said. 'I just thought that, well you know.'

Suzy smiled.

'Our bags are there. We'll need all our things if we're going to come home.'

Eric stepped across a newly ploughed trench and took his wife's hand. Then he kissed it and kissed it and kissed it again.

'Urgh, you two are so gross,' Abi said.

Then they pulled her in and kissed her too.

It wasn't until he was standing by Sally, about to head off to Lydia's, that Eric remembered the other source of his nerves. His stomach plummeted.

'Crap,' he said.

'What?'

'I didn't ask about the eviction. I guess it still stands. After all, the seven days is done, and all I succeeded in doing was ruining two other allotments. I guess they've got all the reason they need to get rid of me now.'

He gazed at the lights and reached out his hand to brush the bonnet. They had had some good memories together, Eric recalled. Great memories. Like the first time his father let him get behind the wheel when his provisional licence arrived. How many teenagers could say that the first car they ever got to drive was a limited-edition Aston Martin DB4? Not many, he was sure of that. Eric had had to get straight As in his GSCEs first, and solid A-level predictions of course. And spend every weekend for the five years before his seventeenth birthday polishing each and every square inch of the car with a six-inch square chamois leather. A deep set, heavily rooted gnawing built behind his sternum.

'I was talking to Penny about that,' Suzy said, bringing Eric out of his daydream.

'Penny?'

'Penny. Penelope. P. Hamilton.'

'Oh, right? What did she say?'

'Not much. She said she hadn't heard anything about it. But she wasn't a member of the committee.'

'Well I'm sure she'll hear soon enough then,' Eric said. And went back to basking in his eternal misery.

Despite awaiting the inevitable loss of Sally, Eric skipped through the next week at work. He left early each morning after he'd brought Suzy her cup of tea in bed and was out the door the minute the clock struck five. Other people managed it; even some of the senior associate directors managed it. It was all a matter of prioritising, Eric told himself, and finally, he was getting it right. During office hours, he'd become beyond efficient. He stuck a tacky plastic mini whiteboard – the type you'd find in a primary school or displaying the daily specials in a cheap sandwich shop – on his back wall and crossed off his to-do list with a thick black line. He got coffee from the machine, rather than heading out, and apart from the one working lunch he couldn't avoid, he ate at his desk or skipped lunch altogether.

Three times that week they cooked at home as a family, which they hadn't done since he started earning enough not to break into a cold sweat at the cost of a takeaway. He helped Abi with her homework on Tudor clothes, and while it was a topic he knew absolutely zero about, he was still more effective at scouring the internet than Abi and therefore maintained the important parental position of omnipotence. It was a great week until the email came through from Cynthia.

Fortunately, the email had come through on the Friday

night, giving Eric only one evening to mull and muse before they drove down together in the Audi on Saturday morning. David Bowie's greatest hits blared out of the speakers as they battled the morning rain.

'This music's so old,' Abi said, crinkling up her nose in disgust as her father bellowed out the chorus to *Life on Mars*.

'Yes, it is,' Eric said. 'And it's stood the test of time.' He continued with his singing at double the volume.

'You're so annoying.' Abi huffed, digging out her iPad, and plugging in her headphones.

Suzy smiled and took Eric's hand.

'We don't mind coming with you,' she said. 'If you want an extra pair of hands? Or some moral support?'

'It's fine,' Eric said. 'I'd rather you weren't there, to be honest. I'm not sure how this works. Or why we have to meet at The Shed. I expect I'm not allowed on the property anymore or something ridiculous like that.' A knot tightened around his kidneys. 'This is stupid. I don't even know why I'm going. What can they say in person that they couldn't write in an email? Unless they've decided I was responsible for the mythical typhoon of Burnham that wiped out Mrs Maddock's damson tree after all.'

Suzy squeezed his hand. 'Perhaps it's positive. Perhaps they want to give you another month.'

'I doubt that.'

'Well, either way, we're only a train ride away if you need us. Or I'm sure Tom could drop us down. Just let me know. We'll be there if you want.'

As they turned the corner and drew up outside his in-laws' house Eric squeezed his wife's hand back. 'Thank you,' he said.

Eric didn't get out the car. He was going to, briefly, then he caught sight of Lydia's glare and her look of daggers aimed directly at him. Suzy may have forgiven him over the lying incident, but it was clear he had a long way to go with her sister. Last time Eric upset Lydia, he ended up being given a crocheted toilet roll doll every Christmas for three years, complete with an almost new roll of toilet paper. Nuances had never been part of Lydia's toolbox.

Griff motioned to the back room as soon as he saw him.

'They're already waiting for you,' he said. 'Do you want me to bring you a Wimpy Git through? Or a bacon sandwich?'

Eric shook his head. 'Just a black coffee,' he said. His stomach never coped well with nerves, and for some reason, he was incredibly nervous. The Cabin was filled with its normal aromas of pig fat and coffee, but the walls and hallways felt exceptionally dark and narrow. As Eric made his way through to the back room he paused, one foot resting at the bottom of the tiny staircase, the other at the top. The *back room*. Despite frequenting the Cabin several times in the last few weeks, he'd not been back to the back room since his meeting there with Christian Eaves. Eric thought back to the letter, now stuffed somewhere in a box with old postcards and passport photos. What was it he said about misgivings? And deluded ideas of success? Eric shook his head clear and focused on the situation. Then he stretched his neck until it clicked and marched forwards into the back room.

With the chairs arranged in one big circle and many of the places already taken, Eric felt as though he'd walked into the world's oddest AA meeting. There were several familiar faces, including Janice, Cynthia, and Rich as well as several unknowns, many of a similar or younger age to himself. The committee was a big one, yet they all had one thing in common. Regardless of their age, race, or choice of breakfast beverage, all the members fell silent when Eric entered.

'Eric, please, come sit down, sit down. Have you ordered some food? Would you like anything? They do a lovely black pudding.' Cynthia ushered him forwards through the chairs.

'I'm fine, thanks,' Eric said. 'I've already ordered a coffee.'

'Great, well sit down then. We're almost ready to get started.'

Eric hovered awkwardly in the centre of the circle. There were three seats free, one on either side of Janice and one next to a face he didn't recognise. After a moment's hesitation, he took the one next to the unknown and quickly quashed his twang of guilt. Today wasn't a day for small talk. There was another moment's fuss when Hank – an exceptionally stocky pensioner with a Sailor Jerry tattoo, a limp, and a three-legged whippet – entered. He politely motioned to his leg when Janice pointed out the available seats beside her, then a moment later caught Eric's eye and winked.

After Hank had settled himself against the window ledge, another, longer silence fell between the group. Eric watched as eyes darted between one another, along with knowing glares and disgruntled tuts. Eric was surprised by how many people he didn't recognise. There was what appeared to be a young married couple with an overly hairy toddler playing with cars around their feet, and several people a generation or two older, most of whom possessed hair of a silvery-grey pigmentation. A few people coughed, some genuinely, others as a more obvious evidence of boredom.

'Well?' A man Eric thought was called Peter was the first to speak. 'What are we going to do? Just sit around here in silence until he turns up?'

'If he turns up.'

'He has to turn up. He's the chairman. And he's never missed a meeting before.'

'He's never done a lot of things before.'

All eyes, Eric's included, fell on Cynthia. She straightened her back.

'What, you think I have some control over him? A likely chance.'

There was a moment's pause until someone said, 'So what are we going to do then?'

The conversation descended into a mass of noise, through which every person was attempting to make their point heard. Eric's head went from one side to another, trying to make sense of the situation until a loud wolf whistle cut clean through them all. Still leaning on the window, Hank raised his hands.

'Look,' he said. 'Is the consensus going to change whether he's here or not?' A resounding *no* was emitted from the mass of shaking heads. 'Right then. In that case, I say we get on with this. No point keeping us all here for no reason. Agreed?'

There were more grumbles, though this time the resounding sound of a *yes* came out from the fog.

'He'll be pissed,' someone said.

'Then you can blame me. But let's get this over and done with. Cynthia?'

Everyone's eyes returned to Cynthia, who this time nodded demurely and rose to standing, her gaze focused solely on Eric.

Eric's insides churned. A juddering sensation vibrated around his appendix and, judging from the motion in his abdomen, his liver had been infested by a welt of hyperactive flatworms. He took a microsecond and closed his eyes. Ripping off the Band-Aid. That's all that was happening here. Ripping off the Band-Aid, blindfolded, using your teeth, while performing a one-handed cartwheel on a marble covered floor.

'Eric,' Cynthia said. 'First, I would like to apologise. After the incident with the digger, I'm afraid a few of my fellow alloties,' she shot some accusatory glares around the room, 'tried to take advantage of your good nature.'

'It's fine.'

'That is very kind of you to say, Eric. I, however, disagree and feel some action should be taken, but that's another matter, not for the here and now.'

Eric's shoulders dropped in relief although his insides squeezed tight. The last thing he wanted was to relive all that again, let alone be the centre of its fallouts. There were already some very disgruntled rumblings making their way in his direction.

'The next thing is the matter of the Unsatisfactory Cultivation Order you received.' Cynthia paused. 'As a committee, we hold the decision on many matters, including Unsatisfactory Cultivation Orders. In fact, all Unsatisfactory Cultivation Orders are supposed to go to the committee. However, in this particular incident, it appears that that step was missed.'

This time it was Cynthia's turn to blush.

'What do you mean?' Eric said. 'How was it missed?'

'Well,' Cynthia's redness was deepening, although she managed to maintain her aura of decorum and calm.

'On this occasion, it appears our chairman deemed it fit to take on the issue independently of the committee,' she said.

Eric took a moment to think through what he was hearing. 'So, what are you saying? That the order doesn't count? Is that what you're saying?'

'Well, it didn't previously count because it hadn't gone to the committee.'

'But it has now?'

'Yes?'

'So now it does count?'

'Well ...'

'Good God, woman. You don't half beat around the bush.' Hank had forced his way into the circle and opposite Eric. 'It's fine. You're fine. Provided you get it sorted in, say, the next two months?' He turned to the rest of the circle. 'Now can we get out of here?'

There was a reverberating concurrence around the room.

'Great,' he said. 'Scout needs his walk.'

He turned to go, his scruffy mongrel at his heel, but turning was as far as he got.

There was a figure standing in the doorway. His fingers were gnarled, and his shoulders hunched, and his stare went straight through the circle and through to the back of Eric's skull. Eric shrank into the chair. He tried to meet the man's eyes, his obscenely green eyes, and to look him squarely and not cower where he sat, but at that moment it was completely impossible.

'Well. It's nice to see how much my opinion counts around here,' Norman said. Then he grunted, spun around, and hobbled back outside.

CHAPTER 21

S EVERAL PEOPLE ATTEMPTED to follow Norman,
but Cynthia stopped them all.

'Let me deal with this,' she said. 'This was my
doing. I called the meeting. I spoke. He just needs a bit of
time, that's all.' There were lots of ifs and buts, hushed voices,
and sideways glances, but Cynthia was steadfast. 'Leave him to
me, it'll be fine,' she insisted.

Eric was not among the concerned do-gooders. If anything,
his sense of jubilation over the decision to let him keep the
allotment – and therefore Sally – was only amplified by
Norman's behaviour. This served him right for trying to set
Christian Eaves and the bailiffs on him. And for goading him
enough to tip the water butt over the plot. After the initial
moment's shock, Eric was practically levitating in his seat
watching the others fret over the miserable bastard's mental
wellbeing. It was a couple of minutes before he managed to
grab Cynthia's attention and gesticulated his farewell. She
offered a smile and nod as he left.

Eric skipped his way to the allotment, and it was only when

he reached the corner of Colombia Avenue that he remembered to call Suzy and tell her the news.

'That's fantastic,' she said. 'As long as you're happy?'

'You know what, I am. I'm glad I get to keep Sally at least. And strangely the allotment.'

'Poor Norman, though. It sounds like a horrid mess.'

'He abused his position on the committee,' Eric said. 'If I were the other members, I'd want him off.'

'You don't know all the details. I'm sure he had his reasons.'

'I know enough.' There was a brief silence in the conversation.

'Well,' he said. 'I'm just hopping over to the plot, making sure he hasn't drenched the ground with engine oil before I get there.'

'Play nice.'

'Not a chance,' Eric said and very much meant it.

As such, it was a stomach-plummeting disappointment to discover that Norman wasn't at the allotment. Gloating was an almost impossible task unless the person you were aiming to aggravate was within visual or auditory range. Still, there would be plenty of time to bask in his triumph later.

Now that the longevity of Eric's relationship with the small patch of ground had been determined, he wanted to get the remainder of the groundwork done. As long as he could get it to the point where the only maintenance required was to pull up a few straggling weeds each week, his part of the deal should prove easy to hold up. Half-an-hour a weekend at most. Unfortunately, with less than a third currently clear and weeds the size of birch trees occupying the remainder, it was going to take a little work to get there. He picked up his fork and got started.

Monday arrived and was its normal hectic self. It hit like a ten-tonne bull elephant and dragged Eric along with it, regardless of how much he wanted to curl up under the duvet and hide. Suzy had an event with her publishing house in Glasgow, which meant Eric had to pick up Abi from school at four. Under normal circumstances, and with his new ultra-efficient routine, it would have been fine. Only things at work weren't exactly normal.

The problem with having a boss like Jack Nelson – who even at the tensest times appeared so calm you'd think he'd just spent a week in a Japanese onsen listening to the entire Norah Jones back catalogue – was that seeing him even slightly flustered was, to put it mildly, troublesome.

On Monday, there was a sense of unease, by Tuesday people were notably agitated, and by Wednesday the tension was so palpable that Greg went home at lunch and reappeared in a pinstripe shirt and tie. Fingers tapped at keyboards with extra force and simple questions were met with snappy retorts. Jack progressed from pacing and hovering to slamming doors and banging his fist against various desks. After thirty-five minutes of marching in and out of his office, traipsing in and around various cubicles, and barking orders at unsuspecting interns, he appeared at Eric's door.

Eric's windpipe constricted.

'Do you mind if I ...?' Jack said as he poked his head into the room.

'No, no, not all,' Eric said. 'Come in, sit down.'

In a dirge-like walk, Jack crossed the office, then hovered, hands on the back of a chair, opposite Eric. It was a solid two minutes before he pulled out said chair and actually sat down. Eric, with his hand having adopted an unexpected quiver, abandoned the email he was writing and focused his full attention on his boss. He swallowed hard.

If anything, the extra lines nested around the corners of Jack's eyes and forehead added to the debonair spirit he carried so well. A touch of Clint Eastwood, perhaps. An older George Clooney. Jack scratched his temple, then his eyebrow, then finally lifted his gaze to meet Eric's.

'Eric,' Jack said. 'You've been at this firm a long time. A very long time.'

'Yes. Yes, I have. I mean I suppose I have.'

'And you've seen a lot of people come and go?'

'Well, I suppose so ...'

'And I bet you've heard a lot of things on the grapevine. A lot of things that maybe people wouldn't like me to hear.'

'I don't know. I don't think so. I mean ... I'm not exactly sure what you mean.'

Eric's pulse rose, sweat forming along his hairline. He really didn't know what Jack meant, and he definitely didn't know where the conversation was about to head, but it was looking less and less likely that Jack had come in to award him the company's very first employee of the month award. Jack leant back on the seat. He took a deep breath in through his nose and rested his fingertips against his brow bone. When he looked back up, he'd aged a decade.

'Sunday was my thirtieth wedding anniversary,' he said. 'Thirty years of marriage to the same wonderful woman.'

'Oh. Congratulations,' Eric said.

'And I forgot it.'

'Oh.'

'Yup.' Jack nodded. 'Thirty years of marriage and I forgot it.'

'Well.' The word came out of Eric in a long, drawn-out gust, expelling the tension that he'd been holding in his lungs since Jack's arrival. 'I'm sure if you do something nice. Buy her a nice present, perhaps? Does she like jewellery?'

Jack shook his head. 'Used that one up. Harry Winston, Bulgari, Cartier. She doesn't even open the boxes anymore. I think this is it. I think I've really blown it this time. She reckons all I care about is the business and the money.'

'What about a trip together then?' Eric grinned as he tried to keep the mood jovial. 'Somewhere special, exclusive. Romantic?'

Jack's head shook again. 'Tried that last year. Took her to Necker, she barely even cracked a smile.'

'Necker?'

'Little island, Richard Branson, and all that. Nice, but what's another beach holiday when she already spends half the year at some resort or another?'

Eric scratched his head. It was clear from this point that Jack had not come in to discuss any matter of impending business doom, yet it was also becoming apparent that he was not planning on leaving until he'd figured some solution. Another email pinged on Eric's screen. The to-do list was mounting, and there was no way of staying late with Abi to sort out.

The silence prolonged past a point of neutral contemplation, and Eric considered telling Jack that a little over a fortnight ago his wife had moved in with her sister on account of his lying and perhaps he'd be better taking his quandaries to Greg, who was clearly far savvier than himself when it came to handling cases of the opposite sex. He reconsidered, however, deciding that perhaps that wasn't the type of information Jack wanted to hear right now. Wishing to speed up the process as much as possible, he did what he often felt he should do in these situations, but never normally managed to master. He channelled his inner Suzy.

'What about going small then?' he said, after a moment's reflection.

'Small?'

'Back to when you first met. I'm assuming she didn't always get twenty-six weeks holiday a year?'

Jack smiled a sad half-smile. 'No, that she didn't. And you're not including the ski-season.'

'Well, why not plan something you'd have done before you had money? Just go for a drive in the car and see where the road takes you. That's what Suze and I used to do, before Abs of course.'

Jack raised an interested eyebrow.

'Go on?'

'You could go to the cinema. Or watch a movie at home with a takeaway?' Eric scoured his head for other ideas. 'What about you take a class together? Like a dance class, or a cookery class?' Jack's head cocked to the side. Eric kept on, not wanting to stop now that he was on a roll. 'Wine tasting? I hear there are lots of wine tasting courses. And brewery ones too. Or you could go on a picnic. Take the train down to the coast, book in at some cheap B&B? What about going to a museum? Or grabbing a load of board games and spending a weekend playing Monopoly?' He paused and noted Jack's somewhat bewildered expression. 'What I'm saying is that I'm sure all you have to do is show her that you're still the same man she married, and she'll forget all about the millions you have squirrelled away in the bank.'

Jack jumped to his feet, nodding his head enthusiastically. 'You know what, I think you're right. I know exactly what to do. You're a genius, Eric, you really are. And that wife of yours is one lucky lady.'

Eric glowed inside and out. 'My pleasure, sir.'

Jack bounded across the room and swung open the door. He was partway to his office when he spun around on the spot and bounded back. 'You won't tell anyone of this conversation, will you?' he said, an unusual air of trepidation in his voice.

'Of course not.'

'Just checking,' he said and disappeared again.

With a new sense of accomplishment and motivation, Eric turned back to his computer screen, finished off composing his last email, then stopped. There was a florist on the way home, opposite Abi's school, or at least there had been a few years back. He picked up a Post-It from the pile and a biro from the pot and beneath a memo about staff turnover scribbled down, *Buy Suzy flowers.*

CHAPTER 22

FEBRUARY MELTED INTO March and signs of spring began to appear. In the city, knitted hats and thick woollen scarfs were abandoned in favour of more lightweight versions, and although Easter eggs had graced the shelves of the supermarkets since the second of January, their presence was now highlighted by the countless adverts of over-smiley people gorging themselves on foil-wrapped goodies. In Burnham, the changes were more subtle; bare trees budded with green, boats began to move up and down the estuary. The allotments were the busiest Eric had known them.

Finally, his plot was clear. It had taken more than a little hard graft, during which Eric had discovered several sets of previously dormant muscles, most of which he'd be perfectly happy never to encounter again. However, when all was said and done, even he had to agree it was worth it. The sixty by forty parcel of land was now a serene patch of smooth brown earth, ready for digging and planting, although until this misadventure Eric had never truly understood the misery of weeding.

Weeding for Eric had previously consisted of blasting the Islington patio with a twice-yearly glug of Weedol and occasionally plucking the stray survivors from the fence line. It had been a chore, but then jobs around the house usually were. Weeding in Burnham was never going to be that simple.

During the previous two Saturdays, Eric had spent over three hours clearing the ground, pulling up every root, stem and leaf he could, only to find that when he returned the following weekend they'd returned en masse and brought with them several of their more stoic friends. Eric considered it a genuine ecological mystery that despite slicing, maiming, and uprooting, they kept managing to reappear. The option of weed-killer was highly frowned upon, not only by his fellow alloties but also by Suzy. Suzy was all about organic; organic milk, organic eggs, even organic shampoo, and she sure as hell wasn't going to let Eric grow vegetables in compost filled with more chemicals than the periodic table.

So digging it was. Abi had started to show more interest in the plot and had even become somewhat of an asset when it came to dandelion extraction, albeit in the hope of stockpiling enough to persuade Eric they had to get a rabbit.

One corner of the plot which proved particularly stubborn when it came to weeds was the patch where the old greenhouse had stood. In a burst of inspiration, Eric decided an easy way to rectify this was to put another one in its place. He also purchased – with a sizeable discount given the greenhouse – a small shed. By the end of March, Sunday mornings had developed into an unnerving routine involving traipsing around garden centres and pining over the excessively expensive accessories one apparently required to grow a batch of carrots.

It was Sunday evening and Eric was lying in bed. Suzy had been out for over an hour beside him. The pages of her book lay crumpled between her face and the pillows as a soft semi-snore buzzed from between her lips. The scent of fresh earth clung to her hair; evidence of their family day at the plot.

'Gotcha!' Eric shouted.

'What? What is it?' Suzy jerked awake and flicked on her light. 'What's wrong?'

'Raised beds.' Eric waved his book at her.

'What?'

'I can do raised beds. We can make them out of old timber, line them, fill them with compost, and boom. Then the rest of the earth we can pave over and nuke with enough weed-killer to flatten the Amazon.'

'I'm sorry,' Suzy rubbed her eyes and stretched before she relocated her crumpled book to the side-table. 'Are you talking about the allotment?'

'Of course, what did you think I was talking about?'

'What time is it?'

'I don't know. Half eleven maybe?' Eric glanced at the clock beside him. 'Twelve forty then. What does it matter?'

'You're right, it doesn't.' Suzy groaned, switched the light back off and buried her head back into the pillows.

'So?' Eric insisted. 'What do you think?'

'About the fact it's twenty to one?'

'About the raised beds?'

Suzy muttered something, almost certainly uncomplimentary about raised beds, into her pillow and drifted back off to sleep.

Still, it was such a good idea that the next morning, and afternoon, it remained lodged at the forefront of Eric's mind.

During the marketing team's meeting, his thoughts were fixated on what type of wood he would use, and where, of course, he could source it. During his working lunch with Greg, he was wondering whether the leftover crusts from his thin-pan goat's cheese and artichoke heart pizza would make for good compost. On the way home, he struck gold.

'What the hell are you doing?' Suzy asked when she glided past the dining room that evening and came to an abrupt stop. Eric was crouched down on the floor among nails, hammers, and various offcut planks. A decrepit wooden door lay flat on the dining room table, the paint chipped and peeling, and emanating a scent reminiscent of blocked drains and day-old kebabs.

'Don't worry, it looks worse than it is.'

'I very much doubt that,' she said.

Noting his wife's obvious disdain, Eric rose to standing and surveyed the situation himself. There were flecks of paint working their way into the beige carpet, and a long streak of mud marked the door's entry route into the room. Four more doors were resting against the wall, a spirit level was on its side propped against a pack of eighteen-inch stakes, and dozens of nails were sprinkled like confetti, marking out a clear silhouette of where Eric had been sitting. Charging by the plug-socket was the old Philips electric screwdriver they'd been given as a wedding present.

'I'll admit, it looks a bit of a mess now, but by bedtime you won't even know I've been in here.'

Suzy didn't move. Deciding it was best to get back to work, Eric started to shift smaller pieces of wood onto bigger ones until he found what he was looking for. A small bag of nails.

'You know we have a garden?' Suzy said. 'We have a perfectly good garden you could do this in?'

'I did think that. But it was already getting dark when I got all this, and I didn't want to waste any more time fumbling around not being able to see properly.'

'We have patio lights,' Suzy stated, and Eric had to admit he couldn't think of a response to counter that.

'What exactly is all this?' Suzy said. 'And where did you get it?'

Eric beamed at the question. 'You're going to love this,' he said.

'Really?'

Eric's smile stretched across his face. It was a face evocative of the expression a teenage boy would use to tell his friends he'd finally gone and popped his cherry, radiating satisfaction and pride from every pore.

'I got them from a tip,' he said.

'Pardon?'

'A tip. That grubby yellow builder's tip. Just down the end of the road. Can you believe that?'

'To be honest —'

'It's saved us a fortune. It's brilliant. I reckon I'll be able to make five beds from this lot. Maybe even more.'

'I'm sorry, you're doing what?'

Eric was about to reply – rather bluntly given that in his mind they'd already discussed the matter at length last night in bed – when Abi bounded in through the door, waving a two-foot-long, matte grey, steel crowbar.

'Is this what you wanted, Daddy?'

'Perfect.'

Eric grabbed the crowbar and jammed it into a gap between two planks of wood. He tensed his biceps and flexed his arm ready to wrench. He stopped and turned to his wife.

'Sorry, darling. Was there something you wanted me to do?'

Suzy's line of sight went from the dining table to the crowbar and back several times.

'No,' she said. 'Nothing at all.'

Despite Suzy's concerns, Eric deemed the dining room a most suitable location for the separating and sorting of the wood and timber, although even he couldn't deny it wasn't ideal for building the actual beds. They needed to be secured into the ground as they were built, and the only way to do that was to be on site. After a brief discussion with Suzy, he decided to book a room at the Sailboat for the following Saturday night.

'I know it was a bit chintzy,' Eric said. 'But even if we stay at your sister's, it'll be ten before we're down there and then we'll have already lost half the day. Besides, I looked on their website and it says they have family rooms, so at least we won't be so cramped.'

Suzy agreed. 'You'll have to take Abi for a couple hours on Sunday, though. I need a bit of time in the morning to get some work done or I'm going to miss these deadlines.'

'That's not a problem. I've got the perfect job. You can go find worms for my compost heap can't you, Abs? You'd like that, wouldn't you, going and finding lots of long wiggly worms?' Abi screamed in delight as her father chased her around the house, wiggling his fingers and making apparently wormesque noises. When Eric eventually collapsed on the sofa from exhaustion, Abi continued to spend next five minutes jumping on the sofa singing 'We're going to eat some worms at the weekend!' to the tune of *Daddy's Taking Us to the Zoo*. Their weekend was decided.

While the old Philips screwdriver had served them well in
their twelve years of marriage – if Eric's memory served him
right, it had hung at least fourteen photo frames in that time –
he decided he needed something with a bit more oomph for
the amount of drilling and screwing he'd planned for the weekend. So, en route to Burnham, he detoured into Chelmsford
and Lewis at Tools4U.

'You have to be kidding,' Lewis said when he saw him. 'You
know you've lost your deposit on everything you've hired from
us so far?'

'Which is why you should be even more grateful for my
custom. You have insurance. You're raking it in. Besides, I'm
not hiring anything today.'

'No?'

'No, my wife is.'

Lewis rolled his eyes.

'And I guess she doesn't need instructions on how to use
these tools either?' he said.

'That'd be like cheating,' Eric replied and waited for him to
fetch the power tools.

It was amazing the difference a month and a few good days
of weather could make. Late Saturday morning, the allotment
bustled with activity, and even Janice was too busy raking
parallel lines in her topsoil to look up and announce Eric and
the family's arrival. Either that or he was now too common-
place to be worthy of her high-level greetings. Suzy decided
she needed to clear her head before she got to work and so
took Abi for a walk along the river in search of seals while Eric
unloaded the car. As well as the Black and Decker cordless
drill, Eric had also borrowed – in Suzy's name – a workbench
and a small jigsaw from Lewis at the shop. It wasn't until he'd
unloaded all the wood and was setting up the workbench that
he noticed Norman.

Eric had kept a peripheral eye on the pathway the entire time, for the exact reason of noting Norman's arrival. As such, he was unsure how he'd slipped past without his notice.

Two months had done nothing to ease the tension between the two, although Eric had made a conscious effort not to engage Norman in any form of eye contact at the risk it may turn into a conversation. Thus far the plan appeared to have worked. As Eric glanced up from his workbench, he accidentally caught the old man's eye across the plot. His stomach dropped. He was left with no option other than to offer a quick, obligatory nod.

'Still here then?' he said to Eric in a gravelly, lung-crackling growl.

'Not going anywhere, I'm afraid.'

'We'll see,' Norman said, then hobbled back into his shed, to return several minutes later with a trowel and a cup of tea in hand.

It was slower work than Eric had anticipated and more physically demanding, but by the time Suzy called to ask if he wanted to meet them for lunch, he had one planter fully built and lined and another four with pilot holes drilled, ready to be assembled.

'I noticed the little cinema in town has opened up again,' Eric said to Suzy as he chewed on his crab roll. 'I don't suppose they've got anything good on, but I thought we could take a look?'

'That sounds like a great idea,' Suzy said. Abi was too busy feeding her roll to the seagulls to reply.

Once lunch had been devoured, it was back to the allotment. Eric finished off one more of the planters before packing everything up and locking it in his shed. It was a cold evening, but a gentle cold. The type that made you feel grateful you had a nice warm coat and thick socks but didn't turn your fingers to ice or cause you to sprint for the radiator as soon as you got inside. The weeds had sprouted yet again, and he spent a scant half hour plucking what he could. It was only a half-hearted effort and more for appearance's sake than anything else. Drilling and sawing may have been the necessities of the day, but it didn't make him look any more of a gardener, unlike Norman who had spent all afternoon on his hands and knees digging around in the dirt, coughing up dozens of alveoli in the process.

The cinema was a pleasant surprise. While the white facade of the building advertised films a good six months old, inside played a surprisingly updated schedule. With Abi the controlling factor, they opted for the latest Pixar movie. A third of the way in, Eric's phone beeped in his pocket. When Abi and Suzy shot him simultaneous glares, he took it out and switched it off without so much as a second glance at the screen.

Abi was practically sleepwalking on the way back to the Sailboat. While Eric carried her up the narrow stairs – trying not to disturb her as he manoeuvred around the bannister and unlocked the door – Suzy went to the off-licence for a bottle of gin and some tonic.

'You know,' she said as they sat cross-legged on the pink satin sheets and clinked their glasses. 'I don't think I've seen you this relaxed for years.'

'Really?' Eric said. 'I can think of how to make me much, much more relaxed.' Then he put down his glass and began to nuzzle.

CHAPTER 23

A S PROMISED, ERIC took Abi in the morning so that Suzy could get on with some more work. With no proper desk in the room, she took herself down to The Shed, where Griff sorted her out with a space in the back and a double-shot macchiato to get her going.

With all the sawing done, Eric just had to assemble the remaining planters. He knelt on the ground, drilled into his salvaged planks, and noted how many of the pieces were tattooed with the hapless doodles of a child with a biro. One of the planks even had horizontal markers and names etched next to the notches. This was far better than buying something prefab, he decided. This planter had a life, a soul. And weren't plants meant to like things like that?

Abi spent a solid hour digging for earthworms. She'd collected quite a few, although the receptacle she was using – a plastic saucer – was highly inefficient in its function. As a result, she spent most of her time moving the same half-dozen worms back onto the plate from wherever they'd managed to slither to while her back was turned. Eric thought he should possibly inform her of the issue but at the same time, it was keeping her quiet.

'Look, Dad. Look what I've got,' she said after a particularly quiet twenty minutes. 'Look what Aunty Cynthia gave me.'

Eric lifted his head. 'Aunty who?'

Abi stood in front of him. Her nails were black with dirt, as were the knees of her dungarees and the end of her scarf. In her hand, she held a little white packet.

'Aunty Cynthia.'

'Sorry.' Cynthia stood behind her, grey roots peeking out from her red hair, an apologetic smile creasing her eyes. 'Aunty Cynthia. Force of habit. We're Aunty and Uncle to all the little ones around here.'

'Cynthia will do fine,' Eric said.

'Of course. Of course.'

'Look, Daddy. Look at what she gave me,' Abi held out her hand. 'They're seeds. Scallywags seed.'

'Scallions,' Cynthia clarified. 'Spring onion seeds.'

'And Aunty Cynthia says I can grow them in the greenhouse. Or I can grow them at home too, but then I have to put them in the greenhouse when they're bigger. That's right isn't it?'

'That's right. You remembered that perfectly.'

'Can I grow them at home, Dad? Can I? Then I can take them to school when it's my turn at Show and Tell.'

'Why don't you put them in the greenhouse? We can bring some pots down next weekend. And then your mum won't get annoyed with all the mess.'

Abi's face fell. 'But then I won't get to take them into Show and Tell. And I'll end up taking something rubbish in, like a doll, or one of mum's books. And Harry Nini will think that's rubbish because he gets to take his rat in and he's taken it in four times now and I've never taken in anything that good, not even once.'

Glossing over his eight-year-old daughter's reoccurring interest in Harry Nini, Eric made one last attempt.

'But we don't have anything in the greenhouse. And it's the only empty greenhouse on the allotment. Your spring onions can be the first things that grow in it. Don't you think that's cool? Don't you want your seeds to be the very first thing that's ever, ever been grown in this greenhouse? Ever?'

Abi contemplated for a second, took another admiring glance at the packet in the hand, then said, quite definitely, 'No.'

When all was done for the day, Eric stepped back to survey his kingdom. Six glorious planters of approximately the same size and nearly straight edges sat flush to the earth below. Even without any soil, or plants, or bean poles, they looked impressive. The multi-coloured stains of the pre-loved wood gave a romantic patina; a vintage feel to them. First stop Burnham, he thought, next stop Chelsea Flower Show.

'So, next week, it's sowing, right?' Suzy said. 'I thought your book said you should have already planted all your beans and whatnots by now?'

'The beans should be okay,' Eric said. 'But we've probably missed asparagus for this year. Shame though. We'll have to remember next year.'

'Next year? Good God, you're taking this seriously.'

'I'm just following my father's orders,' he said.

Abi was currently with another group of children crouched around a small cardboard box.

'I guess we should get her and get going,' Eric said. 'It's a pain I've got to go to work tomorrow. I feel like I've had a mini holiday.'

'Well you've still got all your holiday days racked up,' Suzy reminded him. 'I'm sure Jack wouldn't mind if you rang him now and said you wanted to take a couple of them last minute.'

Eric shook his head. 'No, I couldn't do that to him at the minute. He's been a bit stressed out lately.'

'That doesn't sound like Jack?'

Eric was about to tell her about Jack's missed wedding anniversary, when someone coughed, loudly and with obvious force, directly behind him. Eric swivelled around.

Norman's beard was a truly impressive feature, particularly from this distance. The tight white hairs coiled and spiralled into a thick nest that stretched all the way from his temples to his breastbone, narrowing down into a thin, pristine point. His lips and nostrils were lost entirely to it, and his eyes, though visible, were currently set down, and thus greatly obscured by his massive white eyebrows.

He coughed again, although this time the cough was genuine.

'I wondered if you might have a moment for a word,' he said.

Eric exchanged a glance with Suzy.

'I need to go get Abi,' she said to him. 'I'll see you in a minute, by the gate.'

'I'll only be a minute,' Eric said, then braced himself.

With Suzy gone, Norman continued to stare at the ground. His hands were in his pockets as he shuffled from one foot to the other.

'Did you want something?' Eric said, surprising even himself with the churlishness of his voice.

Norman looked up. He ran his tongue over his top lip, pushing some of the white whiskers momentarily to the side.

He cleared his throat again, with a few more catarrhy coughs, then mumbled with his mouth half-closed.

'I 'spect that maybe –'

'Sorry, can you speak up?' Eric said. 'I'm afraid I can't hear you.'

Norman's eyes flashed, and his nostrils flared widely, although just the once. He closed his eyes then opened them again straight away and began to speak.

'I know we didn't get off on the best foot an' all —'

'With you trying to get me evicted you mean?'

'— and I 'spect I was a bit hasty with my actions, like. But I would like to try to make some 'mends.'

'Pardon?' Eric said.

'I said, I'd like to make amends. Apologise.' He glanced over his shoulder, where Eric spotted Cynthia. She was urging him onwards with encouraging nods.

He turned back to Eric, sucked in a deep lungful of air, held it in his chest, and stretched out his hand.

Eric examined the hand in front of him. It was creased and cracked like no hand he'd ever seen. Every crevice was brown, sealed in years of mud and soil, and there were splits in the fingertips, red and raw and centimetres long. That was before he even got to the dirt that covered them. Eric thought about the situation in front of him. He had no desire to shake hands with this man, particularly when the hand looked like an extra from *The Walking Dead*. But behind him, Eric could feel Suzy watching him, willing him to do the right thing. He held his breath, gritted his teeth, and stretched out his hand.

They had barely touched fingertips when Norman withdrew his hand and plunged it back into his pocket.

'I got you something. For your greenhouse like. Can't be having a greenhouse like that, all new with nothing in. Someone'll steal it. Or smash it. Need to be growing something in it.'

He pulled out a small packet of seeds, not dissimilar to the ones that Cynthia had given Abi earlier in the day.

'Dutch coriander,' he said. 'Start it off at home, I would. Too delicate with the weather being what it's like at the minute. One frost even in your greenhouse'd see it off.'

'Oh,' Eric said, unsure of what else he could say.

'Be best to bring it down 'ere start o' April. When they're nicely sprouted. Then you can put it in your greenhouse. You'll have some lovely plants.'

'Well, I don't know what −'

'Don't want to eat it raw, though. Not like that other stuff. No, you bring it down here come April and I'll tell you the best way to get cooking it.'

Eric took the packet and tipped a few of the seeds onto his palm. They were seedlike; seed-shaped, browny green. He almost expected his hand to start fizzing, not placing it above Norman to douse them with acid or some caustic sap, but nothing happened. He poured them back into the packet.

'A late housewarming, if you will,' Norman said.

What followed was an exceptionally awkward silence in which Eric experienced a peculiar gnawing around his large intestine. His mouth grew dry and his Adam's apple swelled. Norman waited, eyes wide and feet rooted to the spot.

No way, Eric thought to himself. *Not a chance.*

But Norman wasn't budging. Eric's palms grew sweaty. There had to be another way, there had to. But there wasn't. There was only one thing Eric could do, and he hated himself for it. If only Suzy wasn't watching. If only he could just walk away. Swallowing hard Eric took a deep breath and said it as fast as he could.

'Thank you,' he mumbled at his feet.

'What was that?'

'I said thank you.'

Norman smirked.

'I shall get some compost and seed trays and plant them next week,' Eric added for good measure.

Norman shook his head.

'I've got plenty of compost in my shed. And trays mind. Why don't you plant 'em now? It'll only take two minutes.'

'Well, I need to get Abi home,'

Norman huffed away his excuses.

'She can help you. Besides, Cynth has got a few seed trays she wanted to give her for those spring onions. Couple weeks and you'll have a full 'erb garden up 'ere.'

'Well ...'

'Two minutes. Let me get you those trays.' Then he added, 'I can tell you all about the mole fiasco while we're at it.'

It took less than five minutes to get all the seeds potted, and when they left to head back to London, they had four plastic containers of Dutch coriander and spring onions ready to sit on their kitchen window sill.

'Well that was lovely,' Suzy said. 'Give it a few weeks and you two will be thick as thieves.'

'I sincerely doubt that,' Eric said.

CHAPTER 24

THE FIRST THING Eric had felt was an icy blast as the covers were whipped off the bed, exposing his semi-naked body to the air. Next had come the vigorous shaking of the shoulders and the ear-splitting shriek.

'Daddy! Dad! Dad! Daddy! Daddy! Daddy! Dad! Dad! Are you up? Are you awake? Are you awake yet?'

'I am now.'

'It's today, Daddy, it's Tuesday.'

'Really? Are you sure? I thought it was Monday. It's Monday isn't it, Mummy?'

Suzy rolled over and curled herself up into the remainder of the duvet.

'You know what. I think you're right. I think it's Monday.'

'It's not! It's Tuesday,' Abi yelled. 'And you promised. You promised you'd come. You're still coming aren't you, Dad?'

Eric leant over the side of the mattress and hoisted Abi up onto the bed.

'Of course I'm coming. I promised, didn't I?'

April had arrived with its stereotypical showers and less

typical frost, and as such, Eric's lovingly crafted planters remained sparsely populated with compost, old newspaper, and earthworms, but as yet, no vegetation. However, his greenhouse was faring a little better.

A sizeable variety of flora were germinating away in their little plastic pots, and as well as the usual suspects – lettuces (romaine and cos), chard, potatoes, Brussels sprouts, courgettes – he'd also tried his beginner's hand at a few of the more exotic specimens, such as aubergine and artichoke. His expectations were low, impressively so, although with every week that passed, something that could have been akin to anticipation bubbled away inside.

This upcoming weekend – frost depending – was transplant weekend, when everything that could and should be grown outside was going to be moved. In preparation, Abi had spent the last fortnight using the allotment as her inspiration for the Reduce, Reuse, and Recycle project at school. The results were an imposing sight. Along with the stereotypical DIY gardening effects you would expect from a eight-year-old – bird feeder, row markers, hanging baskets, and seed boxes – Abi had also proved herself to be quite the engineer. With the help of Google, Suzy, and Eric, she'd created a drip irrigation feed system out of plastic bottles – enough to place several in each of Eric's planters – and even her own mini polytunnel, created from densely glue-gunned empty coke bottles. Today was Show and Tell at school, and everything was going in.

Abi had been in a fit of excitement for over a week. So much so that on Saturday, Cynthia had had to take her down into town to get her an ice cream so that Eric could get five minutes productive sowing in. Suzy had offered to keep Abi for the morning, but he knew she had deadlines looming and keeping Suzy happy was still paramount on his list of agendas.

Eric's affection for Cynthia had done nothing but warm,

and after his initial misgivings, he'd relented to the title of Aunty Cynthia. The prefix of uncle, however, still made him gag when used in reference to Norman.

It remained a mystery to him how Cynthia had managed to suffer Norman and his indignation for so long. He skulked around from one side of his plot to the next, hacking phlegm over all the beds as he coughed and wheezed, grunting obscenities under his breath at almost anyone who attempted to speak to him. There were a few exceptions, of course, Hank being one. Eric, however, was still firmly off the list. So, when Norman initiated small talk with Eric on the subject of Abi's Show and Tell, he was rather taken aback.

'Taking in all her seeds too, she says.'

'Um, well yes, that's the plan. The ones we've grown at home, anyway.'

'And that'll mean you taking a morning off work then, will it?'

'Well yes.'

'That's something I suppose.'

Eric continued to tell Norman a few facts about Abi's school; highly focused on the arts, and an international exchange programme that ran throughout Europe and South-East Asia.

'A choice of six languages to study from Year One.'

'Sounds grand,' Norman said. 'Can she say deadly nightshade in French?'

'What? Why?' Eric frowned.

''Cos it looks like she's just picked a load from that bush.'

Over by the edge of the allotment, Abi was studying something in her hand.

'*Abi!*'

Eric bolted towards his daughter, trampling over several allotments en route, and leaving great gaping footprints in the soil. Abi had her hand millimetres from her mouth. Dozens of beads glistened black in the sunlight, piled high in her cupped palm. With his heart in his throat, Eric lunged, diving across the air. He swung his arm towards Abi knocking the berries out of her hand a millisecond before they touched her lips.

'Dad! What did you do that for?'

Eric collapsed on the floor, panting. He grabbed his daughter by the wrist.

'You must never eat those berries, Abi. You hear me? Never. Not even one. Not ever.'

'What? Why?'

'They're poisonous. They'll kill you. They could have killed you.'

Abi crinkled her nose.

'Those berries,' Eric pointed to the glistening spheres now scattered on the ground. 'They're called deadly nightshade. And they're very, very dangerous.'

'No, they're not.'

'Abi, I'm not messing about.' Eric pulled himself up to feet. Now that the immediate threat was over the surge of adrenaline transformed into anger. 'You eat deadly nightshade berries and you'll end up in hospital, or worse. You hear me? Do you understand?'

'But they're not –'

'Abi will you please listen?'

'*You're* not listening to me.'

'No. You're not listening to me.'

'No,' Abi insisted with a stamp of her foot. 'You are not listening to me. That,' she pointed to a bush a little way behind Eric, 'is deadly nightshade, although it doesn't have any berries on yet and won't for another four months or so. Those,' she redirected her pointed finger to the black baubles in the dirt by her feet, 'are jellybeans.'

'What?'

'Jellybeans. They're jellybeans, see.'

She pulled out an open pack from her pocket. The crumpled bag was three-quarters full of little red and black spheres. 'Uncle Norman gave them to me. Just before he told me about deadly nightshade. And he said there's a badger somewhere in this hedge too. Have you seen it anywhere?'

Eric returned to his plot. Norman was resting against his pitchfork, his lips pursed in a whistle, a glint of satisfaction in his eye.

So, Eric had taken the morning off work. Jack had been fine about it. Since their heart to heart, nothing more had been said about the state of his marriage, although more than once Eric had knocked on his office door to find him giggling on his phone and using a series of endearments more commonly uttered by a sixteen-year-old girl.

As well as all the recycled articles, Abi also wanted to take in her spring onion plants, which were now proudly sprouting two inches above the soil, and Eric's Dutch coriander, which was demonstrating equally impressive growth. Mostly though she wanted to take in her dad, and Eric had at last relented.

Eric wasn't sure when he'd last stepped past the reception of Abi's school. *Mamma Mia* had taken place in the auditorium and he'd missed the Easter parade a few weeks before due to a meeting. Despite Suzy's insistence that this parade was an important educational milestone for their daughter, it seemed to Eric more of a trident display of parents' arts and crafts ability as opposed to anything to do with the actual children. As such, he suffered no remorse whatsoever for missing that one. As for parents' evenings, he'd told himself that he'd start to go when they actually mattered; GCSEs and above. Before then, there was nothing a teacher could tell him in a seven-minute meeting, cramped on a tiny child's chair in a room that smelt of poster paint, that couldn't be expressed more succinctly in a nice written report.

Show and Tell took place in the Key Stage One library. Only it didn't look like a library, it looked like a living room, or a play centre, or the hybrid mix if a genius child of the future had designed a living room with only play in mind. Rainbow beanbags were scattered across the floor while sizeable TV screens glowed with animated versions of Grimm's fairy tales and Julia Donaldson stories. Along one wall was a bank of computers, while on the other were half a dozen little cubby holes. Three-feet deep and the same wide, each of the cubby holes was padded with cushions, set with dim lights and a curtain, and also fitted with a television, iPod, and a set of headphones. There was a water fountain, a snack desk, and a little plastic box labelled *Ideas*. It was definitely not a library, it was Google HQ in the making. In fact, the only thing that really gave away the scholarly nature of the place was the perfectly procured aroma of pencil sharpenings and the rather voluptuous lady behind the desk who wore her thick-rimmed glasses on a chain around her neck.

Bang on ten, Abi's class arrived. Six other children were doing Show and Tell that day, and four of them had at least one parent there. They, like Eric, had clearly been dragged under duress, although unlike Eric they did not have such an active role in the performance aspect. Instead, they viewed their child's presentation through the screen of their iPhones, while attempting to reply to messages as subtly as possible and make sure they didn't miss the correct time to applaud. While Eric in no way considered himself unbiased, the other children's contributions could be considered, at best, dismal.

There was one vaguely decent attempt in which a boy with a straight fringe and sticky-out ears had recycled an old shoebox to form an elastic band guitar. The neck was made from toilet rolls and he'd even cut out some little cardboard pegs to stick on the end for authentic value. It looked good in the sense that it looked like a pile of absolute crap that an eight-year-old would make as an extended task that meant their teacher avoided any actual marking for a week. Eric was quickly reminded why he hated these types of things.

With the shoebox guitar the highlight, the rest of the offerings failed to hit anywhere near the mark. There was another shoebox, this time marketed as a reusable tissue box. From the clapping and applause the child received, it appeared to Eric that the rest of the audience had failed to grasp the fundamental flaw with the design, being that tissues did, in fact, come in their own box. There was a pencil case made from a toilet roll with one end cardboarded over and no evidence of decoration, and a coke-bottle rocket, imaginatively embellished with fins and blasters, that could apparently fly, only the child's parents wouldn't let him bring in the pump to prove this. Then it was Abi's turn.

Eric's pulse ratcheted up a knot as Abi took to the front of the class. Her arms were stretched wide around the makeshift mini polytunnel as she chose her footing carefully between her classmates. Once at the front, she set the object down on the teacher's desk before dashing back to the classroom to get the rest of the items. After three return trips, she had everything she needed.

'Good morning 2P,' Abi said to the class.

Her eyes darted to her father. Eric's stomach fluttered, and his heart thumped against the wall of his rib cage. He offered her an encouraging smile, but she didn't move. She'd frozen.

'Go, on,' Eric mouthed to her. 'You can do this.'

A thin bead of sweat meandered down past Eric's collar. Pep talks were one of those many facets that did not fall under his capacity as a parent. Pep talks at work were fine, but as a parent, he always missed the mark; a thump on the arm while telling a four-year-old child to buck up their ideas and focus on the big picture was apparently not always the required response. Neither was telling them not be such a wuss.

Abi's eyes still hadn't moved from her father, and several other children were now looking at him too. The one bead of sweat on Eric's neck was quickly joined by others. Channelling his inner Suzy, he shut his eyes, tilted his chin up, and took a deep yogic breath. The air hissed as he sucked it in through his nose. *You can do this*, he said in his head, praying the words would somehow transfer to Abi and she'd get the idea of following his lead. He opened his eyes and smiled.

'You've got this, kiddo,' he mouthed to her.

Abi closed her eyes, took a long inhale, then flicked her eyes open with a glint. A swish of her hair and she turned her attention back to the class.

'At the end of last year,' she began, 'my dad inherited an allotment. Inherited means when you get someone's stuff because they're dead ...'

Abi's speech went by in a flash. She explained in detail how she'd managed to join the bottles together to make the poly-tunnel and how to weight one side of the bird feeders so it wouldn't just spill out as soon as a bird sat on it. She described how the irrigation system meant you could get the water right to the roots of the plants, which was where it needed to be if the plants were going to grow, and when one child asked for a demonstration, she had no difficulty instructing her teacher to go and fetch the necessary water and an empty plastic bucket.

For her *finale* she passed around the seedlings, allowing the students to prod and poke at them at their will.

'Can we eat this?' one child said when handed Eric's Dutch coriander.

'I don't think so,' the teacher said, then looked to Eric as if for confirmation.

Eric shrugged. 'Um, I don't know. It's not fully grown yet. And I think you're meant to cook it first. It's probably better not to.'

The teacher conveyed this information to the child with a look. 'Pass it on for now,' she said. 'I'm sure Abi will bring some in when it's grown.'

At the end of the presentations, the children stood up then, clattering and chattering, went back to their classroom. Abi swung her arms around Eric as she passed.

'Thank you for coming,' she said.

'She was incredible. I mean, she's such a natural speaker in front of a crowd. Did I tell you she sent the teacher out to get some water when one of the children wanted a demonstration?'

'You did,' said Suzy. 'Twice.' She pecked him on the cheek. 'But it's great that you're so proud of her.'

Eric pulled three plates out from the dishwasher, then grabbed a handful of cutlery. He thought he might have over-shared a bit at work too, as for the first time he could remember it was Greg who had to ask Eric to leave his office as he wanted to get some work done, as opposed to the other way around. Fortunately, he ran into Jack two minutes later, who was more than happy to listen to Eric regale him with tales of his daughter's ascension to social science guru.

Abi skipped into the kitchen and hopped up at the table.

'I was just telling your mum how fantastic you were again,' Eric said, laying out the crockery.

'Dad, you don't have to keep going on.'

'I'm not.'

Suzy spooned out the biryani while Eric doled out equal portions of pappadams.

'I thought I might see if I can leave early Friday,' Eric said as he sat down. 'It'll mean working late for a couple of nights, but I thought we could head down to Burnham in the evening again. I seem to get a lot more done that way.'

'Sounds great, only I have to work. I'm behind on this book. I honestly don't know where the time has gone. I thought if you were driving down Saturday, you could drop Abi at Lyd's on the way? You wouldn't mind that would you, hun?' Suzy looked at Abi, who shrugged in response.

Eric shook his head. 'It's fine. I'll take Abi down with me on Friday. That way you get the whole evening to work. Then if you want, you can come and join us Saturday. If not, Abi and I'll just work on together. There's a lot to get on with. We've got a state-of-the-art recycled irrigation system to set up, don't you know?'

Abi beamed.

'Yay! I'm coming too,' she said.

'That's settled then,' said Eric. 'I'll ring the Sailboat and book our room now.'

CHAPTER 25

E RIC'S FATHER-DAUGHTER bonding weekend didn't get off to an ideal start. He had somehow miscommunicated to Suzy that he'd been planning on taking Sally down to Burnham, and while the law was on his side in regard to taking a child in the back seat of a vintage car, Suzy was not. Forty minutes of his afternoon was spent going back and forth via text, email, and finally voice call between himself, Suzy, and Ralph before he finally conceded. It was a tough loss to take, but they could have been there until midnight otherwise. As it was, it was gone three by the time they'd finally packed up the Audi with their plant paraphernalia. Twenty miles of moderately light traffic through London and then, less than half a mile onto the A12, they hit a tailback that left them in stationary traffic for over three-quarters of an hour. Eric could sense a pressure headache developing beneath his temples. He gave Abi her headphones, told her she could watch whatever she fancied, then switched on Radio 4. Rachmaninov did little for the traffic but did at least manage to abate a migraine.

They arrived in Burnham just after six. With Abi and Eric both at the stage of hunger that meant either one of them may have thrown themselves onto the ground, hammering their fists at the slightest infraction, they parked up directly outside the chippy and went straight inside. After food, the evening consisted of an old-school Disney marathon with *The Little Mermaid*, *The Jungle Book*, and one-third of *The Lion King*, all watched in bed on Eric's laptop and thus absolving him of any guilt over not checking his emails.

Abi's eyelids fluttered as he lifted her up off the double bed and transplanted her into her own. *She looks so much like her mum*, Eric thought, brushing her hair out of her eyes. 'Sleep tight, princess,' he said and tucked her up in the duvet.

Saturday was brisk, although in the sun the heat was strong enough to make you want to remove your jacket and perhaps even consider wearing just one layer, long sleeved of course. Out of it and you were quickly reminded that April in the UK was definitely spring and nowhere near summer, and that your vest and cargo shorts should remain well and truly at the bottom of the wardrobe for at least another two months.

When they arrived, Hank was the only person there. Abi wanted to get there even earlier, having laid out all her labels and water bottles before the Disney-athon the night before, but Eric insisted they have breakfast first. While Abi ate a fairly substantial Chubby Little Bugger, Eric had his first Fat Bastard. All ordering was done by pointing at the menu, as even Eric wasn't naïve enough to believe Abi wouldn't pass on every detail of the weekend to Suzy, including a detailed and itemised list of each and every profanity he used.

At the allotment, Eric tipped bag after bag of garden-store compost into his planters, packing it down lightly onto the bin bags and newspaper as he prepared to transfer the bulk of his seedlings from the greenhouse.

In recent weeks, he'd come across the idea of companion planting. It was an appealing concept that involved planting different combinations of fruit and vegetables together in order to deter pests from one another and help maintain an organic crop without the use of pesticides. Suzy was all for it, and while Eric wasn't against it, the only issue was the amount of time he'd spent figuring out the logistics of the arrangements within his six by four raised beds.

Potatoes, for example, were compatible with several vegetables including lettuce, beans, and cabbage, but combative if planted with tomatoes. Whereas onions were ideal planting partners for carrots, beetroot, and strawberries, the effects were far less desirable when placed next to peas and beans. Radishes apparently deterred cucumber beetles while tomato leaves could repel the insects that munched their way through cabbages. But did he really want to plant his radishes next to his cucumbers or would they be better next to spinach, which they insulated against bugs, or lettuce, which would apparently make the radishes a delicious entity in their own right as opposed to an unelected buffer against the harsh insect world that awaits all home-grown, chemical-free vegetables?

Eric had studiously worked out places for most of his items although a few he intended on leaving in the greenhouse until they'd gained a little more growth. For no other reason than sentimentality, he also felt it only fair to give the spring onions and Dutch coriander seedlings a little time to acclimatise in the greenhouse before thrusting them out into the British climate after spending several weeks in a cosy London kitchen. With the plants spread out in their proposed positions, all that was needed was for Eric to pick up his trowel and dig the first little trench.

'Aunty Cynthia! Uncle Norman!'

Abi bounded across the allotment, brandishing her irrigation system as she went. The couple walked hand in hand through the rows. Eric did a double take. He had always thought of Cynthia as a rather youthful pensioner, but from this distance, she looked decidedly old. Her shoulders slumped, and her gait dragged as a heavy bag weighed her down on one side. Still, she shook off the years and smiled enthusiastically when she saw Abi bounding towards her.

'You're down here early,' Cynthia said.

She dropped the bag by her own shed before ambling over towards his. The scent of Dettol and blackberries shrouded the air around her.

'Abi and I came down last night. An important day today. Lots to do.'

'My, my, yes. And this must be your watering invention,' Cynthia said to Abi. 'Goodness me, it looks very technical.'

While Cynthia crouched down to listen to Abi's tales of her school presentation and a detailed scientific explanation of how to use a compass to pierce holes in a coke bottle, Norman cast his eyes over the allotment.

'So, you've started planting at last?' Norman said.

'Just about to,' Eric said. As he spoke the muscles in his neck turned taut, and a strange yet familiar sensation whorled its way through his abdomen. He held his breath and waited.

While the majority of Eric's functioning sense cells wanted nothing more than to tell Norman that he could keep whatever opinions he had about Eric's current horticultural layout to himself, the other part of Eric was in conflict. Seeing his seedlings sprout up through the soil over the last three weeks had been something akin to when Eric discovered he was going to be a father. He hadn't felt a great need to celebrate each shoot with a bottle of Moët and had been much more candid about the exact processes involved than when Abi had asked him how babies were made only four weeks back, but still, he'd done a simple act and created life. He was a miracle maker. The fruits of his labours were burgeoning around, and all he could do was watch and wait in wonder. And yet, until that life was fully grown and slapped up on a plate in front of him – the sentiment had been slightly different in regard to Abi, obviously – a nervous trepidation simmered constantly away in his belly. He'd found himself with a less than hospitable gut these last two nights and was well aware as to the root of the cause. The last thing he needed was the male-midwife of the vegetable patch coming over to tell him that he'd failed as a plant parent before his seedlings were even out of their pots.

'Overpaid for that compost,' Norman said and nudged one of the seventy-five-litre bags with his toe.

Eric decided to take a step back, bite his tongue, and await the verdict.

Norman's eyes scrutinised the freshly composted beds. The hair above his top lip wobbled as he exhaled in heavy grunts. He looked first at the potatoes with their flat, rounded bract, then the lettuce, then the tomatoes. In fact, Eric was certain Norman had examined every single specimen before his gaze finally settled on the greenhouse. He took several strides between the beds, slid the glass door open, then stepped inside. Eric followed, a nervous twitch running down the side of his left leg.

'I thought I was under watering them to start with.' Eric felt an unusual and insatiable urge to fill the silence. 'But then I read up and it said that with herbs, provided they weren't going yellow, I was probably giving them enough. Although I couldn't find anything about this one in particular.' Norman ran the back of his index finger against one stem of the Dutch coriander. He took a toothed leaf between his fingertips then bent down and sniffed.

'They've come up nice,' Norman said, then quicker than a dog in a Vietnamese restaurant swivelled on his heel, marched out through the open door, and disappeared off into his shed.

'It was nice talking to you,' Eric called after him.

By early afternoon, Eric was ready to go home. The middle of his back throbbed from constantly leaning over, his trousers chafed where the sweat had pooled between his thighs, and Abi was doing his head in as she ran in and out of sight chasing Hank's three-legged whippet. In Abi's defence, every time she stopped chasing it, the whippet slowed, doubled back, then pawed at her legs until she started again. Hopefully, Eric considered, she'd sleep the entire journey back. Deciding it would be stupid to stop when there was only one planter left to fill, he began to sow his carrot seeds. He was halfway through the planting act when a polite cough made him halt.

'Mr Sibley?' the woman said.

Eric turned and found himself momentarily stunned.

The voice had come from a petite lady with bright blue eyes, narrow lips, and a fair brushing of bronzer swiped across her brow. With her stature and complexion – and some favourable lighting – she could have easily passed for early twenties, though Eric suspected that she was a decade or so older. Her hair was scraped back in an authoritative manner, and she was the type of woman who, under normal situations, Eric would have found attractive, only in this particular instance he was rather taken aback, not at her sudden presence on his allotment so much as the uniform she was wearing.

'Mr Eric Sibley?' Her expression was neutral as she repeated his name.

Eric fumbled. He wiped his hands on the seat of his trousers, then stretched one out as a greeting, grimacing at the amount of earth under his nails.

'Yes, yes. I'm Eric Sibley,' he said.

His hand hung unmet in the air for a few seconds before he retrieved it and tucked it back away in his pocket.

'How can I be of help? If it's gardening tips you're after, I suspect you've come to the wrong place. I'm a first-timer I'm afraid.'

'Mr Eric Sibley,' the attractive police officer said. 'I am arresting you for possession of illegal substances, with intent to distribute.'

CHAPTER 26

THE NEXT FEW seconds disappeared into a thick, dense haze of brain fog. Eric's mind was numb, yet swimming. He felt both nauseous and faint and downright furious all at the same time. The police officer reached around and unclipped the handcuffs from her waistband. Behind him, Eric heard Abi's shriek followed by much energetic barking.

'You do not have to say anything, but anything you do say may be used in a court of law. Do you understand?'

'What?' Eric shook his head and blinked. 'Now you hold on.' He stepped backwards, catching his heel on the wooden edge of the bed. 'I think we need to take a second here. There's obviously been some mistake.'

The woman remained impassive. 'Mr Eric Sibley, of Albany Road, London? That *is* you? Yes?'

'Yes, but —'

'And this *is your* allotment. One that you inherited from a Mr ...' she took a small notebook out from her pocket and flicked through, 'George Sibley. Is that correct?'

'Yes, but if you give me a minute —'

'And this *is your* greenhouse?' She pointed to Eric's under-plenished greenhouse, the yellow plastic of the tomato grow-bags glinting through the glass.

'Yes, it is.'

'And your daughter,' she glanced down at the notebook for confirmation, 'Abi. She goes to St Andrew's the Apostles?'

'What has that got to do with anything?'

'I'm afraid there has been no mistake, Mr Sibley. I will need you to come with me to the station.' She pulled the handcuffs from her waist and held them out. 'We can do this the hard way or the easy way. There's no need to make a scene.'

A rush of heat burned all the way up from Eric's feet. 'I'm not making a scene,' he said. 'In fact.' He pushed his shoulders back. 'I think I'm being very calm about your accusations.' The officer didn't flinch. The cuffs dangled motionless from her fingers and her eyes remained on Eric, strong and fixed. Eric took this as a sign to carry on.

'You said an illegal substance?' He spoke at half his normal pace if not slower. 'What illegal substance? What exactly is it that I'm supposed to have done?'

The police office smacked her tongue against her teeth.

'I'm afraid talking about this anywhere other than the station goes against protocol.'

'You have to be kidding me?' Eric heard the volume of his voice but did nothing to lower it. 'You want to arrest me, but you won't even tell me why?'

'I've told you.' The officer took a long breath in. She moved to speak, but a fiery blast of barking cut through the air. A chorus of shrill laughter followed straight afterwards.

A rush of adrenaline surged through Eric's bloodstream. This time, his voice came out much quieter. And sounding much more panicked.

'Look, is there somewhere we can go to talk about this, other than the station? My daughter's over there. The last thing I want is for her to see you waving those things at me.' He motioned to the handcuffs. The officer looked at them. She wavered.

'Please,' Eric said.

With a sigh, she tucked them back into her pocket.

'We can talk in your greenhouse,' she said.

'The greenhouse? That's hardly —' Her look rendered him momentarily mute. 'The greenhouse is perfect.'

The greenhouse was substantially stuffier than it had felt that morning. The police officer was wearing a perfume, something fruity and strong, that added to the humidity and, combined with the growing tightness in his throat, made it increasingly more difficult for Eric to think straight. He moved himself to the far end of the shed, trying to find an angle from which he could view Abi, without being too conspicuous.

'Mr Sibley,' the officer was back on task. 'Am I correct in thinking that all the plants on this allotment are owned by you and have been grown by you?'

'Yes, of course.'

'The ones inside this greenhouse, as well as outside?'

'Yes. Well, except the spring onions. My daughter, Abi, she's grown those.'

'Excellent. And could you please tell me what this is that you're growing here? What will these plants be when they are fully grown?'

She pointed to the yellow plastic grow-bags that lined one inside edge of the house. A dozen seedlings averaged four leaves each. Two small, jagged, inner leaves and two large, smoother ones that extended a centimetre or so farther.

'They're tomatoes,' Eric said. 'This end bag here has Gardener's Delight. These here are cherry, and the ones on the end are meant to be San Marzano, although to be honest, I think I may have a few cherry ones in. I let Abi help, and she wasn't very good at —'

The officer lifted her hand to silence him.

'Good. Thank you. And these?'

She redirected her pointed finger to the first shelf.

'They're my daughter's spring onions,' Eric said. 'She'll be planting them outside next week, only she wanted to do it herself and she's been a bit preoccupied today. Also, we thought it might be best to give them a little time to acclimatise to the outside air. You know, like you do when you buy a goldfish?'

The police officer continued to stare at the spring onions, ignoring Eric's question about goldfish which, he realised on later reflection, probably hadn't been the most helpful comment. After a second more of staring at the various pots and plants, the officer reached into her pocket and pulled out her phone. Eric felt the tightness loosen in his gut. Clearly, she was messaging in that this had all be some horrid mistake. A few minutes of her apologising and he could be back to his radishes. He would need to plant fast though, as the clouds had adopted a decidedly purple tint.

'Mr Sibley,' the officer looked up from her phone. 'Do you recognise this plant?' She tilted the screen towards him. A small image took the centre of her phone. Eric leant in. The plant in question was a seedling of vague familiarity, but combined with the ever-increasing temperature and cadaverous odour that he'd just noticed emanating from his underarms, Eric was having a hard time focusing.

'To be honest, I'm probably the last person to ask about something like this. Perhaps we could go outside. If you want an expert opinion —'

'No, Mr Sibley, I want your opinion. Do you think that this

plant, the one I'm showing you on my phone, bears any resemblance to anything you have grown in the last three months?'

'Well, I suppose ...' Eric considered.

'You suppose what, Mr Sibley?'

'I suppose it looks a little like the Dutch coriander.'

Eric studied the photo then the plants. The seedling on the photo must have been at least a week older, but there was the same leaf orientation. The same razor-edged leaves set at right angles to one another. Actually, it looked a lot like it. Eric turned to the police officer.

'Yes. I'd say it's probably Dutch coriander?'

'Dutch coriander.'

'This one here, behind you.'

In an attempt to conceal his ripening body odour, Eric pinned his arms to his side as he squeezed back into the tomatoes and gave the officer space to turn around. With one prodding forefinger, she inspected the coriander, then her phone. Then back again. After one final glance, she reached into her pocket and withdrew her handcuffs.

'Mr Sibley,' she said. 'You have openly confessed to growing the Class B drug, marijuana, in a public space. I have no choice but to bring you down to the station immediately. If you'd like to collect your daughter and advise me as to someone who can take care of her until her mother arrives, I will give you a moment to do that?'

'I ... What?'

'I can assure you I will talk to the judge personally. Clearly what we're dealing with here is a heavy case of drug addiction.'

'A what?'

'Reckless behaviour, obliviousness to the truth, an obvious lack self-hygiene, neglect of children —'

'She's playing with a dog!'

'They're signs, Mr Sibley. I've seen it all too often. Men in powerful jobs. Thinking it's just a way to relax. It starts as a casual thing. Just a spliff to take the edge off the day. Then you can't sleep without it. Then, before you know it, you're skipping work to try to deal your shoddy product to eight-year-old students at your daughter's overpriced private school and spending the weekend turning your dead father's allotment into a crack den.'

'What?'

Eric was standing in a tomato plant, but he couldn't feel it. He couldn't feel anything. His mouth was arid, his chest in a vice, and the only part of his nervous system that appeared to be working were his sweat glands. Even his eyes were having difficulty making sense of the situation. Marijuana? How? This made no sense.

And then it did. Then it all made perfect sense.

He barged past the police officer – pushing her to the side against his ornamental marigolds – and out through the door, sprinting across to the next allotment.

'You!' The tip of Eric's finger was barely an inch from Norman's wheezing chest. 'You did this.'

'Pardon?'

Norman stepped back from his runner beans. His long beard had a splattering of compost in it, darkening the white hair. He stretched himself up to standing, met Eric's gaze for less than a second, then turned back to his plants.

'This is the man.' Eric flayed his arms wildly. 'He gave me the seeds. Dutch coriander. That's what he said. Dutch coriander. This is the man you should be arresting.'

The police officer ambled across the grass, her handcuff swinging wistfully from her waistband.

'Well? Aren't you going to do something?' Eric insisted. 'Take him down to the police station. He's the one who did this. He's the one you need to arrest.'

Eric fought the urge to hurl himself across the allotment, grab the handcuffs, and do the bloody job for her. As she reached the corner of the allotment she stopped, tucked her phone away, and began to re-tie her hair.

'What are you doing?' Eric said. 'Arrest him. Arrest him!'

'You need to calm down,' Norman said.

'Calm down! I'll give you calm down!' Then to the officer. 'Why aren't you doing something?'

The police officer's eyes glinted. The corner of her lips quivered, and one eyebrow tilted up at an angle. She looked from Eric to Norman and back again.

'You're right,' she said. 'He is highly strung.'

'What? Who is? What are you talking about?'

But the officer wasn't talking to Eric. She wasn't even looking at him. She was looking past him and the rows of runner beans, to the scruffy haired geriatric with a smile cracked so wide across his face his jaw could have been dislocated.

'Maggie, my treasure. You did an old man proud.'

The two met together in a wide-armed embrace, the old man absorbing the little officer in a giant, bearded bear hug. Eric watched on, his own jaw barely above his feet.

'Uncle Norm,' the girl said when they broke apart.

'Did you film it?'

'No, I didn't. That'd be more than my job's worth.'

'Ahh, well I'll have to hope I don't lose my memory then. That one's going to keep me warm for very many nights.'

'You? Lose your memory? Chance would be a fine thing.'

Norman's face beamed. His cheeks glowed, and he continued to keep one arm around the officer.

'Eric,' he said. 'I'd like you to meet my niece, Maggie. She's a police officer. And also one of Burnham's keenest Amdrammers.'

'Amdrammer?'

Maggie stretched out her hand.

'We're doing *The Full Monty* at the town hall in the summer. Let me know if you fancy coming. Tickets are selling pretty fast.'

Eric was rigid. Speechless. Every muscle from his toes to his scalp burned, yet at the same time he was frozen to the spot.

'You're his niece?'

'Sorry about that. I can never say no to Uncle Nor. Particularly where a practical joke is involved. Friends?' She kept her hand hanging in the air between them. Eric made no attempt to meet it.

'A joke? Are you telling me that was a joke? Pretending that I'm being arrested? Pretending that I'm growing marijuana —'

'You got off lightly. He was actually going to give you marijuana when he first started.'

'Cinderella 99,' Norman said and kissed his fingers as though talking about some exquisite tasting delicacy. 'Now that would be a present.'

Eric's cheeks burned. His fists were clenched in balls and his nails dug so fiercely into his palms he wouldn't have been surprised if his hands were bleeding. He fixed his glare on Norman.

'You,' he said. 'I'll get you for this. You and all your prize-winning parsnip gang. Don't think you're safe because your niece is in the police.'

It was then, without warning, that something started happening in Eric's intestinal region. It was a cross between a spasm and twitch. Something deep and painful just below his abdomen that caused his diaphragm to lurch upwards and his chest convulse. His pulse rocketed as he attempted to force the motion down, but before he knew it he was doubled over, knees bent, eyes streaming, the uncontrollable paroxysm accompanied by a loud rasping sound that erupted from his lungs.

'You bloody git.' Were the only words that Eric managed to articulate, although they were repeated several times. 'You bloody, bloody, git.' Soon Norman was doubled over too, tears streaming down his tissue-paper skin and pooling in the whiskers around his chin. Maggie, who managed to stay upright for a minute or two longer, soon gave into the urge and allowed her body to be consumed by the convulsions. When Abi turned up five minutes later, the three-legged greyhound hopping behind her, she stared at the three adults and scratched her head.

'Why are you laughing?' she said. 'What's so funny? Tell me. I want to know.'

It was over a minute before Eric managed to control his breathing well enough to stand upright and wipe away his tears. 'One day,' he said, ruffling Abi's hair. 'I'll tell you one day.'

He slapped Norman on the shoulder, hugged Maggie good-bye, and got back to planting his radishes.

CHAPTER 27

ERIC HAD BEEN praying for good weather all week, but the statistics were not favourable. For the last month, it had been as though nature was mocking them. Weekdays had been your stereotypical April weather. Grey, windy, and interspersed with some traffic-seizing showers, but it was nothing you wouldn't expect from the UK in April. Provided you had a brolly and the sense to pack a spare pair of trousers, you were fine.

Weekends were a whole different matter.

In fact, every weekend from the middle of April to the start of June, it poured down. On his trips down to Burnham, the water pelted the windscreen harder than the wipers could keep up with. The car – the Audi, as taking Sally was most definitely off the cards – crawled through rushing torrents that sprouted up from the drains. Eric cursed every second of the journey down. He leant towards the glass, unable to see anything other than headlights in the blurred prospect. Praying for a break between the unending downpours, Eric repeatedly cursed his father and the ridiculous stipulations of his inheritance.

It didn't matter when he went down – Friday night, Saturday morning, Sunday afternoon after a vegan nut roast at Lydia's – and it didn't matter when he got there. Every weekend, the results were the same: monsoon season.

At the allotment, everything was wet. The ground, the air, his planters; they were all soaked. His newly sown seedlings stood limp, bobbing in the waterlogged compost, while rain poured off the greenhouse and shed roofs and gushed in eddying streams towards his little patch of land. Of course, the ground was slanted in a manner that meant the first allotment to flood was his. His rhubarb and carrots were drowning, and his sparkling new greenhouse had already sprung a leak.

Still, at least there was a little escapism.

Without a doubt, Norman's shed was the last place that Eric had expected to find equanimity, particularly with Norman there for company, but there it was. In the weeks since the incident with the Dutch coriander, the two had struck up a firm friendship. The foundations of this friendship, although still a little shallow on the ground, were built primarily on talk of old cars, vegetable growth, and Cynthia's homemade shortbread. If Eric arrived first, he'd do what he could in his Hunter wellies and a Barbour jacket, squelching around in the mud until his fingers reached a state of prunage usually associated with Suzy and the bath. At that point he would disappear into his greenhouse and prune the surplus leaves from his tomato plants until he spotted Norman hobbling up the path. After that, it was a case of waiting to see which dried out first, the conversation or the weather. Eric wasn't allowed in the shed, but the veranda was more than big enough for the foldable deck chairs and cups of steaming tea.

Some days the men had extra company – Hank, Cynthia, a few other names Eric couldn't remember – but mostly it was just the two of them. Their conversation was generally light, although once or twice Eric used it as a chance to unburden some of his work stress over plans of a merger and rumours of jobs cuts. Norman tended to ignore Eric's rants, or else divert the conversation back to the weather and how this was nothing compared to sixty-eight. The one topic they avoided, starkly, was Eric's father.

On the two occasions that George's name had arisen – both times through Norman, not Eric – Eric cast an immediate detour and swerved the conversation off into another direction. Still, the brief mention caused residual shudders to echo down Eric's spine.

As it was, the weather had entirely restricted Eric in his desire to take Norman out in Sally. Each week he'd had to postpone his plans, desperate that the following week would be better when inevitably it was worse. And so, he'd taken a risk.

When Eric received the notification through the owner's club he'd passed the idea by Suzy. When she deemed it a good one, he'd mentioned it to Cynthia. She too gave her approval. And so, weather providing, they were all good to go. Eric went to bed that Friday night with butterflies in his stomach, checking the day's forecast in three different counties on his phone. One day's good weather. That was all he needed.

He was woken the next morning by Suzy. It was an unpleasant awakening as Suzy threw off the duvet and Eric's immediate reaction – besides yelping with shock at the cold – was to grab his phone in order to once more check the weather situation.

'You don't need that.'

Suzy plucked his phone from his hand before striding over to the window and drew the curtains. She was wearing a tiny cotton night slip, and any other Saturday he would have delayed his plans by at least six minutes, but today time was too important.

'Coffee's waiting for you downstairs,' she said, then threw him a towel off the radiator. 'Don't forget to say goodbye to Abi. I told her she could have a lie in, but she'll be gutted if you don't pop in.'

Eric drank his coffee, showered, and dressed, then poked his head around the corner of Abi's door.

'I'm off,' he said. 'I'll see you tonight. Look after your mum.'

'Dad?'

'Yes, pumpkin.'

'I hope Uncle Norman has fun today.'

'I'm sure he will. See you later.'

'Love you.'

'You too, princess.'

The drive down from London to Burnham was all that Eric could have hoped, with empty roads and not a drop of rain in sight, but the cornflower blue skies and spun-sugar clouds did nothing to alleviate the niggling nerves. This was England. Sunshine in the morning may be nice, but it didn't guarantee a thing. Eric had informed Cynthia of their early start at the beginning of the week and she'd suggested he swing by the house and collect him, saving them all a journey to the allotment.

Norman and Cynthia lived on the outskirts of Burnham where the big houses dominated but before the new-builds started. Eric cruised around the bends and passed the

Welcome to Burnham-on-Crouch sign, then signalled right down towards the water. His stomach churned.

It was over a year since he last took this turn. New cars graced the driveways and many of the hedgerows were higher than he remembered, but other than that, everything was the same. The wych elms, the cedar cladding. The oversized windows and red brick chimneys. It was the same as last year, same as the year before, and every year Eric could remember from his childhood. He slowed to park up outside Norman's front gate, hesitated, then kept going for another fifty yards until he reached the last house on the road.

It was impossible to ignore the glaring green *For Sale* sign with its deliberately askew *Sold* placard nailed over the top. Eric climbed out of Sally and took a step towards it. The grass in the front garden had all gone to seed, and the windows were veiled in ochre dust. Through the glass he could make out the shadows of the curtains, though there were no longer the rows of photograph frames sat on the ledge, there from his mother's time. He wondered first how much the house had gone for and second, who it had gone to. The who it was gone to question lingered longer in his mind. A family probably. A well-off one. The type where both parents work, and the kids are brought up by a nanny. Perhaps a family trying to escape the rat race of city life. Perhaps they'd come into their own inheritance lately and that was how they managed to afford it. Behind him, the elms rustled in the breeze. Eric came back to the moment, turned around, got into Sally, and headed back up to Norman and Cynthia's.

Cynthia answered in her slippers. A pink cardigan was draped over her shoulders and a pastel flowered button blouse. For a second Eric thought he may have had the wrong house, and it was only then he realised he'd never seen Cynthia without her sturdy green wax jacket and a pair of wellies.

She frowned, equally confused for a moment, before shaking her head clear.

'Oh, I'm sorry. I completely forgot. Oh dear. It's today, isn't it? Oh, what a nuisance.'

'Is he ready? We've got quite a journey on us. If we can get going now, we can hopefully avoid the traffic.'

Cynthia bit down on her bottom lip. Eric waited.

'To be honest,' she said, 'today's not too good. I'm so sorry. Had I remembered, I would have called you. Saved you the journey.'

'Is everything okay?'

'Oh yes, yes. Fine. Just his cough. Had him up a lot of the night, you see. It's so nice of you to offer to do this, but I'm not sure he's up to —'

'Cynth? Who's at the door?' Norman's holler barked through from the back of the house. 'If it's those bloody internet —'

'No, no. Don't worry. It's only Eric.'

'Eric?' Then after a pause. 'What does he want?'

Eric was about to offer a reply when Norman shuffled out into the hallway. His home attire consisted of plaid flannel pyjama bottoms and a long blue vest that made him almost unrecognisable from Eric's gardening mentor. He walked with a hand against the wall, scuffing his feet against the carpet as he coughed and spluttered. Eric's toes fidgeted in his shoes. This wasn't quite what he'd expected.

'Sorry to drop in on you,' Eric said. 'Cynthia said you weren't feeling great.'

'Nothing wrong with me bar being nagged constantly,' Norman grunted.

'Well, I should probably head back, anyway. Suzy could do with having me at home. Abi seems to be developing her teenage genes five years early.'

Norman grunted towards Eric then peered his head around him. His eyes widened.

'Is that what I think it is?'

With an implausible change of pace, Norman pushed his way past Eric, out the front door, and across the drive. Both Cynthia and Eric did a double take and by the time they'd reached him, Norman was standing barefoot on the pavement in his pyjamas, cheek flat against Sally's bonnet, pawing at the metal work with his hand.

'She gets more beautiful every time I see her,' he said.

'Norman, what are you doing? You'll catch your death. At least go and put some slippers on.'

Norman turned to Eric, tactlessly ignoring his wife. 'Are we going for a spin? Give me five minutes for a cuppa and I'll be good to go.'

After he finished speaking, he promptly broke into a coughing fit that saw flecks of saliva fly out onto the windscreen.

'Well, I'm not sure ...'

'Oh, don't worry about this,' he attempted to wipe the spittle away with the bottom of his vest. 'Had this cough for the last thirty years. It's not killed me yet.'

Eric turned to Cynthia. Outside the house and without the guise of her jacket, she'd shrunk to a person of Lilliputian proportions. Eric imagined her, next to Janice, together in a small house built into the stump of the tree. She looked from her husband to the car, a heavy sigh built between her lips.

'Since when have I been able to stop you doing something?' she said. 'But you need to take it easy, mind? Rest. And none of that junk food either. I'm making you both a salad sandwich to take while you get dressed.'

While Norman showered and dressed, Eric sat at the breakfast bar watching as Cynthia buttered slices of bread and filled them with home-grown produce. It must have been a beautiful house once, and it still was to some degree; it certainly kept with the same fastidious sense of order that Eric had come to associate with Norman. But it was tired. The kitchen was in need of a refit, with its faded lino flooring and veneer edging peeling back from the corner of the cupboards, and from what he saw, the rest of the house was in a similar state. Smells of homemade jams and piccalilli abounded around him, while through the window a view stretched all the way down to the river. Eric sipped at his cup of tea as Cynthia worked. It was peculiarly weak.

'How long have you been here?' Eric asked.

'Forty-seven years,' Cynthia said proudly.

'Wow.'

'Bought it off the plot. We probably should have moved at some point, you know, got smaller, moved closer to town, something like that. But when you're young you don't think about being old, and when you're old, you don't have the energy to do those type of things.'

'Still, forty-seven years, that's impressive.'

She folded aluminium foil around the sandwiches.

'There aren't very many of us originals around here anymore. Until a few years ago, we were still going strong. Then one by one, it's nursing homes and retirement villages. Of course, we've been to a fair few funerals too.'

'I can't imagine you and Norman settling into a retirement village just yet,' Eric said.

'No.' Cynthia smiled. 'Neither can I.'

Her gaze drifted off, and Eric was thinking of some way to break the silence when Norman's voice boomed through.

'Well then, are we getting on the road or not?'

Norman stood in the doorway to the kitchen. His shaggy beard had been brushed straight, along with his mane of hair which was lying flush to his head, glistening with water in perfectly combed lanes. He had on a tweed jacket, which hung well in the arm but a little loose around the middle, and carried a matching tweed flat cap in his hand. Eric stood up and straightened his own collar, feeling decidedly under-dressed. 'I guess we should be getting on then.' He kissed Cynthia goodbye, then turned to Norman.

'I'll be right behind you,' Norman said.

The car show smelt of petrol and hog roast. There was a bouncy castle on one side of the field while on the other side a small stage was set up. As they arrived, a troop of boys were performing what Eric could only assume was a breakdance – disturbingly choreographed – while the poster promised the best Elvis impersonator in the UK as the afternoon entertainment. Following the arm signals of the men in hi-vis, they crawled across the grass and parked up next to a classic red 1955 Spider and a slightly less classic silver Porsche 924.

'It's been a long time since I've been to one of these,' Eric said, dodging the quagmire as he stepped outside. 'I don't think I can even remember the last time.'

"Spect it was around your O-levels. Your dad said you stopped going to things with him after then.'

The comment came matter-of-factly out of Norman's mouth and caught them both by surprise.

'I suspect it was,' Eric said, thinking about it. There was a minute's pause before he spoke again.

'So, what do you want to do?' he said. 'I've got chairs in the back, so we can sit out here, although I hear there's a 1954 300S somewhere in the grounds and a couple of E-types if you fancy going for a wander?'

Norman sucked in a breath with a wheeze. 'I think I'll stay with the old girl for now, if that's all right with you? Although.' He paused. 'I wouldn't mind you picking me up one of those hog roast rolls if you have a mind.'

'What about your sandwiches?'

'You know what? I think I forgot to pick them up.'

CHAPTER 28

ERIC WEAVED HIS way between the metal work and rubber. Norman was right, he thought. It must have been his A-level year the last time he came. After a few more minutes' contemplation, he was certain. Joining a queue for coffee, he raked through years of well-repressed memories. Of course it had been during his A-levels; it had been this time of year too, possibly even this show. He remembered it now because of how fiercely he didn't want to go. Exam season was upon him, and the pressure to get as far away from Burnham and his father was ever increasing. His father had turned up at school unannounced, on a Sunday, and expected Eric to drop everything and go with him.

'I've got work to do. Revision. Exams,' Eric had said. 'They start next week. I can't spend a whole day away.'

'Revision, *pff*,' his dad had harrumphed. 'With soft subjects like you're doing? They're not going to get you anywhere. Anyway. I've told your housemaster you're coming, so you're coming.'

Eric had taken his books with him and spent the whole

time sitting outside the car. Whenever anyone approached Sally, he buried his head deeper into the pages and offered disgruntled grunts as answers to their questions. He ate the bacon butty his father brought, but only because his stomach was growling so loudly he was finding it difficult to read. In the car ride back, he rested his head against the window and pretended to sleep. Four long hours of his revision lost, not including the drive there or back. That was how he had viewed it then.

The clouds were making a play for centre stage, and Eric shivered against them as he took his drink. The coffee was far better than he'd expected for a standard boot-sale food truck, and he made a mental note to come back to the same truck later. While the paper coffee cup heated up his hand, he wandered between the cars. Abi would like it here, he thought. And Suzy too.

Treading down the long grass, Eric admired the paintwork, leather interiors, and restoration projects. He ambled at leisure, moseying about with no fixed pattern or system to his route, revelling in the luxury of no children or deadlines. Once or twice he thought about heading back to check on Norman, but for now, he figured, there was no rush.

It was about fifteen minutes into his amble when Eric realised that he was now part of a strange and apparently obligatory club; one that he appeared to have settled in with remarkable ease and enjoyment.

He also soon noted that he, and other members of said club, followed a somewhat predictable pattern.

First, he would stop by a car and run his eyes over the body, or wheels or some other such feature. Next, an owner would appear by his side.

'Only sixty-five of this colour ever made,' they might say. Or, 'Did all the restoration work myself.'

Sometimes Eric would find himself the first to speak. 'Beautiful looking car you've got there,' he might say, or, 'What year is this?' Or if he were really absorbed, a simple 'Hmmm' of appreciation was all that was needed. They would talk, he would listen, then he would offer his own input, exchanging names and handshakes and pointing people in the direction of Sally. Generally, he'd tell them a bit about her and inform them that he'd be there until four-ish and they should pop over for a gander if they had the time. He was surprised to find he meant it.

It turned out that Eric had had no need to drum up a crowd, as, by the time he returned to Sally, Norman had already amassed quite a congregation of his own. Eric squeezed his way between exceptionally complimentary onlookers and handed Norman his hog roast roll.

'I was just telling them how I used to badger your old dad to let me drive her,' he said. 'Damn git wouldn't let me anywhere near that wheel. Rest his soul and all.'

'He was rather possessive.'

'Possessive my arse. Thought I might drop dead behind the wheel.' He broke into an interlude of coughing as if to confirm Eric's father's reasoning. 'Let me ride in the back often enough. When 'e got that old lad from the garage to take her out. Bit of a squeeze, but I'm hardly one to whinge.'

Eric raised an eyebrow. Norman shrugged and smirked.

For the rest of the day, the two men sat on the foldout picnic chairs making small talk with admirers and sampling the various food trucks on display. Generally, they were as helpful as possible and offered titbits of history about Sally and the DB4 in general. Other times Norman would draw on his family flair for dramatics. Through sheer determination and tenacity, Norman persuaded a young lady that this was the exact car that William had taken Kate Middleton for a drive in on their first date, and an older couple that it was where Fred Astaire proposed to Robyn Smith.

However, stranger than even Norman's never-ending imagination and silver tongue, were the offers of condolence that Eric received.

These condolences came from strangers who had known his father back in the days when he was a regular at these types of events. There were faces that knew Eric by name and apparently had met him and his mother several times in the past. And there were those that knew the car and George but had not heard of his passing. Those were the hardest. Eric smiled and thanked them all for their kind wishes.

By the time they left, the sky had turned opalescent. Between them, Eric and Norman had consumed three pork and stuffing rolls, two bacon sandwiches, four cups of coffee, five cups of tea, and an undisclosed number of freshly fried mini doughnuts. They drove out through the now churned and muddy grass and onto the road, ready for the long drive ahead.

Tiredness laboured Norman's breathing, and though he worried for his comfort, Eric knew better than to ask if he was okay. Still, when they stopped at a garage for fuel, he checked anyway.

'Do you want me to move the seat?' he said. 'I'm sure we can adjust the angle a bit, make it easy for you to breathe.' Norman shooed the idea away with his hand.

'I'm fine. Don't you go getting any ideas,' he said as Eric went into the shop to the pay for the petrol and buy himself a can of Red Bull.

It was only when he got into the car and started to pull down his seatbelt that he stopped. Twisting his neck, he turned to Norman.

'Do you want to drive home?'

'What?'

'I know it's only another half-an-hour to go. But if you want?'

Norman's coughing and laboured breathing subsided entirely into a vault of absolute silence.

'You're pulling my leg.'

'It's fine. You don't have to. Don't feel obliged.'

'Obliged my arse, you can get your scrawny girl's backside out of that seat now.'

Norman flicked his seatbelt off and was standing outside the driver's door before Eric had even managed to get his feet out of the footwell.

'I guess that's a yes then.'

Norman took each corner with the steering wheel firmly between his hands and his lips tightly pinched together. Although his palms were wrinkled and creased, each little bow and curve caused his eyes to glimmer like a child's, and every so often his tongue would flick out while his throat crackled with a cough. Eric sank back into the seat and stared out at the view. There really were some exceptional roads around Essex, he decided. He'd just never really had a chance to look at them before. About five minutes outside of Burnham, he closed his eyes and fell asleep.

When Eric woke, the street lights were glowing a butter-scotch yellow above him. They were parked outside Norman's, the old man wheezing in the driver's seat next to him, the silhouette of his wife moving behind the curtains.

'How long have we been back?' Eric said.

'Only a couple of minutes. I was enjoying a second's peace, but you've ruined that now.'

Eric squinted and blinked.

'Well,' Norman said. 'I'd invite you in for a tea, but Cynth'll insist on making it and her tea tastes like dishwater.'

'That's all right.'

'Easy for you to say. How a woman can cook like she does and still not tell that her tea tastes like weak piss has been a mystery to me these last fifty years. I tell you, I'm giving her one more year and then I'm divorcing her. There's only so much crappy tea a man can take in one lifetime.'

Eric smiled.

'Well, I guess I should be getting back,' he said. 'I didn't realise it was so late. I should have thought ahead and booked a room at the Sailboat.'

'I can ring 'em if you like? Or there's always the sofa? I can sneak you in. Avoid the tea altogether.'

Eric shook his head. 'It's fine. Suzy and Abs are coming down with me tomorrow. Said I'd take them for fish and chips by the river.'

'Sounds grand.'

The two men sat in silence. After two minutes had passed and Norman had not so much as flexed a finger, Eric coughed as subtly as he could manage. Norman jerked upwards in his seat, then stared at Eric confused. Half a second later, the look had gone. He moved his hand towards the door handle then left it there, hovering.

'You know,' he said. 'Last year, when your dad's 'ands 'ad gone, and he used to get that young lad from the garage to take him, I came out with him quite a bit.'

'Did you?'

'Almost every week.' Norman paused. Eric waited. 'He would sit where you're sitting now, rest 'is head against the window and close 'is eyes. Whole drive, didn't matter if it was to the end of the road or all the way up to Scunthorpe, your old man never wanted to open his eyes when he got in the car. Not them last few months. Never fell asleep mind. Wide-awake, just had his eyes closed.'

'I suppose he was tired,' Eric said. 'And he liked to listen to the engine. He always liked to listen to the engine.'

Norman sniffed in a manner that made it clear he disagreed. 'Nah, that's not why he did it. It was you. You were the reason.'

'Me? Why?'

Norman pushed his head back so as to view Eric from the widest angle possible.

'If 'is eyes were closed,' Norman said, 'it was easier to imagine you were still sitting next to him.'

CHAPTER 29

EVEN IF ERIC could have made it down during the week, he doubted he could have kept up with the pace of his harvesting. July arrived and overnight his beetroot, lettuce, and mangetout had sprung out of nowhere. He already had such copious numbers of radishes and courgettes that he'd started taking bag loads into work and leaving them in a basket by the reception to let people help themselves. His tomatoes were out of control, his rhubarb had gone into overdrive, and if he had to have one more meal garnished with Abi's home-grown, organic spring onions he was likely to drive to the nearest garden centre, douse their entire spring onion seed selection in lighter-fuel, and toss a burning match very deliberately in its direction.

The last weekend of the month was Abi's ninth birthday. This year she'd opted out of the idea of a traditional party in some horrific hall with an extortionately priced entertainer, in exchange for a picnic down at the allotment with Eric, their newly extended green-fingered family, and her cousins. The news was both a financial and mental relief to Suzy and Eric, who in their nine short years as parents seemed to have suffered enough princess, pirate, superhero, farmyard, and soft play birthday parties to last them a lifetime. It was particularly good news for Suzy, who last year had stayed up until gone midnight trying to construct the perfect princess castle cake. With its phallic towers jutting out at all sorts of ungainly angles, one could have been forgiven for thinking it belonged at a very different type of party. Abi was pleased with it though.

This year Lydia had offered to make the cake, so there was no baking to be done on Suzy's part at all. Cynthia had said she'd bring a quiche and sandwiches, and Janice was going to provide scones and jam. Eric whipped past Waitrose on his way down and picked up a couple of packs of mini scotch eggs, cheese, and some crusty bread and by lunchtime, they had their picnic blankets spread out under the sun and were well on their way into their second glass of Hank's sloe gin.

'If I'm honest,' Tom said, topping up his glass and ignoring Lydia's disapproving glare. 'I'm a bit jealous of this.'

'Why?' Eric said. 'You've got exactly the same at home. Better. And you don't have a three-hour round trip every week just to go and get a punnet of cherry tomatoes.'

'That's the part I'm jealous of. You can hardly pretend you've spent all day out digging the ground when your wife's been watching you sitting in your deck chair listening to Radio 4 from the kitchen window all day.'

'That's what a shed's for,' Norman piped in.

'Aye, only ours has been recently converted into an outside laundry, so guess who's always coming in and out?'

'There's an answer to that,' Lydia called from over by the greenhouse. 'Clean your own dirty underpants.'

The banter and chatter went back and forth, through midday and beyond. After cake and candles, the children continued to chase Hank's dog, Scout, around and the adults discussed the various benefits of home-grown produce over the shop bought equivalent. Eric had vacated his usual chair on the veranda in exchange for a place on the mat next to the scotch eggs. He glanced across at his wife and caught her eye. 'I love you,' he mouthed.

'You too,' she mouthed back.

He leant back onto the rug and smelt the fresh evening air drifting in. On a normal Sunday, he'd be thinking about heading off at this time. Tomorrow, he'd be back at work and today would seem like months ago. For now, though, he wanted to stay in the moment, the here, and now with his family. In the distance, he could hear Hank telling the children how Scout had come to lose his leg while displaying his own mechanical appendage. The children *oohed* and *ahhed* and asked the type of inappropriate questions that only children could come up with.

Maybe they could look at buying a little place down here for the holidays, Eric thought. There was a static caravan site down by the marina. The places weren't exactly state of the art, and some of the folk looked like they were the result of one too many dalliances with some close relations, but the caravans would be more than suitable for weekends and school holidays. Then again, they could always get a second mortgage if Suzy preferred. Not for a lot, but probably enough for something small. Perhaps he'd talk to her about it later. After all, she'd always liked Burnham too.

At five, the children had hit their limit. Sugar lows struck. Lydia and Tom took their two home after Hugo locked his younger brother in a greenhouse and told him it was an anti-oxygen tank and that he only had four minutes to get out before he suffocated to death. Half-an-hour later and Abi was curled up on the picnic blanket, one arm draped across Scout, the other clutching the personalised trowel she'd been given for her birthday by Janice. Suzy was talking to Hank about the difficulties of having a dog in the city while Eric and Cynthia picked up the remaining few paper plates and cups that had not made it into the rubbish bags earlier.

'You go,' Eric said. 'I can do this.'

'Nonsense,' Cynthia said. 'We're nearly done. Besides. I'll take it with us. We can drop it in the recycling bins at home.'

'Are you sure I can't give you a lift? It'll take me five minutes to run you up there, then I'll come back for the girls.'

Cynthia shook her head. 'No point wasting an evening like this in a car. Not while my legs still work.'

'If you're sure?'

'I am.'

Eric straightened up and shook the rubbish down to the bottom of the bag.

'Well, I think we're done,' he said. 'I guess we better wake the other two up.'

'Seems a shame when they look so peaceful, doesn't it?'

'Like butter wouldn't melt.'

Behind Abi and Scout, Norman was sitting in his chair. His head was tipped forwards, his glass of sloe gin half full on the ground beside him. Eric gathered up the coats and bags, bent down and scooped Abi up in his arms.

'I don't want to go home yet,' she yawned, rubbing her eyes and wrapping an arm around her father's neck. 'It's my birthday. I want to stay with Scout. It's still my birthday,' she dozed. Suzy appeared beside them.

'Scout's got to go home now too,' she said. 'It's time for his bed.'

'Aye, and if I don't feed him soon, he might 'ave my other leg off me,' Hank added.

'You ready?' Suzy said to Eric. 'Have you got everything?'

'I've got the bags, the coats and this one,' he said, nodding to Abi. 'Just need to say goodbye to Norman and we're ready to go.'

Eric turned to Norman. He was no longer sitting with his head forwards, but instead it slumped to one side. Cynthia was beside him, but rather than standing she was kneeling on the dirt. Her face was buried in his lap.

Eric took a week off work and spent the Monday to Wednesday down in Burnham. He didn't know what use he'd be, but he wanted to be on hand, just in case Cynthia needed him to take her anywhere. Maggie was busy with the play and work. She'd said she would drop out, but Cynthia had insisted she didn't. After all, she had said, what would be the point in letting people down, it wasn't going to change anything.

It hadn't come as a surprise to other people. Apparently, the fact that he'd made it to the summer at all had been a bigger one. He had everything in place, funeral arrangements, instructions for his ashes, all deeds, investments, and bank account information ready for Cynthia. He had even included a pamphlet for a local driving school that ran an intensive two-week course and a letter in which he'd said there'd be no excuse for not learning now, not with all the extra time she'd have on her hands. Everything was sorted.

Eric wasn't surprised at Norman's military organisation on the matter of his own death. He was the only person in the allotment who arranged his tomatoes bags according to the average growth height and had a rigid rotation system in place to ensure all areas of his allotment received nitrogen-fixing legumes at least once every three years. Perhaps it was the fact it made him feel so useless he found hard.

'It's easier when you haven't got children,' Cynthia said to Eric as they sat around the kitchen table. Norman had been right, Eric learned; her tea did taste a little like dishwater. He had driven Cynthia down to the church to speak with the minister in regard to hymn choices, only to find, once again, that the matter had been dealt with in advance. Eric was convinced that Cynthia would have been happier to walk the mile down into town on her own, but he had insisted, and so she'd said yes. Then he felt even more guilty. A seventy-year-old woman had just a lost her spouse of nearly fifty years and she was altering her plans so as not to hurt his feelings.

'Don't get me wrong, we'd have loved children,' Cynthia said, back home and oblivious to the insipidness of the tea. 'But at least you don't feel so bad about the fact you've got to move on at some point. I've seen my sisters. The way they fuss over their girls, terrified what will happen when they're not there to look after them. But kids are tough. And Maggie's hardly a baby. Thirty-six and a superintendent. She'll be fine. No, it's harder on us, I'm sure it is.'

'So, what will you do now?' Eric asked. 'If you knew this was coming, and Norman had everything in order, I assume you've made plans?'

A sad smile trembled on Cynthia's creased lips. Her eyes began to glisten.

'Norman was the planner,' she said. 'I was more concerned with making the most of the time together, while we still had it. But I've got some ideas. Some things I'd like to do. Places I'd like to see.'

'Like where?' Eric asked.

'Just places,' she said and smiled again, this time without the tears.

'What do you think she'll do?' Suzy asked when Eric got home that Wednesday night. He had thought about going back again, and had he not missed Abi so much he probably would have done. Work emails were incessant in his absence yet having made the situation clear to Jack, he'd made the conscious decision to ignore them. There was nothing that couldn't wait. No deal he couldn't postpone for another three days. The world wouldn't collapse if he didn't get his spreadsheet of figures to Greg until Friday instead of Wednesday.

'I've no idea,' Eric said. 'Apparently Norman's got family over in Australia or New Zealand. Perhaps she'll go and visit them.'

'What about the house?'

'I think he wanted her to sell it. Move into one of those new retirement properties over by the school.'

'Do you think she will?'

'No idea. It's a lovely place. It could be great, but it needs an awful lot of work.'

Eric went to the fridge, pulled out a can of tonic and topped up their two large measures of gin.

'Abi wants to come to the funeral,' she said. 'She asked if it would be okay.'

'What did you say?'

'I said it would be up to you.'

'What do you think?'

Suzy shrugged. She took a large gulp of her drink. Eric did the same. He winced. There was strong and strong. Suzy spoke next. 'She knows what happened. She knows a funeral's where people go to say goodbye. I think if you're okay with it I am.'

'I'll probably hang around after, just for a bit, if that's okay? See if I can help out at all.'

Suzy took another sip of her drink. When she drew the glass away, she pressed her lips together in a flat straight line.

'What?' Eric said.

'Nothing.'

'No say it. You think I'm interfering, don't you? Poking my nose in where it's not welcome, but I'm not. I'm only trying to help.'

'I know that.'

'Then what is it?'

Suzy placed her glass on a coaster. She tucked a strand of hair behind her ear and drew in a deep breath.

'I think you're doing all this, keeping yourself busy, because it stops you thinking.'

'Thinking? About what? About Norman?'

'No,' Suzy said. 'About your dad.'

Eric frowned and took an extra-large gulp of his gin. He winced again then shook his head and took another mouthful.

'Why would I be thinking about my dad? I already went to his funeral.'

'Well,' Suzy said. 'You have to admit that for quite a while there, your relationship with Norman was pretty similar to your relationship with your dad.'

'That's ridiculous. Norman was Norman. My father was my father. And the only thing the two had in common was being old and having neighbouring allotments. Oh, and loving a car more than people I suppose.'

'That's not entirely true, is it? I mean there's the small factor of Norman making your life a living hell for six months —'

'I wouldn't say —'

'And your desire to prove them both wrong —'

'Again, that's not exactly how —'

'And the fact that deep down all you really wanted was their respect.'

Eric didn't reply. He exhaled in a huff through his nostrils. 'I'm a grown man, Susan,' he said.

'I know that, Eric. But as far as I can see, the one major difference between Norman and your father is with Norman, you got the time to work through your issues.'

Eric went to take another swig of his drink only to find his glass empty. He reached over and grabbed the bottle.

'I guess you've got all that psychobabble nonsense from a book or something,' he said and was kind of grateful when she didn't reply.

CHAPTER 30

THE FUNERAL WAS on the Thursday of the following week. Eric, Suzy, and Abi had all gone down the night before, having reserved their room at the Sailboat in advance. To try to make dinner a less sombre affair, they bought their fish and chips and headed down to the river, but after ten minutes of dive-bombing seagulls and an unseasonable chill to the air, they abandoned the idea and took them back up to the hotel room. Eric dumped their wrappers in the bin by the door and as a result, they arrived at the church the next morning with a subtle yet distinct bouquet of vinegar in their wake.

The church was already three-quarters full when Eric, Suzy, and Abi arrived. All the pews were occupied, though the number of occupants varied from as many as ten to as few as four. Eric shuffled in with his eyes down and cursed himself for bringing Abi. Funerals made him feel funny. He hadn't been to that many, perhaps that was the issue. When you are approaching forty and the only funerals you'd attended were your parents' and grandparents', they take on an even weightier prospect. No child should attend a funeral, not even if they ask, he decided. Eric glanced at his side. Abi had chosen her outfit herself – a knee-length navy brocade dress and dark woollen cardigan. On the plus side, Eric thought, if she did take a turn for the worse, he could always insist that he be the one to take her out for some air. Suzy would understand.

Keeping his eyes down, Eric led his family down the aisle, apologising as they slipped into a pew, two rows from the back.

'Are you sure you don't want to go nearer the front?' Suzy asked.

'It's not a rock concert,' Eric replied. 'Besides. That's where the family are.'

Forgetting his eyes-down-in-churches rule, Eric glanced towards the altar. As if sensing the moment, Cynthia turned around from the front and caught his eye. Eric did a double take. She was a far cry from the figure he usually saw at the allotment and the old lady he'd seen that morning at her house. For starters, she looked at least a decade younger. Her hair was loose around her shoulders, now dyed a glistening champagne blonde and from the look of it freshly permed. More striking still was that rather than donning the traditional black attire expected of the widow in these events, Cynthia had opted for a sunflower-yellow dress, complete with a patterned blue shawl and hat, both of which were adorned with fresh tulips. Had he not been certain of the date, time and persons in attendance, Eric may well have found himself thinking he'd gate-crashed a wedding. Or perhaps Abi's Easter parade.

It was a few moments later that Eric realised Cynthia was not the only one in what he'd have considered inappropriate attire. The immediate family appeared to have coordinated to ensure that every colour of the spectrum was covered, while elsewhere floral patterns and paisleys, men in bow ties and boaters, and women with fascinators, cardigans, and enough fresh flowers to have their own stand at Chelsea Flower Show, graced the pews. The flowers on the altar were not lilies like at his mother's funeral, but massive bouquets of sweet peas, peonies, astrantia, and cow parsley.

Eric turned to Suzy, who also appeared to have noticed their error.

'I think we may be a little underdressed,' she said.

The dress code wasn't the only surprise of the service. There were speeches, many that Eric considered extremely inappropriate, a slideshow of Norman's most revered practical jokes, and the only song sung by the congregation was a Karaoke version of Lou Reed's *Perfect Day*.

Eric's lungs quivered. This Norman, the Norman that people had come to pay their respects to had been so much more than the man Eric had come to know. He had been quick-witted and fashionable. First to laugh at himself and the first to help others. He had been a teacher and a student but also a son, an uncle, and a husband. He had, if these speeches rang true, always been the last to get a drink in, but the first to pick up the tab at the end of the night. Most of all, though, he'd been a family man.

The last surprise came as the casket disappeared. It was a slight click that started it, then a short riff that, although Eric must have heard a thousand times in his life, took him a full ten seconds to place. By the third chorus, every member of the congregation was on their feet swinging their hips and lip-syncing to The Jam's 'Going Underground'. Tears streamed down people's cheeks, with Eric unsure whether the cause was grief or the downright ridiculousness of the situation. As they left the church, Abi was holding her parents' hands, swinging between them as she continued to whistle the tune.

'That was great,' she said. 'Can we go to another funeral tomorrow?'

Eric didn't stay long at the wake. Despite the drizzle, people were already spilling up the stairs and out into the backyard. There were lots of "How long did you know him?" and "Where did you meet?" and Eric wasn't really in the mood for talking about the allotment or his father's death, or anybody's death for that matter. He spotted Cynthia and made a beeline for her.

'I'll be back down at the weekend,' he said, clasping her hand. 'Just let me know if there's anything I can do before then?'

'You've done too much already,' Cynthia said. 'And I'm sorry I didn't mention Norman's *magical not melancholy* dress code to you. I thought you'd already know.'

'It's no problem. I'll see you on Sunday, at the allotment then?'

Cynthia paused. Her bottom lip twitched slightly, then her eyes did a quick scan of the room. Deciding the coast was clear, she moved in next to Eric and whispered in his ear.

'Not a bloody chance. They're a bunch of obsessives, the lot of them. More concerned with the straightness of their cucumbers than anything else. Present company excluded of course.'

Eric laughed. 'But I'll see you soon?' he said.

'Of course you will.'

It was only by chance that Eric saw the email that night. He had switched off his phone before the service then forgotten about it, only remembering when he climbed into bed and went to set his alarm.

He sat upright, pulling the duvet up and over his chest.

'Well, this is it. Jack's announced the meeting's tomorrow. Hartley's coming in too. All directors at nine. Team debriefs after that. All other meetings to be postponed.'

'What do you think it's about?' Suzy folded the corner on her book and put it back on the nightstand.

'It's the restructuring. It has to be.'

'So, what will happen next? You don't think Jack will let you go?'

Eric put down his own book and switched off the bedside lamp.

'What will be, will be,' he said. 'No point worrying about it now.' He only hoped that the lack of light and fact he was facing away from his wife may have been enough to convince her he wasn't lying straight through his teeth.

CHAPTER 31

EVERYWHERE ERIC LOOKED people were huddled in little groups, whispering to one another. Eyes darted frantically around the room, all making sure that nobody was in possession of a tiny snippet of information that they did not yet have.

It was a scorching day. Shirt collars clamped around the men's necks. Most of them had loosened their ties; several had removed them altogether. The women fared little better in the tailored dresses and shirts, although Eric did spy one or two who had sensibly opted for something looser and a little more aerated. He was infinitely envious.

'Perfect bloody timing.' Greg was sitting on Eric's desk, chewing on the end of Eric's favourite ballpoint. He stopped, studied it for a second, then moved to place the pen back in Eric's pot.

'It's fine,' Eric said. 'You keep it.'

'Sweet,' Greg said, pocketing the pen. A split second later, he pulled a new pen out of the pot and was chewing on that.

'I asked Emily to move in with me last night,' he said with a look of gloom.

'You did what? The intern? I didn't even know you were dating.'

'Well. We weren't and then we were, and then it turns I actually quite like her. Anyway, it won't matter. She's hardly going to want to stay with me if I don't have a job.'

'It won't come to that.'

'It might.'

Eric stayed silent. He didn't want to offer too much false optimism; he barely had enough for himself as it was.

At eight fifty-five, Eric and the other directors huddled into the boardroom, each one adhering to their own, individualised tics. While Greg was busy gnawing his way through an expensive-looking fountain pen, one of the senior associate directors was unabashedly chewing his nails and spitting out the off-cuts. There was also shoe-tapping, lip-picking, and handwringing to add to the mix. Eric realised his own foible was to stare intently at every other person in order to pick out their idiosyncrasies while avoiding any admission of his.

Jack Nelson and Alistair Hartley were both smiling as they entered. Jack, who was wearing a bottle green suit, took his laptop over to the screen and made eye contact with each person in the room. Hartley sat down and got his phone out.

'So,' Jack began. 'Let me start by saying thank you for your patience. But I'm not going to beat around the bush. Let's get down to the reason we're all here.'

The meeting was a first in that every senior and associate director remained absolutely silent until they were certain Jack had finished speaking. The nail-biting had stopped, as had the pen-chewing and the people judging. No one knew where to move or look and certainly not what to say.

'I know you will all have a lot to discuss,' Jack said. 'And I shall catch up with all of you later. For now, I'll let you think over what we've just said.'

With that, they left.

It was Greg who was the first to speak, finally breaking the minute-long silence that had engulfed them.

'Did anybody manage to follow that?' he said.

'I think it means we're screwed,' said one of the associate directors.

'Not all of us,' someone else chipped in. 'Just some of us. Just some of us are screwed.'

Eric kept his thoughts to himself as he too tried to decipher exactly what they'd all been told.

Yes, there was to be a restructuring. Yes, there were to be job cuts. Yes, they were to be part of the process. No, even though they were directors, it did not mean they were safe. Yes, they would answer all their questions. No, they wouldn't do that now. Yes, every situation would be viewed in a personal, case-by-case scenario. No, they couldn't discuss that with them now either. Yes, there would be one-on-one meetings. No, the order that these meetings happened wouldn't mean anything. Yes, they would be required to fire people. Yes, it would probably get unpleasant. Yes, this was all extremely necessary in order to bring the business forwards.

Eric's insides churned. Fifteen years at *Hartley and Nelson*, and he'd fired exactly four members of staff. And each one had been deserved. The thought of calling someone into an office to tell them that he was stripping them of their entire financial security was enough to make him nauseous. Then again, perhaps he was already out the door. Perhaps Nelson and Hartley had already deemed him unstable, and he'd be one of the first to pack his bag, collect whatever little bundle of redundancy they deemed him worthy of, and trundle off down the treacherous road of unemployment. Fortunately, it wasn't too long a wait to find out.

The meetings for the directors were to start after lunch. While the majority of the possibly condemned huddled together in the communal area for moral support, Eric waited at his desk, blinds drawn down. His stomach was in a bad enough state already. The last thing he wanted to do was drive himself mad seeing who had been called in first and second, how long they took, or how ruffled they looked when they reappeared.

At 5.00 PM, when he still hadn't been summoned, Eric messaged Suzy to tell her that he'd be late home. She replied to wish him luck. He then messaged her again at seven to apologise and wish Abi a good night, and yet again at eight to tell her not to wait if she wanted to eat without him. Suzy replied to all the messages and said she'd wait for him to get home before she ate. She then sent another message immediately afterwards to say that she'd order food early though as the delivery time at the Sichuan could be hellish on a Friday night. When his phone buzzed for the third time, Eric almost ignored it until he glanced at the screen and saw Jack's name flashing up behind the glass.

Come in when you're ready, it read.

There was little that could rival the view from Jack's office. As nine o'clock approached and the summer sun sank low into the horizon, Eric stepped into the room and drank in the scene. Through the windows, the sun clipped the roof tiles and cast them in a cloud of berry pinks and indigo. Below them, the Thames glinted and reflected every colour it was offered. It was a perfect scene; peaceful, serene, intelligent. But for some reason, while gazing at the plush white carpet and aged leather desk, Eric transported himself back to the little office of Christian Eaves. This was it, the furthest away from

Burnham that any man could get. And it wasn't just the furniture or the carpet or the view. Jack's office smelt successful. It smelt of polish and wood and the air had a minty – almost caustic – tang that was impossibly far removed from the sea-blighted offerings of the east coast. This office was everything Eric had dreamed of, and from where he stood, he felt a very long way away.

'Why don't you sit down?' Hartley said. Eric turned to Jack, who offered one sombre nod.

'That's crazy,' Suzy said, chewing on a spring roll. 'Insane. I mean. Not that I doubted you, but wow. Really, wow.'

Eric chewed on his chow mein. It was after ten when he got home, and Suzy had reheated the noodles for him in the microwave. They tasted okay, but the texture had altered to something resembling polystyrene foam tubes. He munched the mouthful the best he could, then swallowed.

'Education is where they want to focus, apparently. Schools, colleges, universities. Apparently, they want to slim down and specialise.'

'So, Director for Education. How does that feel?' Suzy said.

'Bizarre,' Eric admitted. 'Jack wants me over in Norwich next week, then Glasgow, and Birmingham over the weekend. Not exactly sure how I'm going to manage that.'

'You'll find a way if it's what you want to do.'

'I know,' said Eric.

CHAPTER 32

AT FIRST, ERIC thought Greg was the reason he couldn't sleep. Despite sending him three messages asking how his meeting had gone, he'd heard nothing.

'He's probably out celebrating,' Suzy groaned. 'That's what people do at this hour. Celebrate, or sleep.'

'Maybe,' Eric said.

While Suzy shuffled about under the covers, Eric's mind continued to race.

'Maybe I'll just give him a quick call,' he said and climbed out of bed.

It took two gin and tonics and several episodes of *QI* for Eric to decide not to call Greg. Calling someone at three in the morning, even if you did have their best intentions at heart, was not something a man like Eric did. Forty-five minutes later, he was staring at the ceiling wondering how he'd never noticed all the cobwebs up there before and whether it would be a good time to try to get them.

Two hours later, he gave up trying to sleep. Suzy was out cold next to him, offering scarcely a murmur as he switched on the bathroom light and grabbed his unwashed jeans from the laundry basket. He wrote two notes – one for Suzy, one for Abi – pinned them to the fridge door, and got a cab round to Ralph's.

Given that it was barely dawn, Eric hadn't expected a response when he texted Ralph to inform him he was taking Sally for a drive. In truth, he only sent the message so Ralph didn't freak out when he woke up to find the garage empty. As such, he was surprised to find his former housemate standing outside the front door, a wide-awake baby bouncing on his hip while tugging at his newly formed beard.

'Nine-month sleep regression apparently,' Ralph said. 'Before that, it was the six-month and the four-month one before that. When's he not in a bloody sleep regression? That's what I want to know.'

Eric tickled the baby under the chin. It gurgled happily.

'I won't be gone long. Perhaps if I get back early enough, we can go for a spin?'

'That'd be great,' Ralph said. 'First time I'll have had a nap in the last seven years.'

'I'll try my best,' Eric said.

If anything, the journey muddied Eric's thoughts further as opposed to clearing them the way he'd hoped. It was only when he started the engine and checked the side mirrors he remembered that the last time he'd driven Sally, Norman had been in the passenger seat. Together, they'd twisted through the lanes around the back of Burnham discussing their possible entrants for the autumn show while ridiculing Eric's disastrous attempt at making tomato chutney. It had been a short spin, less than fifteen minutes. Eric had been in a rush, but Norman had been in a grump all afternoon, whinging over the weeds and cursing the insects, all the while whining about how it was too hot and too hard and too everything. Eric had thought that maybe a drive would help bring him out of the funk. And it did a bit.

Now Eric wished it could have been longer, that they could have laughed at more of his gardening failures, that he could have asked him a bit about the past. As he drove past the sign and the old garage where they held Sally after George's death, Eric took the right turn, down the cul-de-sac lined with elms, and parked up outside Norman and Cynthia's bungalow.

A blue *For Sale* sign punctured the newly mown lawn. Eric felt a stab in his gut. Obviously, Cynthia wanted to move out quickly; the place must be red raw with memories. Still, Eric thought, she might have wanted to give it a little time first. Then again, if Norman had anything to do with it, he'd probably placed the listing the week before his funeral.

A glance at his watch told him it was far too early to call in and pay her a visit. Eric put his foot down on the clutch, twisted the key in the ignition, and took another glance at the doorway. He was about to pull away when Cynthia dashed out into the drive, dressing gown slipping off her shoulders, madly waving her arms.

'Eric, Eric!' Realising he'd seen her, she slowed to a walk, then stopped, panting. Eric cut the engine and climbed out the car.

'Sorry,' he said. 'I didn't mean to disturb you. I didn't realise the time. Thought I'd pop in later instead.'

Cynthia dismissed his apology.

'I'm glad you did. I'm heading out with Maggie this afternoon. She's got the day off, so we're going to check out some old folks' villages together. I take it you've noticed my news?' She motioned in the direction of the *For Sale* sign.

'I did,' said Eric. 'Is this his doing or yours?'

'Oh, this is all my doing. He'd have approved mind, but no, it's me who wants to get out of there. Can't even clean my teeth without seeing him in that bathroom, combing his beard.'

Eric laughed.

'That'd be enough to make anyone want to move house,' he said.

Eric stopped, took a moment, then moved towards the car. 'Well, I should be getting on. I want to get as much time in as possible.' He paused then added. 'Actually, I have a bit of news too. I got a promotion at work.'

Cynthia clapped her hands then reached around him for a hug. 'Oh, that's wonderful. Well done, you. I hope it means you get to spend a little more time with the family?'

'Well, I'm not sure, exactly,' he said.

'Oh, I'm sure you've got it all worked out. A smart lad like you.' She stopped and scanned him up and down. Her eyes widened as a sudden thought struck. 'Hold on one sec. I have something for you. Can you hang on a minute?'

Without waiting for his reply, Cynthia dashed into the house. She hurried back out a few moments later although her hands were seemingly empty of whatever it was she'd gone to retrieve. It was only when she uncurled her fingers and reached out her palm towards Eric that he saw the key.

It was an entirely unspectacular specimen. A little under an inch long, flat and flimsy with a thin loop of wire attached to the top. It was the kind of cheap-looking key that you'd get with any hardware shop padlock.

'It's for his shed,' Cynthia said. 'He wanted you to have it. Well, what's inside it anyway,' she added. 'I think he decided it would be easier to leave the actual shed on the plot. Of course, if you want it, I'm sure it wouldn't be a problem.'

Eric couldn't speak. A large, obtrusive lump had forced its way up his throat and was causing difficulty breathing.

'He's given me his shed?' Eric said.

'Only if you want it. I think he thought you'd find the tools useful. There's a lot of other junk in there too, mind. Might have found yourself more work than you bargained for. But I'm done with that place now. I've got my memories and they're more than enough for the next few years, so if you come across anything you don't want, either you pass it on or you bin it. Either will be fine by me.'

Eric nodded. His eyes were still fixed on the key, uncertain what would happen if he moved them. In a swift motion, Cynthia tucked the key into his top pocket and tapped it there.

'Well,' she said. 'We should both be getting on. And just because I'm taking a break from the allotment, doesn't mean I'm going to stop cooking. You get too many carrots, you pass them this way. I'll have a vat of soup and a half a dozen cakes for your freezer by the end of the week.'

Cynthia retreated to the front porch where she stood and waited, then waved until Eric had driven out of sight.

Eric was grateful the drive to the allotment was short. His legs had become decidedly wobbly and the lump in his throat had swelled so large that it was causing his eyes to water. Here was a man he'd known for less than a year. A man who had caused him torment and torture and insufferable frustration, and yet in one large swoop all that had disappeared. Norman Kettlewell had thought of him. He had thought of Eric beyond his own life in a way that his father never had. There were no conditions to this inheritance. No rules he had to abide by. True, it was only a shed, not an eight-hundred-grand house, or a five-hundred-grand car, but it was Norman's palace and he'd bequeathed it to Eric. Eric's flood of gratitude was hit by a sudden surge of anger towards his father. So much for thinking the twisted inheritance would bring them closer together.

The allotment was empty and the large metal gates pulled

closed. Eric pushed them apart. It had been a long time since he'd been the first person there. Those were the days when he'd arrive as early as possible in order to leave as early as possible. When work was at the forefront of his thoughts and Suzy and Abi somewhere around the back, along with important dental hygiene and renewing car insurance. A sadness swelled inside him; it would be like that again soon. In early, out early. No time to stop and natter over the compost heaps or indulge in lingering brunches at The Shed. He would have to be as productive as possible from now on. Only fourteen months, Eric told himself as he plucked a raspberry from a bush. He could manage fourteen months of juggling. After that, he'd have it all: the car, the job, the perfect house. Fourteen months and his life would really be complete. Although even as he said it to himself, he had great difficulty believing it.

The air smelt of greenness; of wet grass and dewy moss and freshly harvested vegetables. The powder-blue sky was littered with grey-white clouds, making the greens even brighter and bolder. Eric shut the gate and began to take his normal path towards his own little patch. It was well trodden and muddy and he could walk there with his eyes closed, but when he reached the first crossroad – straight ahead for his, left or right for who knows what – he stopped. Nine months he'd been here, and yet he'd made no real attempts to visit the other plots. He knew some of course – Norman's, Hank's, and Janice's to an extent – but had no real idea what lay beyond those little boundaries of turf, turnips and six by fours. Fighting against the power of practice, Eric turned right.

There was much of a muchness of course – runner beans, greenhouses, large blue water butts, and sheds with little brass padlocks – but there were also hidden gems among the sprouts and parsnips. Whole plots laid to wildflower. Not uncultivated, not full of weeds, but bursting at the seams with thyme and foxgloves and honeysuckle and lavender, the scents of which spilt upward and tickled Eric's nose as he leant in and sniffed. There were giant greenhouses again filled with flowers, but this time of a more cultivated variety. Roses, lilies, varieties that Eric had assumed you could only get at a florist, super-market, or at a push, a garage service station, but had never assumed you could actually grow yourself. There were several beehives, birdhouses, and even some garden ponds. Each plot had a story and personality, and at each one, he found some-thing different to admire. When he'd exhausted every route possible and was certain that he'd at least glanced at every plot that the Arcadia Road Allotment had on offer, he arrived at the plot with the neat rows all labelled with plastic markers, the turf trimmed to an even more exacting level and the toma-toes ordered according to height.

Already the grass was growing up around the corners of the beds.

'Ten minutes with the secateurs and I can sort that out,' Eric said to himself. Then removing the key from his pocket, he stepped up on the wooden veranda of Norman's shed.

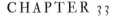

CHAPTER 33

INSIDE THE SHED large pots and plants obscured the light from the windows and caused a damp sticky heat to fill the air. The space smelt of ash, with a heady, woozy undertone that took Eric a second to place.

'Cinderella 99. What else.' He lifted his eyes up to the roof and said, 'If this is some kind of elaborate plan to get me arrested again, I'm going to use your ashes in a punching bag.'

Eric strained around until his eyes found the light switch. Hoping that Norman was as particular about his electrical skills as he was the rest of his allotment, Eric flipped his switch. A millisecond later he stood in the light, squinting but thankfully not electrocuted.

On the wall nearest the door were Norman's tools. Each one hung on its own specific nail, the outline drawn onto the wood behind it, indicating the exact angle from which it should be hung. Below the window was the plant life. Most of them were seedlings, but a few plants were more substantial. Eric ran his fingers between them. They were familiar, but nothing more than that. He'd need a couple more years at this before he could tell what plant was what from a two-and-a-half-inch sprout.

In the corner sat a small kettle while a half-sized fridge buzzed rhythmically below it. Inside was a blue and yellow cake tin. Eric picked it up, flinched against the cold, and shook it. When it rattled, he opened it to find half a loaf of Cynthia's carrot and walnut cake, green spores of mould beginning to flourish on the surface.

The last side of the shed was more like something you'd find in an office than a gardener's retreat, and Eric needed to take a step back to view it in its entirety. The desk featured a set of shelves loaded with pictures and frames and four drawers set beneath them. Sitting in front of the writing area was a heavy wooden rocking chair, complete with a padded cushion. Maybe Eric could get a rocking chair at work, he wondered. Maybe that would make evenings away from the girls more bearable. He picked up the cushion and turned it over in his hands. It smelt of lanolin and earth and hard work. There was nothing exceptional about it, and it was probably harbouring a dozen unknown pathogens, but it caused an ache to spread through the upper region of Eric's torso. He put it down on the chair, took a step to the side, and turned his attention to the picture frames.

The largest images faced out. There were wedding anniversaries and birthdays. Photos of Norman and Cynthia smiling, centre frame, cutting into cakes, surrounded by grinning children and adults. There were graduation photos of people Eric could only assume were nieces and nephews as well as Christmas shots around the tree and one or two christenings. Eric recognised a few faces – faces from the funeral – and Maggie featured in several, but mostly they were strangers to him. He continued to browse though, trying to place dates by the length of Norman's beard, or the style of the women's dresses and men's hair.

Behind these images were stacks of cards. Certificates. Mostly they came from the village show but there were a few with *National*, written in bold letters in the title. Best in show, second place, highly commended; carrots, cos lettuces, kohlrabi, cabbages. Largest onion. Three salad vegetables on a dinner plate. It appeared that every item in Norman's harvests had at some point been placed and prized. And not just him. Cynthia was there too. Her carrot and walnut cake appeared numerous times, as did her elderflower wine and her pickled shallots. Eric glanced at the dates. Two thousand and five. Nineteen ninety. Nineteen eighty-four. He flicked through, seeing how far back they went. Nineteen seventy-nine. Nearly four decades of knowledge and green fingers, commemorated by nothing more than slips of paper. Eric wiped the dust from them and placed each one back where he had found it.

The top drawer of the desk was filled with nails and screw plugs, but in the second one, Eric found more photos. He blew them clean, causing a billow of dust to fog up the air in front of him. The papers they were printed on were no bigger than post-cards, and the sepia tones had faded with time. On many, the edges had bent and torn, and little speckles of dirt veiled the image like a veneer. Eric turned the top print towards the light.

The picture had been taken on a seafront, with a pier behind and a carousel off to the right. The couple in the centre had their arms around each other, although the young girl had her eyes closed, scrunched shut as if caught unaware mid-sneeze. He put the photo to the back of the pile and began to work his way through the rest. There were hundreds of mono-chromatic and tea-stained images. Some had stuck together with damp, many faded so much they were indecipherable, but still, there were countless left for Eric to look through and muse upon. Mostly they were images of Norman and Cynthia. A young Norman and strikingly beautiful Cynthia, both with long hair, thin waistlines, and wrinkleless faces that lifted out of the paper with their smiles. There were animal shots; a black and white cat lying on a window ledge beneath a hanging basket; a shaggy-furred dog with its tongue hanging out and a patterned bandana around his neck. One by one he worked through the pile, absorbing everything he could until the image of Norman and Cynthia at the carousel reappeared at the top.

There were only two more drawers left. In one was a toolbox. Rusted, grey, and locked with another cheap little padlock. Eric gave it a light shake, and a jangle rang out from within. No doubt more nails and screw plugs. He opened the last drawer.

The photo inside was face up but stuck at a jaunty angle which made it impossible to see what was on it until Eric had pulled it all the way out. The layer of dust on the frame was thin and the glass itself mottled with fingerprints as though it had been looked at recently. Twisting it towards the light caused his heart to lurch. Eric had seen the photo once before, all those months ago. Even so, it caused the tears to prick behind his eyes.

The photo was taken in front of the town hall with the clock tower clock clipped off the top. It consisted of three rows of people, several holding certificates, several more holding fruits, vegetables, and flowers, all arranged underneath a dated banner decorated with drawings of fruits and veg.

Eric ran his eyes along the back row. Hank stood at the side, his right leg out of view but Scout's tail just made it into the shot. Next to him stood Penelope Hamilton – from the excavator incident. Moving to the middle row, Janice, Cynthia, and another lady who was holding the most impressive spray of flowers stood in the centre between another dozen faces. Norman was on the front row, sitting on a chair. Several certificates were propped up against his feet and a few more on his lap, their corresponding prize winners next to them. However, for the first time since Eric had entered the shed, Norman was not the focus of Eric's attention.

Guilt struck behind Eric's sternum. It was solid and fast and caused his lungs to constrict and eyes to water. Still, he didn't change his gaze. His father was laughing. The flat cap on his head pulled firmly down. Eric had not once seen his father wear a flat cap, yet there it was.

From the date on the banner, Eric knew this was the last show he could have done. September, only a month before he died. Eric stared at the image of his father. Had he really looked that old? Not that Eric ever remembered. Perhaps it was because he was sitting down. People always look older when they're seated, Eric convinced himself. It's the way their posture slumps. His cheeks had hollowed too, sunken in and sallow. His hands were crossed on his lap, his fingers and wrists bent at strange looking angles. So, it wasn't just talk, his hands really did go.

Trying to ignore the intensifying heat building behind his eyes, Eric took the photo and placed it flat on the writing desk. He would keep it, he decided. Abi would like to keep it. Glancing back down, he saw that once more, the photo was refusing to lie flat. Assuming it was some problem with the frame, he turned it over to check the back.

Something stiffened behind Eric's belly button. His stomach twisted and churned while his eyes were locked on a small white envelope stuck with masking tape to the back of the frame. The name *Eric* was scribbled across the front.

Gently, Eric peeled the tape away and ripped open the envelope. Inside he found a small metal key.

The smell of soil and thickness of dust had become too much for Eric, and he carried the toolbox outside and onto the front of the veranda. He lowered himself into one of the chairs only to realise almost instantly that it was Norman's chair he'd sat in. He jumped up, wiped it down, and moved across to his usual place.

Eric's hands were back to shaking as he pinched the padlock between his fingers and racked his brain for what could be inside. Seeds? he thought, then dismissed the idea. Why would anyone keep his seeds under lock and key? Eric's pulse answered. Illegal seeds? He swallowed hard, held his breath, and turned the key.

EPILOGUE

I T HAD BEEN ten years since Eric and Suzy had last shared a spliff, and he was certain it must have been more exciting back then. It had to be. Right now, all he was feeling was sleepy, clumsy, and like his nostrils had been held against a biofuel exhaust pipe. Still, there was only the one joint tucked in the bottom of the toolbox, and by the end of the evening all evidence of Eric's adult dabbling in narcotics would be over and done with.

'Do you think it was for the pain?' Suzy said, drawing in a long deep drag then blowing it out over her shoulder, and out through the open window. 'At the funeral, a lot of people said he was in pain.'

'I think they said he was *a* pain,' Eric attempted to clarify for her. 'He was definitely a pain.'

Suzy passed him the glowing roll up and rested her hand on her husband's knee. She leant in with a slight sway.

'But truthfully, how do you feel?' she said, 'About everything?'

'About everything? You mean the weed? Or the fact that I can see two tiny Erics in your pupils?'

'Eric ...' Suzy shuffled back accordingly.

Eric sighed. He offered the joint back to Suzy, who shook her head. He dropped it into a half-empty tonic can and flopped down on to the sofa.

'Truthfully? I have no idea. I mean, how am I meant to feel? It's nice, I suppose. Finding out my father isn't a complete and utter bastard and didn't entirely despise me.'

'He didn't despise you —'

'But that doesn't change the fact that he was an arsehole for most of my life. And even when he was dead.'

Suzy glanced down at the floor. The toolbox was open, the contents scattered out on the carpet. She riffled through for a second before selecting a tea-coloured newspaper scrap.

'Local Students Perform Outstanding Charity Concert,' she read.

'You didn't tell me about doing this,' she said, reading down the column to find Eric's name.

He shrugged. 'It wasn't anything big. It was just a local thing, I can't even remember what it was for. Probably an old people's home or something.'

'It says here it was for the Life Boat rescue.'

'That would make sense.'

'And your dad obviously thought it was a big deal, he wouldn't have kept it otherwise.'

'Well, he seems to have kept everything else.'

The contents of the toolbox were a walk through Eric's childhood. There was his hospital bracelet, impossibly small and written in the type of curved handwriting that tran-scended modern day penmanship, along with a photo of the three of them, standing on the hospital steps. Baby Eric's eyes were invisible in his full throttle wail and had there been colours to the image, Eric suspected his face would have glowed in phosphorescent purple. There was a letter Eric had no recollection of writing, in which he'd told his parents all about his first day of school, a picture of him sitting on his mother's knee, reading books, and another of him standing on a stool in the kitchen, reaching up to stir some giant bowl on the worktop. There were several other photos too, half a dozen of them out in the garden and various ones involving birthday candles, but most of the photos had a running theme.

Eric could map his age from toddler to teen, sitting behind the rim of Sally's polished steering wheel. Unlike the others in the photo, she had not aged a day, but in each one Eric's face glowed as he gripped the wood and gazed out of the windscreen, grinning. Sometimes his father was beside him, other times he was on his own. There were photos in the summer, a seascape and seagulls drifting in the background behind them. There was Eric in his school uniform, with his tie hanging loose and his hair sticking out at wayward angles. There was the day that he'd passed his driving test, where he stood on the driveway, one hand resting on Sally, the other holding onto a slip of paper, pouting in a sullen sulk. He could remember that one being taken. He was meant to be meeting friends to celebrate with, but his father had insisted they get a photo first. They had gone out in the cold only to discover that the camera was out of film, so he'd had to wait forty minutes for George to go into town, queue up in the post office, and get some film. Eric's mood had been made even more unbiddable by the fact he wasn't allowed to drive Sally there on his own. A little thing like insurance irrelevant in the mind of a hormonal seventeen-year-old boy.

Photos took up the majority of the toolbox. There was also his mother's jewellery; nothing fancy, her engagement ring, now dated with its gold floral setting and tiny diamond, and a few other pieces with it, like a locket which Eric opened to find a picture of himself and his father. There were bank account details. Accounts not specified in the will, for they were not in George's name. There was one in Eric's name – small, but not insubstantial – and two in Abi's, which Eric had to get Suzy to double check the figures on twice before he was satisfied his eyes weren't playing tricks on him.

And then there was the letter.

'Right,' Suzy said, standing up with a slight wobble. 'I'm going to bed. What are you doing?'

'I'll just check we're all locked up. And have a bit of a tidy up first,' Eric said as he stood. 'You go up, I'll join you in a minute.'

'Don't be too long,' she said and kissed him on the forehead.

Eric strolled around the house. He checked the back door and kitchen windows and, on finding the living room still humming with the scent of weed, opened all the windows as wide as possible. Heading back into the kitchen, he poured himself a large gin and took a seat at the dining room table.

He sat in silence, making no motion for the television, or paper or even the letter. After a couple of minutes, he downed the drink, shut the windows, and went upstairs to Suzy. It was time they talked.

It was the right decision. He was positive it was, and if he'd needed any clarification on this matter, it came when he told Jack the news. Losing his professionalism for only the second time in Eric's company, Jack pulled Eric towards him and slapped him hard on the back, then pulled away with tears in his eyes.

'I couldn't be prouder of you,' he said. 'I couldn't be more pleased.'

'I'm not sure how I'm meant to take that,' Eric said.

'Oh, I think you're barking. Completely barking. And you'll be back in six months without a doubt.'

'Thanks for the vote of confidence,' he said.

Jack slapped him on the back.

They had three sets of people view the house the first day it went on the market. Within five days it was sold, and six weeks to the date they had the movers at the door.

'You sure you're not going to regret this?' Suzy asked him for the hundredth time. The sun was out although the chill was enough to make them keep their jumpers on. The scent of peonies drifted in from somewhere up the road. Abi was at Lydia's. She was going to stay there for a few days until they could get the place in order. Eric took Suzy's hand in his and lifted it up to kiss her knuckles.

'No,' Eric said. 'But then who says regret is a bad thing?'

Suzy and Eric may have rekindled their love... for now. But when Suzy's mum turns up without her dad, it is clear who is going to have to be the responsible one. Grab your copy of Peas, Carrots and a Red Feather Boa and enjoy a new generation of family drama.

AFTERWORD

A brief history of allotments:

With roots spreading all the way back to the Saxons, small parcels of land, known as allotments, have long been a way for people to grow and enjoy their own produce. Varying in size and located throughout the UK, allotments – which can consist of anything from just a single plot, to hundreds of plots gathered together – are leased from local councils or parishes, with tenancies costing anywhere from a few pounds to substantially more.

Allotments became most prominent during the Second World War and the "Dig for Victory," campaign, where their numbers rose to over 1.4 million. Nowadays, numbers are not so high. While it is estimated that less than ten percent of those original plots are left, they are still tended enthusiastically by those 'alloties' that remain.

Often hidden behind housing estates or on the outskirts of

towns these are places where a discerning few choose to opt out of the consumerism that arises with vast super markets and convenience stores and instead choose to sow and harvest their own produce. And they do so in the company of quiet, like-minded individuals, all sharing tips on pruning and pest control over cups of tea and homemade cakes and cider. For many it is refuge from the hectic-ness, noise and commotion of the modern world. A place where an Englishman's shed is his castle, hidden full of treasures and capable of providing all the sustenance a person could need.

NOTE FROM HANNAH

First off, thank you for taking the time to read **Peas, Carrots and an Aston Martin,** Book 1 in the Peas and Carrots Series. If you enjoyed the book, I'd love for you to let your friends know so they can also enjoy the misadventures of the Sibley family. I have enabled the lending feature where possible, so it is easy to share with a friend.

If you leave a review **Peas, Carrots and an Aston Martin** on Amazon, Goodreads, Bookbub, or even your own blog or social media, I would love to read it. You can email me the link at Hannah@hannahlynnauthor.com

Don't forget, you can stay up-to-date on upcoming releases and sales by joining my newsletter, following my social media pages or visiting my website
www.hannahlynnauthor.com

ACKNOWLEDGMENTS

Massive thanks must go to Emma and Jessica for helping me get this book edited.

To my parents, for introducing me to gardening, with their hanging baskets, herb gardens, and out of control hedgerows. To my in-laws, John and Chrissie, who are always willing to read my early and often scrappy drafts. In fact, thank you to all of you who take the time to read early drafts and offer valuable feedback, especially the eagle-eyed Lucy, Kath and Niove, as well as support and encouragement.

To Sally, for cementing my love of vintage cars – I hope wherever you are, you are being well looked after and well driven. Obviously, to my long suffering and patient husband, who, along with everything else he does, drove me around countless vintage car shows in search of the elusive DB4 as research for this book.

Lastly, thank you to every reader who has taken the time to read my work and listen to my stories.

ABOUT THE AUTHOR

Hannah Lynn is an award-winning novelist. Publishing her first book, *Amendments* – a dark, dystopian speculative fiction novel, in 2015, she has since gone on to write *The Afterlife of Walter Augustus* – a contemporary fiction novel with a supernatural twist – which won the 2018 Kindle Storyteller Award and Gold Medal for Best Adult Fiction Ebook at the IPPY Awards, as well as the delightfully funny and poignant *Peas and Carrots series*.

Her latest works include retellings of classic Greek myths and saw her win her second IPPY Gold Medal for the first book in her *Grecian Women Series*, the heart-wrenching *Athena's Child*.

Born in 1984, Hannah grew up in the Cotswolds, UK. After graduating from university, she spent ten years as a teacher of physics, first in the UK, then in Thailand, Malaysia, Austria and Jordan. It was during this time, inspired by the imaginations of the young people she taught, she began writing short stories for children, before moving on to adult fiction.

Nowadays you will most likely find her busy writing at home with her husband and daughter, surrounded by a clowder of cats.

Printed in Great Britain
by Amazon